MORE THAN THEY COULD CHEW

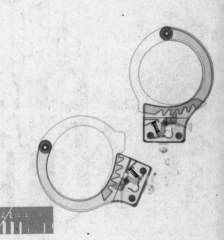

Rob Roberge

PERENNIAL
DARK ALLEY

An Imprint of HarperCollinsPublishers

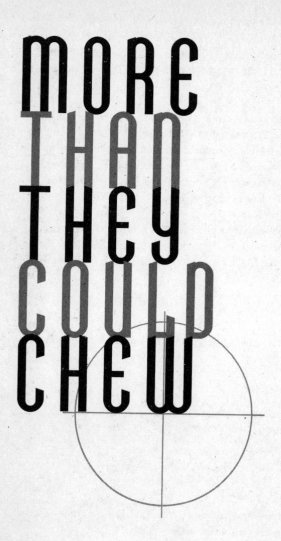

MORE THAN THEY COULD CHEW. Copyright © 2005 by Rob Roberge.
All rights reserved. Printed in the United States of America. No part of
this book may be used or reproduced in any manner whatsoever without
written permission except in the case of brief quotations embodied in
critical articles and reviews. For information address HarperCollins
Publishers Inc., 10 East 53rd Street, New York, NY 10022.

HarperCollins books may be purchased for educational, business, or
sales promotional use. For information please write: Special Markets
Department, HarperCollins Publishers Inc., 10 East 53rd Street, New
York, NY 10022.

FIRST EDITION

Dark Alley is a federally registered trademark of HarperCollins Publishers Inc.

Designed by Nicola Ferguson

Library of Congress Cataloging-in-Publication Data
Roberge, Rob.
    More than they could chew / Rob Roberge.—1st ed.
        p. cm.
    ISBN 0-06-074280-1
    1. Witnesses—Protection—Fiction. 2. Organized crime—Fiction.
3. Alcoholics—Fiction. 4. Extortion—Fiction. I. Title.

PS3618.O31525M67 2005
813'.6—dc22
                                                          2004048857

---

05 06 07 08 09 WBC/RRD 10 9 8 7 6 5 4 3 2 1

For Gayle—if I went into all the reasons why,
this would be longer than the book itself. Thanks, Bud. Love.

Acknowledgments

Thanks to my mom and dad, Ceci and Leo, who've always been incredibly supportive and loving, and have been a great example to me my whole life. To my great friend and big sister, Dianna, and her very cool kids, CR and Nadia. Thanks to Joe, Grace, Gwen, and Joe Jr. To Katie, François, Diane, and Darrell, who read this in manuscript and helped it and me a great deal. To my agent, Gary Morris, and my editor, Mike Shohl, who've both made this a better book than it was before they saw it. And thanks as well to all my friends who've helped me so much and who are, lucky for me, too numerous to list here. I'll have the pleasure of thanking you all in person.

DAY 1
CHRISTMAS DAY

Long Beach, California

Exile on Main Street

"That's one of the tragedies of this life—that the men who are most in the need of a beating up are always enormous."

—Preston Sturges, *The Palm Beach Story*

Nick Ray will let you down, is the way my ex-wife Cheryl puts it. Nick Ray is not without his charms, she'd tell you, but he's a sucker bet. In a fixed race, he'd find a way to finish second. Ask me, she'd say, and I'll tell you about a loser.

I am Nick Ray and I was once, and not so long ago, viewed by myself and others around me, as a young man with potential. No one would have picked this. No one, I'm betting, would've picked me as the desk clerk at a rat hole like the Lincoln Hotel, a place full of people with too much past and too little future.

Even Cheryl, who, for a number of years, made it her life's business to be disappointed by me, wouldn't have guessed I would end up at the Lincoln, but that's where I am.

The Lincoln Hotel sits on the corner of Long Beach Boulevard and Broadway. There is, as the sign announces, a bath in every room. The sign was painted the last time the hotel was totally renovated, I'm guessing sometime during the Eisenhower administration, since the lettering on the sign is in the same style as the lettering and graphics from the first wave of television commercials.

The plop-plop-fizz-fizz guy. Steve Allen holding a box of Post Toasties, telling you he'll be right back. Drive-ins. That lettering.

You're watching a rerun of *Kraft Mystery Theater* and Fred MacMurray just paused in front of a hotel and lit a cigarette. He looks around to see if Richard Widmark put a tail on him. He exits the shot, the building all that's left of the scene. That's this building. It might as well be in black-and-white.

The building cannot be torn down, it received historical status from the state of California a couple of years ago. It can, however, be wrestled, foot on throat, from Mrs. Carlisle, and it will be in a few months. The state of California's like those cops in Penn Station at three in the morning. They're rapping on the seats. They're exercising their authority.

Move along. Doesn't matter where you go but you can't stay here.

This has added a jittery quality to normal day-to-day life at the Lincoln. It's made Hank Crow, the other desk clerk, angry as hell. Hank's an old-time socialist who looks like Ossie Davis and there are stories he has to tell you. He's locked arms with Paul Robeson and Woody Guthrie, he's had Emma Goldman's tongue deep down his throat, and she only took it out long enough to harmonize about the circle being unbroken. Hank Crow did his part—he walked the picket line while the Weavers tapped their feet, plucked their revolutionary banjos and sang and this was all back when the country was young enough for something like hope. Just ask him, and Hank will tell you these things.

Listen to Hank Crow and learn this and learn it well: if he had a hammer, he'd hammer in the morning and if he had a monkey wrench, he'd show those bastards downtown, and if he had a pipe bomb and a thirty-ought six, he'd say good-bye to this world in style and take a few of the screwheads with him.

Hank's still angry enough to care and I end up feeling vaguely guilty that I've never had that passion about much of anything in my life. I have lived thirty-three years and I have only learned what I don't want to do with the rest of my days. I've never had much of a plan—I came out west because the weather was nice, I came to Long Beach because it was the cheapest beach city in Southern California, and I took the job at the Lincoln because I got free rent and I didn't have to do much of anything at all.

Me and Hank work the desk on the first floor and we sit behind bulletproof yellowing Plexiglas and we have one of those push-pull drawers you used to see at drive-thru banks to handle monetary transactions. Our desk is huge and pink and it has three buttons near your left leg. The one on the left buzzes people in. The one on the right is wired to the cops. The one in the middle doesn't do anything. I press it sometimes when I'm bored.

On the first floor is the lobby, which was probably nice once, with the metal ceiling that once had impressively hammered designs that now looks like a world of broken knuckles behind forty years of quick slap paint jobs.

The Lincoln was built in 1921, when Long Beach was the pride of the golden coast. Three years earlier, on what had been the land where Fatty Arbuckle and Buster Keaton shot two-reelers, they'd struck oil and Long Beach had its greatest real estate boom. The town flourished, the old Pike Amusement Center ran for miles on the beach. The Old Pike was the pride of the West with the centerpiece being the Cyclone Racer, the biggest and fastest wooden roller coaster on the coast, a coaster that danced and hairpinned its biggest curve a hundred feet out into the water.

In 1933, an earthquake rocked downtown hard and ugly and there wasn't much left standing. The city rebuilt the tourist center of the Pike, which had started its steady decline into navy-port sleaziness. The city council put up breakwaters that stopped the waves so the navy could have a safe harbor for the marine yards flourishing in the war-machine money. The city found out waves were important—the lack of motion killed sea life and coughed and hacked the garbage onto the shoreline. The waves were gone, the tourists stopped coming. The "New Pike" debuted after the war. By the late seventies, it was nothing but a gang hangout and the city ripped it down and started putting up parking lots and office buildings. All that's left of the Pike now is the gambling game "Lite-A-Line," a tattoo parlor in the basement of a brownstone on Chestnut Place, and a portion of the walking subway tunnel that connected the Pike to Cherry Park. It's blocked off on one end by the Hyatt Hotel's basement, but you can still sneak in on the end up by Cherry. Homeless people sleep down there in the tunnel that was built to keep tourists cool when they walked from one end of the world's greatest amusement center to the other.

The 1933 earthquake didn't do much to the Lincoln. There are surface cracks in the walls of the basement, but beyond that, it stayed healthy and upright. And because of this, it's one of the oldest commercial buildings in the city. This is why despite, at last count, ninety-plus code violations, it hasn't been bulldozed and forgotten like the wrecked dream it is. Instead, the city is supposed to turn it into some business, maybe condos or artist lofts, they haven't decided.

After the New Year, we have forty-five days.

How did I get here? The short answer is that I drink. The long answer has a lot of names and details and explanations, but pretty much boils down, reduces itself, to the short answer. I drink. I have my rules: I don't drink until I pass out, I don't drink and drive, and I'm not sloppy. But I don't get much done when I'm drinking, and I chose the drink over the life of achievement. People think all people who drink are sloppy losers, but that's not always the case. Some of us are a little quieter about it.

A lot of roads may lead to the Lincoln Hotel and places like it, but there only seemed to be a few kinds of people living there. We all like to think we're so different from one another, but we're pretty much alike. If you don't believe me, go to an AA meeting sometime and then come back and tell me on a stack of Bibles that you could pick one sad-sack narrative from another by the end of the night. People get defined by what they lost—not who they are. You're the guy who lost the wife, the woman who lost the kids, the blank who lost the blank. It becomes a kind of Mad Libs of pity, regret, and sorrow:

"It all started [adverb] and then, before I knew it, it had turned [adverb]. I thought I was in control, but soon I lost my [noun]. And then I lost my [noun]. But still, I thought I had it under control. I still worked at [job]. Then I lost [noun] and [noun] and [noun]."

And fill it in—after a while, only the names of the heartsick husbands, wives, and lovers change. And, once you've had any experience with pissing your life away, you realize there's absolutely no difference between a Lamborghini and a Pinto. You're still walking.

No one with anyone they could count on ended up here—there were no moms or dads knocking on the doors of the Lincoln. This was a place for bill collectors, bail bondsmen, officers of the court, johns, and parole officers. Seems like every woman here had a restraining order on someone from her past who kept trying to be someone from her present. No one got excited about the mail. No one looked forward to the phone ringing. Bad news had a habit of stumbling through these doors and poking its nose in your business.

But there were, roughly, three groups here. You had your old men and women, as planted as buildings and as stagnant as death itself, ghosting their way down your halls. You'd hear faint coughs and you'd see grocery and liquor delivery kids coming and going to know some of them were still alive. The hallways outside their rooms stank of age and disinfectant. About once every couple of months, we'd get a smell and Mrs. Carlisle would have me call the coroner's office.

Then you had the second group—the criminals and recently paroled. Mostly small-time, usually drug- and alcohol-related, and mostly male except for the two hookers who shared 3A/B.

But me and the Man with the Maggot Arm, aka Maggot Arm Joe, were here for the same reason—to heal up, do some court-order rehab, lick our wounds, and move on with whatever we could collect of our lives. He'd fallen further than me—he was a hotshot young black lawyer who'd become a drug addict and pissed it all away. We were starting over—which made us true Americans, to my mind. We were beaten, we were lost, but we had the golden coast and the palm trees and all the promises of the West and ahead of us were, if not better days, at least different days.

Most importantly, we would, it was understood, at least by us, move on. Joining us in the temporary crowd was Jeanine Clark and her seven-year-old daughter Molly, who were in 2C, which overlooked the parking lot and, beyond that, Long Beach Boulevard and Broadway.

It's Christmas night and I see Jeanine and Molly's room as I cross the street on my way home from the liquor store for the poker game me and Maggot Arm Joe are having in his room up on the fifth, and top, floor. Molly, the kid, waves from the window and I kind of lift and lower the bag full of bottles and cans in response. In their window is a dinky Christmas tree with a single row of blinky lights, the kind of tree you get at Pick-n-Save. Fake, sad, and small, and it only serves to remind you of the inherent sadness of Christmas in a place like the Lincoln.

I go inside, check the desk for messages, and see, thankfully, that no one wants anyone at the Lincoln Hotel. Southern Culture on the Skids' *Dirt Track Date* tremolos and twangs out of my CD player, but doesn't cheer me up the way it usually does. I had the afternoon and evening off, because of the holiday, but I'm still on graveyard shift and on call in case of an emergency. And this is not out of the question. The suicide lines ring off the hook this time of the year. Around the holidays, sorrow kicked in to an extra gear and hearts gave out. Plus, holidays are big times for repo men. Thanksgiving, they came to take Hank Crow's television and he chased them out into the street, half naked and screaming.

Hank's supposed to be at Maggot Arm Joe's place tonight. But this isn't because he's a social beast, but because he's been watching a postage stamp of a TV for the last month and this guy Sergei's supposed to hook him up with some fifty-inch monstrosity for a great price.

Sergei's this half-Dutch/half-Russian criminal who used to live here before my time and found it to be interesting enough to come back around now and then, like one of those big men on campus who keeps coming around when each year's new freshman class comes in. He flashes money in dangerous enough ways to get himself killed someday, but that's his business, not mine.

Sergei's loaded and he doesn't mind losing it. Like big Vegas gamblers, losing gives him a public forum to show all the little people how he doesn't give a fuck. He's rich enough not to care, and it's extremely important to him that you see how little he cares.

Normally, seeing Sergei is entertainment. But tonight, I have business to discuss with him and Maggot Arm Joe.

Last week, I had to buy a cheap computer that would have Internet hookups so I could e-mail this woman I see, Tara Norwood, and set up our meetings without her lover Jenny getting wise to the whole thing. I found a bunch of old 386s for sale at this downtown surplus military place, bought one, took it home, and plugged it in, seeing how I could streamline it to just do e-mail as quickly as possible. I went into DOS to try to clean it up, and I stumbled into this huge directory of files. One after the other, mostly names, followed by aliases and then this registry for their new names and their new addresses. Under each person's name is a long entry titled NEW IDENTITY. I scrolled down, name after name, list after list until it clicked on me that I was reading some government data. The first entries, with the names and aliases, listed crime.

Mostly drugs, various client crimes, murders, and some jury tampering. The second entries, with the new identities, had entire made-up histories of total white-bread, mayonnaise lives. Ivy League schools, army service, and everything else Mr. and Mrs. Joe Friday would salute the flag for.

It falls on me in a Newton's apple thwack—I'm looking at government witness relocation files. I search through the rest of the drive, and only find a couple others like this. The rest are memos, various field reports from what looks to be FBI agents.

All this shit from the eighties and early nineties. Much of this I can't make heads or tails of, but the bunch of names and addresses of criminals who turned state's evidence and who are now in the witness protection program could be worth something.

The 386s were going for fifty bucks a pop. I took every bit of money I had and bought nine of them.

When I get the rest, I learn they're all former United States government, FBI, and DEA 386s. All sorts of security warnings come on when you boot them up. And the government, from what I've been able to find out, auctioned them off dirt cheap and in bulk to legitimate businesses. Whoever was supposed to wipe the hard drives clean before the big auction didn't, and the computers are still full of information that the U.S. government would rather not have made public.

Mistakes were made.

Heads have rolled.

I've extracted some of the information from the hard drive into some word documents. An easy-to-read list.

Much of their information is useless, yesterday's news, like the top-secret documents of Ceausescu's government that

11

people used to wipe their asses with once there was no such thing as Ceausescu's government.

But the big fish is I've got the witness relocation protection lists from 1980 through 1996, when the computers were sold.

I figure this might be valuable to someone. But I have no idea how it could all come together in a way that would give me money, give me a chance to be the kind of person who might impress Tara Norwood to leave her lover and come with me to a new life somewhere else.

I'm a loser. I'm not a criminal. Sergei is a criminal, and Maggot Arm Joe represented some of the slimiest fish in the sea and knows how and where they store money. I need to figure out a way to make this something I can cash out on.

The way to make any machine reliable is to have as few parts as necessary. The fewer the movements, the fewer things there are to go wrong. Just me, Sergei, and Maggot Arm Joe.

My thinking is I can get this done with me and the two of them and cash in my chips and start a new life.

Your Troubles Will Cease and Fortune Will Smile upon You

At first, I called him the Man with the Maggot Arm. And for a while, I didn't know the Man with the Maggot Arm's real name, which, it turned out later, was Joe Cole. He was introduced to me as the Man with the Maggot Arm and that's the way it stayed, until some of us shortened it to Maggot Arm Joe.

Maggot Arm Joe is called that because of some special experimental treatment that he's undergoing. He was a lawyer, then he was a lawyer/junkie, then he was a junkie/lawyer, then just a junkie. Near the end of his run with the stuff, he missed what was left of a vein and nailed muscle tissue deep and mean enough to have an infection stubborn and relentless as a Buffalo winter.

They tried everything, but his right arm stayed infected for eight months, his whole stay at Terminal Island, a local prison known simply as "Terminal" around here. After eight months at Terminal, he got paroled and got placed here, which is typical, as we have, as Mrs. Carlisle puts it, an "understanding" with the some paper pushers downtown. Part of his parole is state-sponsored NA meetings that he has to attend three times a week. On Friday mornings, he goes to his parole officer, whose receptionist is the woman I see, Tara Norwood. I don't get to see Tara enough. She dates Jenny. Jenny the lawyer. Jenny the success. Jenny is, as Maggot Arm Joe likes to point out, the anti–Nick Ray.

I'm Tara's slumming-on-the-side person. Tara helped get me the job at the Lincoln a year ago. Her boss got Maggot Arm Joe into the Lincoln; before that, he was at some halfway house sponsored by the Scientologists, and it wasn't, to hear him tell it, helping much.

The courts are paying for this experimental medical treatment for the infection that wouldn't go away.

The treatment, it's called Maggot Therapy.

They lanced the wound and this left him with a festering hole the size of half a golf ball in the crook of his right arm. The tissue was dead and there was no way that hole was going to close on its own, so they went with the maggot therapy. The logic was that only healthy tissue heals, but that they had to get rid of the dead tissue. They could cut it out, but then they'd have to enter and violate the muscle—they'd have to cut healthy flesh, which they'd rather not do. The surgery would cause a longer recovery time, and he would have lost motion in his right arm. So they opted for the radical treatment.

Maggots eat dead tissue, but they won't touch live tissue. So Joe Cole became the Man with the Maggot Arm and then became Maggot Arm Joe because five weeks ago, they wrapped his arm thick with rolls of gauze that had specks of larva on them. For the last five weeks, they've grown fat and lumpy as risotto under the gauze. He gives me updates on the progress, says the dead tissue's almost gone and that it'll all be over soon.

*　　*　　*

We're in Maggot Arm Joe's apartment when Sergei struts into the room, wearing a cream-colored lace shirt and these shiny-looking brown pants. You can see his nipples and some garish chain that sits between his thick pecs. Sergei's pumped up—steroid-stacked, Muscle Beach big. The chain's thick as a thumb, too thick to be jewelry, unless you're some idiot rapper with the fashion sense of Elvis Presley. He carries two shoe-box-size gifts and puts them on a dresser and turns to us.

He smiles and a gold-capped tooth catches the light from the bulb that hangs from the cracked plaster ceiling. He holds his arm toward the boxes like he's one of those *The Price Is Right* women saying "all this could be yours." "I bring cell phones. What are we drinking?"

"What the fuck are you wearing?" Maggot Arm Joe says.

Sergei looks down at his clothes as if the question's insane. "This six-hundred-dollar shirt."

Maggot Arm Joe shakes his head. "It's *lace*."

Sergei nods.

Maggot Arm Joe says, "It's a fucking lace shirt. You can't be wearing that out. Look at you."

"How much *your* shirt?" Sergei says.

Maggot Arm Joe wears a red flannel shirt. "What the hell does that have to do with anything? It's a shirt." He pauses. "It's not lace."

Sergei holds the fabric between his fingers. "No six-hundred-dollar shirt, is it?"

"Of course not," Maggot Arm Joe says.

Sergei lights a cigarette and waves him off. "Then I don't listen. You shop at Gap. At Target. You know nothing." He turns to me. "I am listening to man with bugs inside him. I think of that—it makes me creenge."

"What?" I say.

"Creenge—you get disgusted, you make face." He pauses. "You creenge."

"You mean *cringe?*" I say.

He slaps me on the back. "Yes. His arm with bugs, it makes me creenge."

And I think, *Well, sure. Of course. It makes me creenge, too.*

"What we drinking?" Sergei says.

I tell him we're drinking Guaro and he gives me a funny look.

"Guaro," I say. "It's Costa Rican."

"What is it?" Sergei says.

Maggot Arm Joe takes a drink and scrunches his face. "Grain alcohol, sugar, and nitroglycerine."

"You joke me."

"Nope." I give him a drink.

"Where you get nitroglycerines?"

"Lenny," I say, but Sergei still looks confused. "Mechanic Lenny. Drag racers use it as part of their fuel."

Sergei shakes his head like he's never heard of anything as crazy as drinking fuel and takes a drink. "I thought you were not supposed to drink on parole," he says to Maggot Arm Joe.

"You've seen him drink," I say.

"Beer is no drink."

Maggot Arm Joe says, "I buy clean piss from a kid in the parking lot." He shrugs. "I'm not supposed to consort with criminals, either."

Sergei points to me. "Nick Ray not criminal."

"I think he meant you, Sergei," I say, toasting him with my mason jar, thinking that I really shouldn't be drinking Guaro. It's too strong and I need to keep control. Warmth spreads through me with the first sips. Tingly. Good. "But thanks."

"Me?" Sergei says. "I am in business. Not criminal."

Maggot Arm Joe says, "You break laws, Sergei. You break laws, you're a criminal." He pauses. "Trust me. I studied this. They gave me a degree."

Sergei shakes his head. "I break bad laws. Gandhi break laws. Martin Luther King—he break laws."

Maggot Arm Joe lights a cigarette. "You steal as an act of civil disobedience. This is what you're telling me?"

"Fuck you and your big words. I can use big Russian words. Big Dutch words. So fuck you, smart man." Sergei takes a mason jar of Guaro. He points with his drink hand. "I not criminal—I read the silly Marx and Engels. I redistribute the wealth."

"That you do," Maggot Arm Joe says, and clunks heavy glasses with Sergei.

"It's just Marx now," I say. They give me curious glances and I tell them I was down at the Borders and saw new editions of the Communist Manifesto with just Marx's name on them.

"No Engels?" Sergei says.

I shake my head.

Maggot Arm Joe says, "When did Engels become Roebuck?"

"Who did Roebuck write with?" Sergei says.

Maggot Arm Joe shakes his head. "Forget it—let's order some food."

We order Chinese, the only restaurant open downtown. We're talking about Christmas, or avoiding talking about Christmas, since this is no way to spend one, when Hank Crow walks in, lumpy as dirty clothes, and starts in about the TV.

"Please," Sergei says. "I eat. We talk later with business."

And it's later, after we've eaten, after Sergei has talked

business about his hot TV with Hank Crow, after several mason jars beyond common sense of Guaro, that we've settled into a game of Texas Hold 'Em with Sergei and Hank Crow way down and me and Maggot Arm way up.

"You will like TV, Hank Crow," Sergei says as I deal a new hand. "You like your porno, no?"

"Shut up," Hank says.

Sergei holds his hands apart like he's holding a watermelon above his head. "Penis as big as marlin on this screen. Tits like medicine ball. Make you very happy."

Hank looks over his two cards. "Shut the fuck up."

Sergei leans toward me. "Porno people love this TV."

Maggot Arm Joe says, "Your bet, Sergei."

Sergei throws in five dollars like we were playing with corn nuts.

"Two-dollar cap," I say. "You're playing with poor people."

Sergei shrugs. "I take exchange rate." He points at the five. "That's two to rest of you."

I win and I'm up over twenty dollars. We go another round with the cards and bet again. Sergei's getting drunk, and he's getting sloppy. He throws in one of those new hundred-dollar bills and acts like it's an accident, like he meant to toss in a dollar. I hold it up. "Man, our money's ugly," I say.

"All money's ugly," Hank says. He tosses his cards in. "And I'm out of it." He pushes himself back from the table and looks at Sergei. "When do I get my TV?"

Sergei shrugs. "When it comes, boy brings it to you." Sergei watches as Hank Crow slumps out of the room. I watch Hank, thinking of how he reminds me of a grown-up Pigpen, the *Peanuts* character who always trails a lumpy cloud of dirt.

He also makes me think of me, of what I could be if I slip here and there. A couple bad days at the perfectly wrong time, they lead to a life like Hank Crow's, I don't know much but I know that. Hank Crow had dreams, visions for a new and wonderful America where people shared with one another. The wealth distributed to all. He believed in this enough to have his head kicked on picket lines. He was split open to die by his own government. Now his friends are all dead and all he wants is a fifty-inch television. That couldn't have been the plan.

We crush some amphetamines on the table and snort them up through Sergei's hundred-dollar bill. I unwrap it to look again at the new bill, the one with the big, bubble-headed circle, the one with watermarks so it's harder to counterfeit, and the crushed white powder dandruffs its way over Ben Franklin's face and over his shoulders. I lick it and feel the racing numbness on my gums.

"You lick my money?" Sergei says.

"Sorry."

He waves it off.

With Hank Crow gone, I can make my pitch.

"I came into something that might lead to some money," I say.

"Good for Nick Ray," Sergei says, and slaps my back. "Make you your own dollars to lick."

I snort this acidy snot that stings its way down my throat and look over at Maggot Arm Joe, whose face hovers in a desert heat-wave kind of way. I make a mental note to switch to beer when this jar of Guaro's out. Maybe stop. I can work with the healthy buzz of alcohol, but I need to make my pitch here and stay on top.

"No crime," Maggot Arm Joe says. "I need to stay clear of the law."

"You drink rocket fuel," Sergei says.

"Drinking rocket fuel's not a crime," I say.

Maggot Arm Joe tilts his head, makes an I'm-sorry-but-you're-wrong face. "It is. Controlled substance."

"This isn't about drugs," I say. "But it could be worth money."

"How much?" Sergei says.

"I have no idea," I say. "But you want money? You want to leave this shit-hole Lincoln Hotel life we lead?"

"I don't live shit-hole life," Sergei says.

"But you want money?" I say.

Sergei looks confused. Like it's the dumbest question on earth. "Always."

And I'm not just selling them on the idea, but myself. I can see it in Maggot Arm Joe and I can feel it tingle through my whole body like a first kiss. Money. A ticket out. A new life.

"I'm listening," Maggot Arm Joe says.

I say, "I have a bunch of computers and I need to move them."

"Stolen?" Maggot Arm Joe says.

Sergei lights a cigarette. He takes a drag and flicks a hint of ash off his lace shirt.

"No," I say. And then I explain all I've been able to find out.

"Witness relocation?" Maggot Arm Joe says. He scratches his arm and I get queasy seeing the gauze give a little. I wonder what makes the maggots stay in there. Then I remember, it's the dead tissue. But what about when they're done? Do they bust out? Do they go looking for dead flesh? Or do they just curl up and die in his arm?

Sergei nods. "The witnesses. They send them to Flagstaffs. To Sioux City. To little horse-hole towns, no?"

"Gallup, New Mexico," I say.

"Don't make fun, Nick Ray." Sergei looks at me hard. "No such places as a Gallup. Don't make fun." Stories float around the Lincoln and one of those stories has Sergei putting both of some loser's hands, one at a time, down a garbage disposal many, many hours before Sergei put him out of his misery. Sergei's skin is ugly—pocked and mean looking. There's a scar over his eyelid—it's from a tattoo he had removed, he says, and it's discolored and gives him a crunchy-looking heavy lid—like it's peppered with cysts. All this makes him look like what he is—a violent man who can't be trusted.

Be nice, I tell myself—the difference between life and death can be the difference between Sergei thinking I respect him or not. Even stupid people tend to know when you think they're stupid.

"Not making fun," I say. "Gallup, New Mexico, is a real place. It's a shit hole." I take a drink. "No joke."

"To Gallup, then," Sergei says. "They send them there, too."

Maggot Arm Joe says, "How'd you get the computers?"

Sergei snorts some of the speed. He sniffs, wipes a streak of snot on the back of his hand. "There are things you don't ask a businessman. Things you don't need know. Right, Nick Ray?"

I almost tell them I bought them at the surplus story on Anaheim, but I catch myself—they think I'm connected in some way, and I need to keep myself valuable.

"Right," I say.

"I'm not sure," Maggot Arm Joe says. "Sounds like trouble."

Sergei says, "Who would want this information?"

"The people on list—they would like this," I say. I've

thought it through—this is the way to make money without anyone getting hurt.

"They're criminals," Maggot Arm Joe says. "They're criminals who betrayed other criminals. They're less ethical than the average criminal. You think you can trust them? I'll tell you now you can't. I know those people."

Sergei says, "There's the people who they rolled on. They would want list."

"No dice," I say. "That would get people killed."

"So?" Sergei says.

"I just want to make money. If we sell it to the people on the list, they'll just be happy to have their info."

"So you're comfortable being a blackmailer, but not a killer?" Maggot Arm Joe says to me.

"Fuck you," I say, even though he hit it dead-on.

"I am comfortable as blackmail or killer," Sergei says. "Sounds good. Much money for all."

"You're better off doing business with businessmen," Maggot Arm Joe says.

"Not an option," I say.

"I know these people," he says.

I say, "I know you do. That's why I'm talking to you. But they're my computers and it's on my terms."

Sergei snorts the last of the speed. He takes out a clean hundred-dollar bill and hands it to Maggot Arm Joe. The rumply, snotty one he scrunches into my breast pocket.

"I love this, Nick Ray. What a Christmas miracle, no? America. Land of the miracle?"

"Right," I say. "So you're in?"

He shoves another bill in my pocket and claps. "Many,

many more. We do this fast, we make much money." He claps, rubs his hands together zippy-fast like Paul Newman when he's taking Robert Shaw for all he's worth in *The Sting*. He flashes his gold tooth and looks around the table. "Fortune cookie?"

"You?" I say to Maggot Arm Joe.

"You won't consider going straight to the money end?"

"No."

"We'd make more money that way."

"We'll make plenty this way," I say. "No need to get greedy."

"I don't like it."

"It's still a lot of money," I say. "Or it could be."

He sits, tossing it back and forth in his head. I hear Christmas music from a building outside. There's no way I can do this without him—Sergei knows criminals, but he doesn't know the ins and outs of the white-collar guys the way Maggot Arm Joe does.

"I'm in," he says.

I breathe out and it's only then I realize I've been holding it in.

"Fortune cookie!" Sergei says.

I find the fortune cookies. Sergei takes his and the one that would have been Hank Crow's—"a tip for the porno TV," he says. I open mine and Sergei asks what it says.

I read out loud, "Your Troubles Will Cease and Fortune Will Smile upon You."

Sergei loves it. He gestures to the sky, arms spread. You know this gesture. It's kitsch. Glorious crap. It's a LeRoy Neiman print on Limited Edition Burger King cups. The winning touchdown. He's Rocky standing over what's left of

Apollo Creed. It's America in its huge ugliness. He's overdramatic. He's the World's Tallest Thermometer. Big and silly as those forty-eight-ounce-you-eat-it-and-it's-free Texas steaks.

He's been watching the religious channels—he loves them. He's a criminal, but what he really wants, you can see it, is to heal the sick, to kick away those crutches that are no longer needed, to crush the sad blind man's sunglasses. He was lost and now he's found, Sweet Jesus. And why not? This country was founded by criminals and religious lunatics and they still sit in Daddy's Chair. Why not Sergei?

He laughs. "You see, Nick Ray. Listen to cookie."

By the time Sergei comes into what little I have of a plan, it's too late for me, even though I have an immediate smack of regret. Even though it is my idea, it seems to have a momentum all its own after I say the words and make my pitch.

I'm not a criminal. I'm an ex–film editor who drinks too much and doesn't like to work for a living. My head is Ping-Ponging between this seeming like a pot of gold dumped into my lap, or simply just a really bad idea.

But bad ideas, like ugly people, get a whole lot more attractive at the end of the night, and you'll side with them over being alone most every time.

And between the speed and the Guaro, I'm buzzing and humming like a tube of neon and anything would sound like a good idea.

A friend of mine recently told me about this study where they had someone cut in on someone in line. The person who'd been cut in on would have none of it, wouldn't stand for it. But, if the cutter gave them a reason ("I need to go ahead of you, *because* . . ."), that changed things. People need the "because," it satisfies their desire for an ordered cause-and-effect-ruled universe.

So I ask Sergei and Maggot Arm Joe, criminals tougher and more dangerous than me, because I am drunk. Most of my bad decisions have been made after I was drunk. Or, I get involved with them because I need money to change my life. The best reason, though, is still the one my ex-wife Cheryl would give you: Nick Ray is a loser, a stoop, a man with an uncanny knack for clutching defeat from the jaws of victory.

In the Nighttime

I'm at my desk on the night shift.

You know the story. You know the results, anyway.

The suck and drain of hot poison corroding its way down, down, into the earth.

These are things you cannot fix.

Chernobyl. Three Mile Island. The useless land that spits and gurgles out sad parodies of vegetation, the tainted meat—the off-the-scale lymphoma counts. The blank look of thirty-year-olds given death sentences for them and their families by their government.

They, the accidents, happened at night—happened between 4 and 6 A.M. And if you've ever worked this shift, these hours, you know why. Between four and six, the world changes into something beyond foreign and it doesn't matter how often you're there for it, it will stay as foreign as it was the first time you felt it. An everlasting Gobstopper of despair and loneliness. It never gets smaller and it never lessens in intensity.

People make mistakes at this hour and I know why.

It's dark out there and you feel young and weak and alone.

At night, we are all small. It's physical. The world is huge and you shrink into yourself.

Work the night shift and you'll come to understand this and more.

You read books, all night-shift people try, and you'll read, over and over, people saying that it's silent, that's the word they'll use, *silent,* when the people stop talking. But it's never silent.

Work nights and you'll find how much noise there is when people think things are quiet. There's nothing so loud as the quiet. The clank of pipes that've churned for years. The running pats of rat feet in the wall. Their chewing—you can hear it through cracking plaster that spiderwebs its way up and down the wall. Listen. Hear the bugs' antennae tick the tile. Realize how busy things are in your aloneness. Hear the wind kick leaves into corners. Hear bags roll their way down the street. Listen, at 1 A.M. when Phil, the guy at the porno video place next door, closes up and scrapes his security cages over his door. Listen to the glass in the front door settle and crackle as it does every night.

Listen to the hum of wires and the hiss of tires as they drive by. You listen to this, and you understand why people talk, why they tell their stories on talk radio all night. They talk to block this out, this noise they mistake for silence. They talk to push it back, push it away. Talk talk talk.

First-time caller, longtime listener.

I have a question and I'll take my answer off the air.

Blah, blah.

I turn off the radio. The click, like everything else, seems loud. I try to focus on blocking out the noise.

And if you can block all of this out, you'll feel and hear the swoosh of blood through your body. You will hear your heart. You will hear you. And you'll start to think about that heart, about how much it can do, how it just keeps thumping its way through these nights, through these days, and you'll wonder how much it has to go and will you have time to do whatever it is you were meant to do. Or will it stop? And will you know silence then?

These are the thoughts that lead you to miss that blinking button on reactor five. The thoughts that cause you to miss the downshift and put your truck in the ravine. This is what happens between four and six in the morning.

The Ghost of Christmas Past

I'm thinking about this computer deal. A momentum of negativity floods me.

Christmas night, five years ago. I'm on a bus. A Greyhound. Going west on Route 80 through Pennsylvania. I was leaving Buffalo, New York, I was leaving a life, a job, friends, and Cheryl, my wife who'd grown sick of waiting for me to become a better person than the one she'd been stuck with. We started out okay, but we turned as rotten as British teeth. I was that thing that clings to you in the water, I was kelp in a wave. I was a briar. Stuck and unwanted and serving no purpose.

I leave Buffalo with a friend who's on his way to Duke University for their Ph.D. program. He drops me in Scranton and rides on.

I am on this bus and the bus swings into the passing lane. And then, and I *felt* this as if it had been me at the wheel, the bus started to drift. It lost control and spilled. The sounds are metal ripping, heads wetly thumping on things, suitcases a little drier in their thumping. There are screams. And here's what I think:

This is how it ends. This is how, this is where, my life will end. I'm calm. I'm not happy or sad, nothing big, I'm empty, accepting. I'm okay. It's a feeling I'd never had before.

But it didn't end, not that night and not for me, anyway. There were deaths. There was a class-action suit that I didn't want anything to do with. I moved around. Florida. Tennessee. Connecticut.

I quit drinking for four years.

When I didn't drink, I had some plans, some ideas about what to do. I thought about going back to school, but I couldn't think for what. Then I came out to California and thought I'd try to save up some money and go to school for film restoration. I'd been an editor's assistant, and I liked the quiet time, assembling images and sound and making a coherent world out of all of those options they drop in your lap. Editing was okay, but all I could ever get was TV work— nothing noble. No documentaries that pried the innocent from jail, or indie films, or anything that wasn't a waste of time, ultimately.

But film restoration: that seemed like a decent and not disgusting or corrupt way to make a living. You'd be preserving culture, fighting the ravages of time. There are even awards for it, a noble pursuit, in its way. I had this image of me bent over some silent film that was almost history, saving it with my latex gloves and X-Acto knives and obscure chemicals. People, when I told them what I did, would be interested, impressed.

But I wanted to drink. When I'm drinking, there's not much beyond my next drink, which is why I have to keep a governor on it until we cash in on this deal.

And what straight people don't get, can't get, really, is that it takes an enormous amount of tunnel vision to be a full-time drinker. So I thought about school, and I thought about drinking, and school took focus and it took faith and determination, and the drink took a walk to the corner.

I thought about alcohol every day. People say that, they say like "not a day went by that I didn't . . ." and fill in the fucking blank of what they've been thinking about. But I'm telling you the truth. I thought about it every day. It wasn't dramatic, it wasn't a big deal. It was there, like something in your line of vision, like a bum knee that reminded you of itself.

It was a car that pulls severely on the freeway. You notice it every day. You don't think so much about it, but it's there and it affects you and after a while you do think about it and you realize how tiring it is to always be pulling that car back to the middle. You realize you're fighting, all the time, to keep it from where it wants to go. You get tired of pulling against the pull. You let it go.

I started drinking again a year ago because I wasn't sure why I'd quit.

And things, predictably, have gotten worse. And now I am making this deal with Sergei and I feel something slipping as sure as I felt that bus.

This is how it ends.

I am, at times, afraid to die, but never when it seems as if I'm about to die. But now, this moment is announcing itself as trouble, as the end. And that feeling smokes its way through me again.

I'm okay.

Then I shake it off, thinking, these thoughts are normal. Not good for you—but normal. There's no such thing as luck, and premonitions are for fools. I turn on the radio and try to think about something else.

In the Nighttime II

I think of calling Tara, but think better of it. Jenny could answer. This is the holidays and I'm not supposed to make demands on Tara's time when I know she's got responsibilities at home. Jenny takes off for Michigan tomorrow morning for a couple of days, so I'll get to see Tara tomorrow night. I sit, trying to decide if I actually miss her, or if I don't want to be alone tonight. I settle on a little of both.

Tara does not, I'm pretty sure, love me. She loves me, but doesn't *love* me. We're friends. I could very easily, and may already have, fallen in love with Tara—but I'm not sure how much of that is because I know it's doomed.

Tara and Jenny have been together awhile, but there's a problem and I'm Tara's short-term solution to the problem. I'm safe. We go way back. Know each other from art school, when I thought I was going to be a director, and she was going to be a fine-art photographer.

Which she is.

And Jenny and Tara have their problems—I don't ask much and Tara doesn't tell much. I'm the last guy she slept with before she started sleeping with women, and I seem to have gotten grandfathered in. She's a lesbian, more or less, but still sleeps with me.

Tara calls herself a sexual thrill seeker, an adventurer. Sex is her Mount Everest, her marathon. She lives for the endorphin kick of pain and exhaustion during sex. She likes to be out of control and she likes to be hurt. She's asked me to use alligator clips on her nipples, on her labia, while I went down on her. She's had me whip her ass with everything from a hairbrush to various-size riding crops. Most of what she asks for I do, even if it bothers me, even if it feels like something you shouldn't be doing to someone you love, because it's something you do for someone you love if it makes them happy and you shouldn't be listening to anyone else, anyway.

Last week, we were at a doughnut shop on Seventh Street called Angel Food Donuts, because Tara needed to take a picture of the sign for this book she's putting together on signs that are in the shape of the product they're selling. Mimetic architecture. She's doing this for fun, but I figure it could sell. Fortunes have been made with less of an idea in the world, but that's not where she's going with it. She just loves signs that are in the shape of their products and wants to go cross-country taking pictures of them. She likes to interview the owners and they talk, they talk a surprising amount, about their signs, and she takes notes. They love her, these sign owners, but most people do. She has that knack.

The Angel Food Donut sign is in the shape of a doughnut on a twenty-foot pole. The pole is white and the doughnut is shit brown and Tara's kind of upset because the paint job is new and before it was all rusted and covered in bird shit that made it look glazed. One side reads: ANGEL FOOD DONUTS.

The other side reads: ANGEL FOOD DO-NUTS.

Tara's bending down taking pictures from a few angles. I ask her how many signs she has now and she tells me twenty-seven.

"In L.A. County?" I say.

She takes a picture. "Yup. I'm thinking of limiting the book to California."

"Sounds good."

She shakes her head. "But then I'll lose Vegas," she says. "Lot of great signs in Vegas. Plus, the Arizona sections of Route 66."

"Save them for a sequel," I say.

She takes another picture and says she's done. We go inside and ask to talk to the owner about the sign and the counter boy, who looks to be about twelve, says that the owner isn't there.

"What do you think of the sign outside?" Tara says.

"What do you mean?" the kid says.

"The do-nut sign," she says. "What do you think?"

The kid looks overwhelmed. This is a face reserved for high school physics. He looks pained, like he had no idea that the world could be this confusing outside a classroom. He says, "We sell doughnuts."

Tara thanks him and buys a dozen, she always buys something from a place she's photographing, and when we get to her car I ask her if she eats doughnuts and she tells me she feeds them to the birds on the beach.

Once, I asked her why she likes pain so much.

"It gets me somewhere," she said. She seemed mildly put off. She said, "People test their bodies all the time—bodybuilders. Triathletes. Nobody calls them freaks."

"Everybody calls them freaks," I said, and smiled.

"But people admire them in a way. Like that woman who swam the English Channel—she gets greased down in gobs of white lard. She swims in forty-degree water for days. She gets stung by poisonous sea creatures. And she gets in the papers, talks to Mary Gross on NPR—it's endurance—it pushes the limits of what humans can do." She took a drink. "It's *ennob*ling."

"So that's you—you're the woman who swims the English Channel?" I said.

"All she did was go from France to England," she said. "I get multiple orgasms."

This is our agreement, though we don't talk about it much. She tells me her fantasies, and we end up, sooner or later, playing them out. She usually writes me a story. She does it at work, and it's on L.A. County Parole stationery, or in an e-mail, but she writes me a story that turns her on and the way it's developed is that we end up acting her stories out. Sometimes they're about her being tied down. Lately some of them involve her tying me down. Trust me, she says, I'd never *really* hurt you, and she smiles the sweetest smile I've ever seen. Being with Tara has taught me I'd do anything she wanted, just to be with her, and think I get the better end of the deal.

After the Angel Food Do-nut sign, we got back to my place and I asked her what she wanted for Christmas.

"Nothing," she says.

"Really?"

She pauses and looked out the window. "You'll think it's sick."

"Sick?" I say. "What's sick?"

She pauses. "Even I think this one's sick. And it's my fantasy."

I kiss her cheek and she leans away, but lets me. "Sick-away. Sick-appalooza."

"I'm serious," she says. She tells me about this thing she's read where you eat a bunch of laxatives the night before. Sleep on it. Empty yourself out in the morning. Then give yourself a series of enemas the next day until you're really empty and what comes out is pretty much what went in. Then you keep giving yourself enemas one after the other until your body clicks into some reverse and you convulse and vomit out your mouth what you just put in your ass.

"It's supposed to be incredible," she says. "Multiple orgasms. Total loss of control. Total pleasure breakdown."

"You read about this?" I say.

"Yes."

"There's a place to read about this?"

She looks mildly hurt. "I shouldn't have said anything."

"Sorry," I say. "We'll do whatever you want."

"I'd do it myself, but I could pass out. You can't be in control and lose control."

"No problem," I say. "It'll be fun."

"You're just saying that," she says. "It's not fun for me if you're just doing it to be nice."

"Really," I say. "If you'll enjoy it, it'll be fun for me."

"I'd do it myself—but it's better if I'm forced to go through it."

"I'm forcing you?"

Tara says, "In my fantasy, someone's forcing me."

The "someone" hits me sour. I know if Jenny'd do this, I'd be alone. "Forced it is."

She kissed me and left the next morning before I got up. There was an envelope on my desk. Inside was a note that read, "Thank you so much. You don't know what this means" and a $700 check with a list of things to buy:

Five 2-liter enema bags
A Kiddie Pool
2 liters of lemon juice
PVC Straitjacket—small
Video Camera

I thought the $700 was a lot, that I'd have money left over to give back to her. I got a nice video camera from this guy who sells stuff out of his trunk and figured there'd be plenty left. But kiddie pools and straitjackets are both more than I'd ever figured. But, still—I got it and it's waiting for her.

Tara and I have one rule. I don't tell her I love her and/or bring up her leaving Jenny. In return, she doesn't ask me to quit drinking and make something of myself. But it nags me that if I did quit drinking and try to make something of myself, maybe then I could break that rule and ask her to leave Jenny and be with me.

DAY 2
DECEMBER 26

Welcome to Sergei's

At 6:30, after a night of cataloging a life's worth of failure and regret, I slosh my way over to Sergei's apartment. I have that edgy hollowness you get when you've been up all night drinking stale coffee. There's a chemical burn inside me from the Guaro and the speed and I feel like shit. I need a drink, but try to avoid one. I pop a couple of uppers before I go—cheap trucker speed. I'm not sure how much trouble this will be, but I know that if I get too much sleep I'll see it for the loser deal it is. You need to risk to profit in this world, and I need to shuck and jive my better self into thinking this is doable.

I buzz downstairs and he lets me in. I glide up the quiet elevators, walk through freshly painted halls with clean corners, and make my way to Sergei's door. I wonder for a moment why someone who lives in a building this nice would want to get involved in crime and then I catch myself and remember that's what pays his rent.

Sergei opens the door naked to the waist, wearing these slick dark green pants. He sees me looking at them and starts to walk away. He stops and spins like a runway model, poised for my approval.

"Lizard," he says. "Very thick skin, these lizards. Make warm pants. Nick Ray get lizards pants when this goes down."

"I don't want lizard pants," I say, and he looks hurt and confused. Like most people, Sergei lashes out with hatred and violence at things he doesn't understand. I try to take a step back, soften the blow. Unring my bell. "I'm not a lizards-pants kind of guy."

That seems to do it; he's not hurt anymore. Sergei's moods are jerky. You're with him, you can never settle in and let things happen. He's an edge-of-the-seat guy. Jumpy as an EKG. Talking with him is like bumper cars.

The buzzer sounds.

"Your Maggot friend," he says, and goes to the intercom.

I sit on the couch. On the glass-topped table in front of me is a small pile of powder that looks like crystal meth, the polyester of drugs. At the side of the table are a bunch of IDs. I pick them up.

All of them are Sergei; at least, all of the pictures are him. There are nine of them with nine names. None of them have the name Sergei on them. A couple of them are California, but there's a bunch from other states. I wonder if I know his real name and it gives me a jolt. Should you get into something illegal unless there's absolute trust?

He grabs them from me.

"Don't look at that."

"Sorry," I say. That doesn't seem to do it. He stands over me tensed and poised. "I didn't see anything," I say.

He nods. Taps his temple with the same chunky hand that's holding the nine IDs. "Good. Nothing to see, right, Nick Ray?" He flashes the gold canine tooth.

"Right," I say.

"Nick Ray, look at this, though," Sergei says, and runs to his kitchen and back. He hands me a diploma big as a vinyl place mat and almost as thick. It's a Ph.D., awarded to Sergei in the field of political science.

"How did you get this?"

"Buy. Can buy many—save all trouble of school."

"You bought a Ph.D.?"

He nods. "Thought about master's, but went extra mile." He takes a sip of coffee. "Nick Ray want Ph.D.?"

"I'll pass."

He shakes his head with what seems like genuine sadness. "No ambition, Nick Ray."

Maggot Arm Joe comes in and says to Sergei, "What the fuck are you wearing?"

I tell him it's lizard.

Sergei holds one finger up in a friendly correction. "*Thick* lizard." He looks at Maggot Arm Joe. "Three thousand dollars. What do you think?"

Maggot Arm Joe shakes his head. "As long as it's thick lizard, it's a good deal." He points to the table. "Coke?"

Sergei says, "Meth."

Maggot Arm Joe goes to the kitchen to get some coffee. He calls back, "You've got three-thousand-dollar pants and nickel-and-dime drugs, Sergei." He comes into the living room with his coffee. "You've got it backward."

"It's not what's outside, but what's inside?" I say.

He toasts me. "You got it."

Self-Storage

Sergei drives us to this storage garage the Lincoln Hotel rents out for when we auction off evicted people's stuff. It's where I've been keeping the computers.

We pull off Studebaker Road into the Mr. Storage lot. Sergei's SUV, wide as a snowplow and about as economical, is the only car, or whatever it is, in the lot. They're closed for the day after Christmas, but I've got an outdoor access key, so we don't need any help getting to the computers.

Sergei says, "I am surrounded by spondees."

"What?" Maggot Arm Joe says.

"Spondees. Names with one-syllable each. Nick Ray. Joe Cole. Hank Crow. I am surrounded by spondees."

I'm fiddling with the keys in front of the big orange door.

"Shut up," Maggot Arm Joe says. "I hate it when foreigners know the language better than me."

Sergei turns to him. "I not foreigner. More American than you. I love this country. I have three green cards." He squints against the sun. "I am many Americans, right, Nick Ray?"

"I wouldn't know," I say. I undo the lock.

"No," he says, and slides the door. "That's right, Nick Ray.

You know nothing. Keep knowing nothing. Keep you healthy."

"Loud and clear," I say.

Sergei looks at us before stepping into the storage unit. "Spondees," he says. "My lot for life."

An old Datsun B210 pulls in next to Sergei's SUV.

"Trouble?" I say.

Sergei looks, frowns, shakes his head. "Just some person visiting their things. Like us."

Inside, it doesn't look like much. Or even the potential for much. There's a beat-up piano, the kind families two generations deep in tone-deaf, ham-fisted nonplayers give away when Grandma dies, leaning against the left wall. Against the right wall is one stack of four banana boxes next to one stack of five banana boxes. There are my nine 386 hard drives, one per box, laid flat and horizontal like flight luggage. I open the top box and see the computer metal that's faded nicotine brown. The storage area's cramped and the outside light doesn't reveal much.

"You got a monitor?" Maggot Arm Joe says. "I'd like to see what's in these."

"Not here," I say.

Sergei shakes his head.

But I know, whether or not these look like it, they are my future. They will be my good or bad luck, and whether they look cruddy and innocuous or not, they will lead to one extreme or the other. I run my finger along the cool metal.

There's a crunch on gravel outside the storage unit, and before I know what's happening, Sergei's standing at the entrance with a gun in some guy's face. I had no idea he had a gun on him, and my heart hiccups in my chest. The guy looks to be in his midfifties, maybe sixty. He looks like my dad, if my dad was scared crazy. He puts his hands up like we're robbing him.

Sergei says, "You have no business here."

The guy doesn't say anything. I make a move toward Sergei and Maggot Arm Joe grabs my arm.

"You are here why?" Sergei says. He holds the gun the way the kids in the movies do these days, the handle out to the side, and I wonder if he got that from the movies or if the movies got it from people like him. It doesn't matter how he holds it, though, he's a foot and a half away from the guy and he'll probably blow through the back of his head at this range.

"I was checking my food," the guy finally says. "Next door? Unit seventy-one?" He holds up a key between his index finger and thumb.

"Food?" Sergei says. "In storage?" He starts to put the gun down and me and the guy release deep breaths.

"Food," the guy says, and you can tell he's not sure whether he should go on or not. His hands are still up.

"Who puts food at Mr. Storage? Don't lie to me."

"Vac-U-Seal food." He pauses. "For terrorism."

Sergei holsters his gun. "What the shit are you talking about?"

At first, the guy's still nervous. His voice is rushed and cracky, but a while into his explanation, it becomes a pitch. The world's going to hell in a handbasket and the smart people, it seems, are locking themselves in basements with Vac-U-Seal food. The gun seems, for him and Sergei at least, forgotten.

You've met this guy. He's at the bar yapping about how the government's going to put chips in our hands. Chips in our brains. He's got theories on JFK and MLK, he knows things about J. Edgar Hoover they'd never put in books. The government doesn't let us see in Area 51 and do you know why? Of course you do, any fool can see that there's something to hide. Where's the sealed Operation Blue Book information? Where's the truth about those nuclear tests? And where, and don't think they don't know, is the rest of Kennedy's brain? He wants answers, damn it. And no one's talking—at least no one's saying anything he wants to hear. His life is fear and synchronicity and fallout shelters. He yearns for an audience, even one that just pulled a gun on him and almost blew his head off is okay. Sergei seems hooked.

The guy's going on about how much those bastards in Washington know, what they're not telling us, and so on. Me and Maggot Arm Joe roll eyes at each other while the guy rambles on about terrorism, about the lies of the Bushes, about how the entire developed world's food supply's going to be contaminated by our government or someone else's, that the world's going down, down, sinkhole down, and someone better be prepared for the calamity. This is fire and brimstone, this is Book of Job, and he shall be cast out and have no name in the street and we're talking pestilence and suffering and worldwide starvation.

Dust-bowl sorrows that would have left Woody Guthrie awestruck and mute. End-of-the-world shit. World War II was a roll of Neco wafers next to this. This guy's got bad news he wants to share, he's Nostradamus in Bermuda shorts and you better listen, friend.

Sergei says, "Your government. They know nothing about this?" When the government lies to him, Sergei calls it "your" government. When he lies to them, they're his government.

"They know plenty," the guy says. "That's just it. Haves and have-nots. They used to need have-nots as workers, but now computers are replacing the need for humans—there's too may of us. They want to kill us—you need to see. Medical science gets better—allows us to live longer, so what happens? Congress votes down nationalized health care. They won't let us sue the fucking HMOs that would rather see us die of cancer than pay for a test. They want us to fucking die. There are too many of us."

And here I'm a little frightened because the last one made sense to me.

The guy says, "Do you think they really don't know how to shut off a nuclear reactor? That they don't know how to fix this fucking terrorist problem?" He gives the three of us his business card. It reads:

Mel Collins
Vac-U-Seal Foods
Foods for the New Millennium

"You have this food here? No refrigeration?" Sergei says.

"That's the thing," Mel Collins says. "You don't need to." He leads us toward his storage unit. Things are happening too fast; the shifts have menace and I can't seem to gain a fix on the situation. If everything would slow down, I'd be okay, but I've been up all night, watched Sergei pull a gun on this guy, and now I'm walking into an infomercial.

"This is the vacuum pack," Mel says, handing a vacuum tube to Sergei and one to Maggot Arm Joe. "And this is the food dehydrator." Sergei nods.

Mel Collins throws a hunk of dried meat at me. I catch it,

ready for it to feel like a canned ham, but it's as light as balsa. Mel Collins says, "How much do you think you're holding?"

I give him a look that says I don't get it.

"How much weight?" he says. "How many pounds of meat is that?"

I've been a drug addict, I know my ounces, my metric weights, if need be. Metric was supposed to be the thing of the future back in the seventies. By the turn of the century we'd be zipping quietly from town to town in our electric cars. We'd pull into a charging station and ask how many kilometers it was to Dallas. But it didn't work out that way. The future of the past is rarely the present. Only Ed Begley Jr. has an electric car and only scientists, addicts, and narcotics officers can tell a kilo from a pound and do the math in their heads. So how much does Mel Collins's dry meat weigh? I shrug, raise and lower it a couple of times. "Five ounces."

He shakes his head. "Not even close," he says. "That's twelve pounds of meat—dehydrated and Vac-U-Sealed. And here's the thing. When you want to eat it, the process is reversible. It'll *be that same* twelve pounds of meat again."

Maggot Arm Joe takes the meat from me. "Really?"

Mel Collins says, "Well, no. That's a minor distortion. Eleven pounds. You lose some."

"Where?" Maggot Arm Joe says. "Lose it where?"

"In the process," Mel Collins says.

"No," Maggot Arm Joe says. "Physically where?"

"In the process," Mel Collins says.

"A process isn't a place," Maggot Arm Joe says. "Where does the pound of meat *go* when it's lost in this process of yours?"

Mel Collins looks confused. Sergei steps forward. "I take six-month meat," he says. He looks at us. I shake my head and Maggot Arm Joe says he'll pass.

Sergei says, "Wait outside while we do business."

We walk a hundred yards or so away. I light a cigarette and sit against the nubby bark of a palm tree. Maggot Arm Joe stands above me. There's spaghetti sauce dried on his running shoes. I hear the sound of cars revving their way onto the 405 and the 22 behind me.

Maggot Arm Joe takes a deep breath and lets it out slowly. "So we're together on this? Me and you?" He pauses. "You know we can't trust Sergei."

"We have to," I say.

"Maybe you have to," Maggot Arm Joe says. "I trust no one."

"Then how are we *together* on this?"

"In not trusting Sergei."

I wonder if he's had this talk with Sergei—the "We can't trust Nick" version. I feel hurt—little-kid hurt. Not-picked-for-kickball hurt. "You don't trust me?"

"Nothing personal, dog. Just business."

This is a finger poking at me. This is something I should address, but I don't know what to say without ending things, so I don't say anything.

Sergei and Mel Collins come out of the storage unit. I see Sergei shake hands. Maybe he's saying how sorry he is about holding a gun to Mel Collins's head. Just business, he's probably saying, too. You understand.

I lean my way up the palm tree until I'm standing. Me and Maggot Arm Joe shake hands. We're together, whatever that means, not trusting each other, if things go south with Sergei.

Sergei walks toward us. Mel Collins gets in his car and takes off.

Sergei says, "Let's take computers out."

"Why?" I say.

"Mel Collins saw things. He could talk—the computers—they should not be in there if people look." He looks at Maggot Arm Joe. "You take three. Nick Ray take three. And me."

"But all nine are mine," I say.

"Partners or no deal," Sergei says.

Fuck. He could be bluffing. "No," I say.

He throws his hands up. "Okay, then. Good luck with computer, Nick Ray."

"That's it?" I say.

"No trust, no deal," Sergei says.

"Why can't we just put the info on disks?" Joe says.

I say, "Big disks—bigger than the A-drives now. No one has those anymore." I look at Sergei, staring at me. I fold my hand. "Okay," I say. "We take three each." I make sure I grab the one with the silver duct tape that has most of the witness relocation lists in word documents. The other ones are gibberish, unless you know you're way around DOS. So long as I have the one I've already made some sense of, I'm still holding the cards.

He claps. "Much happy. See? Much better." He slaps me on the back.

"It's got five and a quarter disks?" Maggot Arm Joe says.

Sergei nods. "Must carry machine."

*　　*　　*

Later, we're in the SUV headed back to the Lincoln with the computers in the back. I say, "You don't trust Mel Collins?"

"I trust Mel Collins to deliver meat," Sergei says. "That is all."

When we get to the Lincoln, I drag my three computers up the stairs to my room and I'm asleep before I can even think about the events of the day.

Benny the Mole

I wake up about 4:30 or 5 in the afternoon—the funky gray/blue night swells into my view. I have to be at the desk at 11 P.M.—though I don't expect much traffic tonight.

I drink one beer. It slides into me, filling all the cracks and soothing the damaged nerves. The first drink of the day is a beautiful thing. Like a warm, smooth, lubricated hand job to your whole body. Peace. I wonder if this is what the monks on the mountains get—this feeling. I think about a second drink, but the alcohol's just for medical reasons until we get the money. Just to keep myself moving smoothly. And then maybe I can think about quitting and seeing what Tara thinks about a life with the new Nick Ray.

I go see Benny the Mole at the pawnshop. A few months back, I hocked some stuff, including a Harmony flat-top acoustic guitar, my old computer and monitor. The computer was good—I would have bought it back when Tara wanted to hook up via e-mail, but I couldn't afford it back.

It's full of my film-editing software, Adobe and Vegas Video and a couple others, and I let it go for some short-term money. I have no use for that computer, but I want my guitar back.

The Mole is Benny Wynn—and Benny Wynn runs the pawnshop that his mother owns. The Mole is called the Mole because he blinks all the time to keep the floating dirt and dust out of his eyes.

It's a condition he took back from being an oil-rig worker in Saudi Arabia. The story people tell, which may or may not be true, has Benny Wynn becoming Benny the Mole the minute this rig he was working on went up in flames. Burned all the hair on his face and the front part of his head. His hairline starts near the crown of his head now. No eyebrows and no eyelashes. He blinks—both eyes at once—every few seconds. The oil fire was sometime back in the late seventies. Since then, he's run his mother's pawnshop and no one calls him the Mole to his face.

I open the door and a buzzer goes off in the back room where the Mole and his mother watch TV. The mother's near deaf and I did the Mole a favor a few months back by running some wires from the TV to a speaker that I mounted right behind her head where she sits in this fat-assed recliner chair that smelled like old urine and cigarettes and bologna. A chair that smelled like a subway stop—like a tenement stairwell. She's sitting there now—I can see her—with the speaker I hooked up screaming at her from behind her head.

The Mole comes out.

"Wasn't sure you'd be open," I say.

"I'm not, really," he says. "Sometimes you get some late shoppers."

"A day late?"

"It happens."

I look around. There's the jewelry in the cases. The fine instruments. The Mole's got a soprano sax with ivory inlays over gold plate. It's beautiful. I stare at it for a moment—wondering what led to it ending up here. Only someone who knows how to play loses an instrument that good. Whoever it was, they had to know how low they'd sunk to let go of it. There's a mahogany-topped Martin R-17 hanging above the gun rack. An Epiphone. A nice Gibson Hummingbird. A couple of mid-sixties Harmonys, including the one I sold him. He hasn't cleaned it. Hasn't even added a new set of strings—it's still got the broken B-string dangling the way it did when I brought it in.

I know that Martin, I used to have one. It's the only non-collectible guitar Martin ever made. A total Edsel of an arch-top guitar. I used to have a couple of other guitars I see. I lost them all in bad decisions and desperate moments. The way you lose things. Or, at least, the way I lose things.

I've lost stuff, things, quickly in my life. People, I lost more slowly.

Behind the Mole is the gun rack. There's a kid, maybe thir-teen years old, looking at the guns the way we looked at fake guns when I was a kid, like it's the greatest toy in the world. But a thirteen-year-old can't, I suppose, be bothered with toy guns these days. They have real problems and the cops just might shoot them for carrying a fake pistol. Why not get the real thing? A depressive funk starts to settle on me, one of those you get when you really think about thirteen-year-old boys getting shot and shooting one another. The Mole tells the kid to move on, that he can buy a gun when he looks eighteen.

I shake myself out of it for the moment.

"Shopping?" the Mole says.

"Not really."

"I'll give you a deal," he says. "It's Christmas."

"Yesterday," I say.

He shrugs. "It's the *season,* is what I'm saying."

I tell him I want my Harmony back.

He blinks—his whole face makes a fist of itself. The scar tissue's a different color than his skin—it's pinker and lumped up like cauliflower heads. It looks painful. His face fists up again and releases itself. "Sure," he says. "Slow going on old guitars. Fucking eBay is killing me. I never should have taken it off your hands."

"I'll give you a hundred and twenty for it," I say. This is what he gave me for it.

Benny the Mole blinks two or three times. "A midget came in here. This is not now—I'm talking maybe fifteen years ago. A midget comes in and says to me that he wants this gorgeous nine-foot Brunswick pool table. Perfect slate—nice felt. He tells me there's two grand in his pocket—cash. I ask him how he can play—I mean he'd need a phone book to get eye level, you follow? He tells me that's his business. I ask again why he wants it and he tells me again it's his business and not mine. He puts the cash on the glass." Benny the Mole raps knuckles on the glass counter that I'm leaning on. "I didn't sell him that table. Cash on the counter and I said no. Do you know why?"

"I don't know," I say. "You hate midgets?"

"Because he would have sawed the table's legs. Things have integrity. Money has integrity—and I won't let any midget with a roll of bills destroy the inherent integrity of things, you follow?"

"No."

"I let you have that guitar for what I gave you and what am I?" He holds his palms up in some parody of wonderment and puzzlement. "I'll tell you what I'm not. I'm not a businessman. The rules—in business—must apply to everyone, or else the system's integrity is compromised."

"You didn't even add new strings," I say.

"What I did is my business."

I hear his mother wheezing in the next room in between commercials.

"How much?" I say.

"Two seventy-five," he says.

"You only gave me one-twenty," I say.

"What am I running? Charity?"

I make a face.

Benny the Mole says, "Don't try to make me feel bad for earning an honest buck." He waddles back along the counter and grabs my guitar. He puts it on top of a box that was once used for some black, greasy auto parts. The box smells like burned motor oil.

"Two hundred," he says. "Merry Christmas."

I pay him, pick it up, and walk out.

The Garage People

I'm looking through the second of my three computers, the one with the silver duct tape—the one with relocated witnesses *A–F* in a nice, clean word document. There's so much shit here—information I can't believe anyone ever wanted to record—but it *is* the government. And I found them—the unfortunate *A*s through *F*s that will make me rich enough to leave this life. I feel mildly sorry for them, but sense a certain them-or-me vibe that melts the sharp corners of my guilt.

I scan them down by location and find that, no surprise, none are in Long Beach or Los Angeles. What's wild, though, is that there's a whole nest of them down in Orange County. I MapQuest a few of the ones in the nicer neighborhoods.

The information on these hard drives only goes back to 1986; anyone relocated and protected prior to that is probably in some file in the bowels of some building, dusty and forgotten.

One not dusty and not forgotten, and not very far away, is Mr. Frank Carr. Mr. Frank Carr—he had the "Mr." legally added so that people would have to address him as "Mr."—Mr. Frank

Carr got in over his head with heroin and turned evidence against, among others, a Spencer Durrell, a major player in Vegas and a major drug dealer, who also dealt in various chemical weaponry and anarchist cookbook goodies, to read Mr. Carr's reports.

Mr. Frank Carr is now known as Timothy R. Shay and he lives in a development of hilltop town houses in the Anaheim Hills. I run a Web search for him and find out he does custom tile work in high-end kitchens and bathrooms.

On the follow-up paperwork to Mr. Frank Carr's case is the information that the feds botched Spencer Durrell's case and only put him away for two years. He's in Vegas, and to hear what they say about him is that he's as mean as rickshaw and talking to him is like cutting meat with a spork. Useless and futile. The physical description is that he's five-ten and wears an eye patch over the right eye and to have that eye patch walk through your door is like having death incarnate come calling and he'd probably love to know what became of Mr. Frank Carr. And I'm hoping Mr. Frank Carr will pay handsomely for that not to happen.

It's 7 P.M. when I tell Sergei the specifics, names, directions, and so on, of what I've found.

It's 8 P.M. and we're headed east on the 22, driving out toward the Anaheim Hills under a crooked smile of a moon, and we decide we'll ask Mr. Frank Carr for ten grand to get his name off our list.

I'm in the backseat.

"Nick Ray," Sergei says from behind the wheel. "You must talk tonight."

"In what sense?" I say.

"You must do talk," he says. "Do the talk."

"Do the talk? You mean talk to Mr. Frank Carr?"

Sergei nods.

Maggot Arm Joe says, "And what are we saying?"

Sergei says, "You not talking—you upset people."

"How?" Maggot Arm Joe says.

"You act like you think you're smarter than other people."

Maggot Arm Joe lights a cigarette and cracks his window. "I *am* smarter than other people."

Sergei nods. "But you need to show them." He looks over at Maggot Arm Joe. "That bad for business. Nick Ray blends. Like blending lizard."

I'm nervous, but Sergei's confidence buoys me a bit. Unless I'm reading it wrong, I think being called a blending lizard is meant to inspire confidence.

"Chameleon, you mean?" Maggot Arm Joe says. "Nick's like a chameleon?"

Sergei says, "You see? Nick Ray would have just nodded and left it at blending lizard. I talk—people understand. No need for you to make correct." Sergei simultaneously puts the blinker on and turns into the next lane without looking. "Look out," he says in a calm voice. The car next to us swerves and the driver lays on the horn for a good five seconds. Sergei cuts him off, smiles, and waves: "Fuck you, mister." He looks back at me. "That lucky little man. Lucky we have somewhere to be."

We get to the bottom of Stagecoach Road and wind our way up toward Mr. Frank Carr, aka Timothy Shay's house. At the top of the hill, we take a left on Ruby Lane. I point the house out to Sergei and we park down the street in a guest spot. The guest spot is at the end of the dead end, and we have to pass four houses on the left and five on the right before we get to where we're going. I worry about being spotted here and then I catch myself: *We're not killing anyone,* I tell myself. *People can see us. It's okay.*

This calms me and it's a good thing, because plenty of people *do* see us. We're not hard to miss. I look out of place most places. Maggot Arm Joe's probably the only black guy in this neighborhood, and Sergei's wearing a black leather suit that looks straight out of Elvis's '68 comeback special.

The street is lined with old men sitting in their garages. Some sit on couches drinking beers. Some at card tables with empty seats around them. All of them wave and nod as we pass. We wave back.

"What the shit is going on?" Sergei says.

"They're garage people," Maggot Arm Joe says.

"Garage is a kind of people?"

"Retired people," Maggot Arm Joe says. "Retired *men,* actually. They sit in garages and watch the sun go from one end of the sky to the other. It's a whole culture."

"How do you know this?" I say.

"My father's a garage person," he says.

"Where?"

"Right around here," he says. "Tustin. In Orange County."

"You never mentioned him," I say.

Maggot Arm Joe points to his maggot arm. "We've kind of lost touch. I'm not his favorite reminder that life has some curveballs."

I think of my own parents. We've had our troubles, but I should give them a call. It *is* the holidays. Maybe we can say something to one another without setting something off.

"This is it?" Sergei says, pointing to the right.

I look at the number and nod. We single-file our way up the walk.

A woman who looks like Martha Stewart, like Sydney Barrow, like blond money itself answers the door. I smell something freshly baked, sweet with cinnamon coming from the kitchen. We tell her we're there to see Mr. Shay and she gets him. We meet the family.

Mr. Frank Carr's transition to Timothy Shay is so complete, so smooth, that I wonder if the wife and kids came with the house as part of the government's program. You've seen these people. You're buying a cheap frame at a Rite Aid. The family in the frame, that's who I'm looking at, trip their way through piles of yesterday's torn wrapping paper.

"What can I do for you guys?" Mr. Shay says, looking at us with mild confusion. Mild confusion, until he gets to Sergei in his black leather suit, then he seems to realize we're not good news.

Sergei looks at me and it becomes clear that this is what he meant by me doing the talking. I stumble for a second, not sure what to say.

"It's about a tile job," I say.

"I've got an office," he says. "A Web site." He starts to lean back into his perfect house, his perfect life. The door inches toward closing.

I say, "It's a tile job for a Mr. Frank Carr."

That stops him.

"He's a friend of ours," I say. "Mr. Frank Carr."

His face opens, whole and vulnerable. He's been hoodwinked. Bamboozled. Never saw it coming, but should have known. We stand around quietly shifting the weight from one foot to the other while he recovers from our sucker punch.

"Come in," he says. He leads us to a heavy wood-paneled room and tells Mrs. Shay he'll be out in a while. It's about a job, he tells her, and these men can't wait. He closes the door and doesn't sit down.

"So how much do you want?"

"Ten grand gets your name off the lists," I say.

He looks at me, not saying anything.

Sergei says, "Ten grands stop us from sending the information to Durrell."

He nods slowly. "Ten gets me everything and I never hear from you again?"

This seems way too easy. We must have asked for too little. But it's too late. We'll just jack the price up on the next guy. "Sure," I say.

"It's a deal then," he says. He slides over a legal pad that has THINGS TO DO across the top. "Give me an address and give me a time. Try to make it a weekday." He pauses. "It's easier for me to be away then."

I can't believe how well this is going. I figured there'd be some struggle, some name-calling, some threats hurled back and forth, but maybe that's shit for the movies. This is business. This guy's willing to pay.

Maggot Arm Joe says, "You don't seem to have much of a problem with this, Mr. Shay."

Sergei gives Maggot Arm Joe a dirty look.

"I try to worry only about things I can control," Shay says. "I don't see me holding the cards here."

"That's it?" Maggot Arm Joe says.

He shrugs in a weary way. "I had the fight kicked out of me a long time before I met you three." He takes a deep breath and lets it out quickly. "Now. I have accepted your terms, and it's time for you to go. Give me the address where we can end this."

I write my address and the phone number of the Lincoln on the pad and slide it across the table. Sergei grabs it.

"Which address?" he says, and looks. He says, "I have better phone for you to call." And he writes his cell number, for reasons I can't quite see, and I wonder if he doesn't trust me. He puts the pad back on the desk and slides it over to the man who used to be Mr. Frank Carr. "Yes," Sergei says. "That proper address."

I'm doing quick math in my head, thinking about a bunch of Mr. Frank Carrs willing to shut us up, thinking about a fast three hundred grand split three ways. I look over at Sergei and get a quick shiver, knowing he's violent, and there's Maggot Arm Joe, who's smarter than me and pretty much said he's in it for himself—a bad set of circumstances when there's $300,000, or more, on the table.

And it's settled. We make nice with Martha Stewart on our way out, we'd love to stay but we can't, just a quick business trip. On the way back to the car, all the garage people wave at us. We wave to them all twice—once on the walk to the car and once on the drive out of the neighborhood. When we go past his house, I see the man who used to be Mr. Frank Carr watch us roll by from behind the curtain.

Twenty Bucks and Some Uppers

I walk in the front door of the Lincoln. Hank Crow's at the desk.

"Any messages?" I say.

"That strange little girl you see came by."

"Tara?"

"You see other strange little girls?"

"Not to my knowledge," I say. "Define *strange*."

"The little black girl with all the earrings."

"She's Hawaiian," I say.

"She looks black to me," Hank says. "You sure we're talking about the same friend?"

I point to my ear. "About ten earrings all the way up?"

Hank Crow says, "That's her—those ears look like you could hang shower curtains off them."

"Tara," I say. "What did you tell her?"

"Told her you were out with that Russian criminal friend of yours," he says. "Then I let her in your room."

"She still there?" I say.

"She is, unless she zipped down the fire escape." He looks at me suspiciously. "What the fuck you got a kiddie pool for?"

I can't think of anything to say. "I don't," I say.

"You do. I saw it in the box. That little friend of yours got all excited." Hank Crow mimics a little-girl falsetto that sounds nothing like Tara. "'Oh, he got the kiddie pool, he got the kiddie pool.'" Hank snorts. "Seemed like she was about to bust."

"Listen, Hank," I say. "How about pulling a double tonight?"

"Why should I?"

"Because it's Christmas?" I say.

"It's not," he says.

"It's the Christmas season," I say. "The season of giving."

"It's Kwanzaa."

"I don't mean disrespect," I say. "But isn't that a made-up religion?"

"What the hell do you call Christmas?" Hank Crow says.

"Fair enough," I say.

"An all-nighter?" He thinks for a minute and looks up at me. "You in love, son?"

"Something like that."

"Something close?"

"Something very close."

He shrugs. "Get me twenty bucks and some uppers and thank me."

I tell him it's a deal.

Smart Chicks Ball Better

I take the stairs a couple at a time. There's an envelope on my door with my name on it. I open it—on top is a handwritten "thank you" from Tara. I look at the page—it's one of Tara's done-at-work fantasies, typed single-spaced on Los Angeles County Parole stationery:

Her Christmas Fantasy

She doesn't eat for 48 hours. 24 hours before coming over, she takes several laxatives and then cleans herself out with as many enemas as it takes until she's empty and drained. She lets herself into the apartment. Then, she's to wait, naked, until he comes home. When she hears him outside the door, she turns the video camera on.

He walks in the room.

"You think you want this?" he asks.

"Yes, sir," she says.

"It's important that you remember, later, when you've lost control—when you feel me inside of you, controlling you—it's important that you remember that you wanted this."

"Yes, sir. I want this."

"You've begged for this?" he says.

"Yes, sir."

"It's disgusting," he says.

"Yes, sir," she says.

"But you can't control your desires, can you?"

"No, sir. I can't control my desires."

"And you want this?"

"Yes, sir," she says.

"You need this?"

"Yes, sir," she says.

"What do you need?" he asks.

"I need to lose control. To feel possessed. To feel like I have no say in what happens to me. To be told what I am—to be forced to feel how weak I am in the face of my desires."

"That turns you on?"

"Yes, sir."

"And you're weak now? In the face of your desire."

"Yes, sir."

"And you'd do anything to feel the way you need to feel, wouldn't you?"

"Yes, sir."

"Thank me for this."

"Thank you, sir."

He tells her to fill five enema bags with hot water and set them up in the living room. She obeys. She's told to stand in front of him and step into the straitjacket. She obeys and is bound into it—arms tied across her body. He runs a chain around her waist and padlocks it in front of her. He puts restraints on her ankles. He tells her to kneel and he caresses her head.

"Are you ready?" he asks.

She tells him she's ready. He has her lie on her back in the pool. He connects the ankle restraints to the chain at her waist so that her knees are brought up toward her stomach. Her legs are spread. He inserts the enema tip in her ass, unlatches the clamp, and sits back.

"You begged for this."

"I begged for this, sir."

After the second 2-quart bag is emptied, she begins to spasm. He reaches down and begins gently caressing her cunt. He tells her that she must warn him if she's about to come. Every time she warns him—he stops. She begins coughing—but nothing comes out. First, it's a dry cough, then wet, then she turns her head to the side and vomits out the clear water. Several more quarts are emptied. She vomits them back out. He teases her until she's convulsing, weakened, broken by desire and begging to be released, and then he lets her.

I read Tara's story a couple of times. This really isn't something I would have thought of, but she becomes so strange, so filled with joy, whenever we do one of her fantasies, that the turn-on is infectious. We haven't yet repeated one of her fantasies; they're new every time and I'm struck with a memory of when I was a kid:

I'm ten, maybe twelve, and I find a stack of porno magazines under my dad's bed. One of them, I remember, had a centerfold of Joe Louis's daughter. Another one, the one I'm reminded of now, had a cover story titled NEW STUDY SHOWS: SMART CHICKS BALL BETTER. I didn't give it much thought at the time, but frequently as an adult, having sex with a smart woman, it pops back into my head.

I wonder for a moment about what L.A. County would think of the amount of time she must put into these, how many hours at her desk are spent typing away at her fantasies.

I open the door.

The lights are off and I flick the switch but the lights don't come on. It's then I see the ring of candles around the pool, which is inflated and in which is Tara naked and facing away from me. My futon bed is turned into a sofa, so there's space in the middle of the room. I lock the door and dump my keys on the bookcase by the door.

"Nick?" she says.

"Yes?"

"Is this okay?" she says. "This one?"

"Yes," I say. "It's okay."

Later, I'm amazed things pretty much went just like in her story. The only differences from the story:

1. We had to have her on her knees facing down instead of on her back. When she first started puking the water up, she started to choke on it, so I turned her over.
2. The straitjacket also locked through the legs. We had to leave that strap loose.
3. Right after she first started puking, something red came out and I got scared as hell, thinking it was blood, thinking it was something from inside her. I told her we

were done, sorry, but it wasn't going to happen. She told me it was a Gummi Bear that she'd put up her ass so she'd know when she stared vomiting that it had gone all the way through her. She needed, she said, to know that she wasn't puking stomach bile; that would be unsafe. If, when she started puking, the red Gummi Bear came out, that meant she was vomiting the enema water and that everything was okay. The Gummi Bear was a safety precaution.

4. We had to move to the tub, which was harder on her knees and more difficult to fuck in, but the pool was filling up and emptying it would have been an annoying interruption.

We're on the couch, watching TV.

Tara's wrung out and messy and tired, but she's about as happy as I've ever seen a person after sex, or after anything else, for that matter. The clear vomit, we did this for a couple of hours and we must have run over twenty liters of water through her, is kind of caked and dried on her cheeks. I start to wipe her cheeks and it flakes off.

"You want something to eat?" I say.

She shakes her head. "I'm fine."

Neither of us says anything for a moment and my mind drifts.

"What are you thinking?" she says.

"Wondering what Mr. Thomas would say about my life decisions." She gives me a quizzical look and I explain that Mr. Thomas was my high school social-studies teacher and he had this monthlong exercise where we were paired up, boy/girl/ boy/girl, and given lives. I was with Carol Stone and we were supposed to have some jobs at some factory, some of the same blue-collar dead-end shit that killed all our fathers and mothers, and the trick to the class was you got a job, a mortgage, and all the rest of the standard responsibilities in life. It was all made up, picked out of a hat and meant to teach you about the way adults lived. Some people did well, some got the shaft. In that way it was supposed to be a life primer. And, I suppose it was.

Carol and I had trouble with our budget and we ended up divorced. I joked about it in class and Mr. Thomas tore into me, yelled at me in front of the class that someday, some fucking day, my wise-ass mouth would get me in trouble and someday I'd be faced with those life responsibilities and I would have to make some decisions. I tell Tara that I was laughing because there wasn't a slot in his hypothetical life-choices class for a guy who drank too much and a lesbian who had an enema fetish and what hard life choices they might have to make.

"Too bad," she says. "You might have passed."

I don't tell her about the drunk's trouble with criminals. I stay clear of whether or not our drunk is in love with the lesbian with the enema fetish.

I kiss her head gently until she falls asleep.

In the Nighttime III

Later, Tara's asleep and I'm listening to some late-night talk show. The topic is circumcision. There are pros and cons. There are callers on both sides. It seems strange to have an opinion, beyond your own cock, to me, but people are pretty fired up. A doctor calls in, says he's an expert. The host asks how.

"I reconstruct foreskins," the doctor says. "Many young men make a mistake—they're nineteen, maybe twenty, and they're at that age when they want the same hair as their friends, the same clothes as their friends—"

"The same *penis* as their friends," the host says.

"Ex*actly*," the doctor says. "I reverse the process. Give them back what they've lost."

"Is it the same?" the host says. "The restoration?"

"I like to tell my patients this: only God can make a rose and only God can make a foreskin."

I picture this guy walking through his life saying this, I wonder how many times he's said that to someone, *Only God can make a rose and only God can make a foreskin*. I think about his kids, how often they've heard this at dinner or something. His wife must cringe and wish him dead now and then.

"So it's not the same?" the host says.

The doctor pauses. "It's never the same. But I do my best."

Another guy calls in and says he hates his parents because of his circumcision. The host tells him to make it quick, his hate, because time is running out on the show. Tomorrow, she promises, she'll be interviewing a guy who talks to vegetables. I take the headphones off until the voices are a distant buzz. The headphones vibrate in my fingertips every time someone says whatever it is they have to say.

Tara's chest rises and falls a little. She sleeps so quietly that I get scared every once in a while and I have to check close to make sure she's still breathing.

DAY 3
DECEMBER 27

Enter Mookie

Tara takes off around one in the morning. I'm out of smokes and I stay up most of the night chewing Nicorette and listening to the insectian buzz of the streetlights outside my window and thinking about drinking.

Around 6 A.M., I get tired of thinking and head down to the street to find someone to talk to so I can take my mind off me and my troubles. I start to go to Wang's Everything's a Dollar Chinese Food/Doughnut House, but I realize I'm tapped out. Benny the Mole last night set me back to my last twenty cents. Broke as I am, I usually have enough for something at Wang's, but now I can't even get coffee. I'm kind of shaky and I need a meal, so I set out for Sergei's, figuring we're in business and we're about to turn a quick ten grand, he can buy me some hash browns.

But Sergei's not at home. I check in at Wang's and he's not there either. I stop back by the Lincoln, but no luck.

He's gone.

He's playing DB Cooper with me. He's swept away and swallowed whole by the natives like Michael Rockefeller.

He's Amelia Earhart—gone over to the other side and living as a geisha.

Where did he go?

It hits me that this may not be funny. I can't really trust Sergei and I've put myself in a situation where I *have* to trust Sergei. Where could he be? Not off with Mr. Frank Carr? He could pocket the ten grand all by himself. But, if he was going to screw us, it would make more sense to wait until after the basket fills up a bit, and then screw us. If this is a score, it's a big one. But he might have gone to Carr and gotten the ten grand? He wouldn't. My head spins.

I can't be thinking like this.

I need sleep. I need food. Money for food.

And my head's doing this ugly dance when Mookie the Fisherman comes up and nearly bumps into me with his shopping cart that has two white five-gallon buckets and two deep-sea fishing poles sticking out. Mookie lives by the riverbed, he sleeps tucked in between the spaces the pillars carve in the freeway overpass. They bust him out every couple of months and he has to find a new place to live, which makes no sense to me, since it's not as if it's a place that's being used for anything else.

They arrest him and he pinballs north and south. Last I heard he was under the Pacific Coast Highway exit overpass. Sometimes, he lives in the old Pike Subway. He's told me there are still some of the old arts-and-crafts booths down there, still a couple of the human-pulled carriages they zipped the rich back and forth on. On the overpass, you can see his stuff, his and a few other people's, if you walk up by the river. There's sweatshirts and blankets all laid between the supports and you look for those if you need to find him.

"Better watch out, Nick," Mookie says as he pulls his cart to a stop. "Don't want a hook in your ear."

I'm not sure I heard him right and I don't say anything.

He points to his fishing poles, halved and bent over, but with the sharp lures and hooks sticking out. "End up in an ear—got to cut the ear."

"I follow," I say.

"Ear ain't like no fish mouth," Mookie says. "Ear don't grow back."

"Fish mouths grow back?"

"They do," he says, and he looks up at the sky like he's on some game show and the category's *things that grow back*. "Fish mouths, genital warts." He pauses, stumped. "Fifty-one percent of a worm."

"What?" I say.

"You can cut a worm up to a half and the back half'll grow back," Mookie says. "Down to fifty-one percent."

"But if you cut, say, fifty-one percent, there's still forty-nine percent on the other side—wouldn't that grow back?"

He shakes his head. "I'm talking the head side. Fifty-one percent and the head, and you're in business—the worm grows back." Some fish thump against the side of one of his buckets and I can see their angry silhouettes shadow-flash through the white plastic in the sunlight.

I point to them. "Can you eat those?"

"Nope." Mookie dips a hand in, comes up with a fish that's gray as concrete and lumpy as wet stucco. "Toxic from the navy dumping all that shit in the harbor all these years—plus the Japanese tankers. Pretty much poison—these fish."

"Why do you keep them?"

"Sell 'em as bait—Bondo Bob at the pier gives me a buck a foot."

"What does he use them for?"

Mookie looks at me like I'm an idiot. "I told you, man. They's bait."

"But if they're poison, won't eating them make the big fish poison?"

Mookie shakes his head. "You know what happens when you ask these kinds of questions?"

I don't say anything.

"You don't get a dollar a foot for your catch, I'll tell you that."

Mookie starts to push off east toward the pier.

"Can you lend me a couple of bucks?" I say, and right away feel like shit for asking Mookie—he needs what he has. I make a mental note to get it back to him with interest.

He holds up two fingers like the peace sign. "Two things they'll say about Mookie. Mookie never showed up late and he never lent money," he says. "They'll carve that on my headstone."

"C'mon, Mookie."

He considers me for a moment. "Thought you had some big-money thing cooked up with that Russian fellow."

"Where'd you hear that?"

"From the Russian—from Stalin's mouth."

I shake my head—I'm having trouble focusing, but I know that if Sergei's talking about this, there's no way that could possibly be anything but very bad news. "I don't know what you're talking about with Sergei," I say. "But I need a couple of bucks for some coffee and food. Can you help me?"

"You look bad."

"I feel bad," I say.

"Tell you what," Mookie says. "I'm covered on the fish—don't need any work—I'll hook you up with some work with Bondo Bob." He smiles proudly. "I been knowing Bob long enough to set you up."

"Set me up with what?"

"Work," he says. "You ain't too proud to work, are you?"

I shake my head and we go up to the pier to see if we can, as Mookie puts it, wrestle me up some food money.

Live Bait

The work I'm not too proud for turns out to be riding a bike with an igloo cooler mounted on it, restocking Bondo Bob Lopez's "Live Bait" machines all over Long Beach. A live-bait machine is, if you haven't seen one, pretty much like a Pepsi or Coke machine, except that it's stuffed with live worms and live shrimp. It's also a bit of a misnomer, since there's some dead lumps of mackerel and mackerel chunks on dry ice. The mackerel are apparently good if you want to get the big fish. According to Bondo Bob, these chunks make the halibut and the tuna go nuts—they forget what was on that little dust-speck brain of theirs once these mackerel are dropped in the water. You'll need another bucket for your fish. You'll need to hire a helper, hell, you'll need to rent a backhoe to carry them home, the way Bob tells it.

But here's how the machines work:

You're out driving, out in the world, and it hits you that you need live bait.

You drop in a dollar, and you get a squirrelly handful of live bait. He's got ten machines all over town, usually outside of liquor stores.

The worst part isn't, as you might suspect, the loading of the live-bait machine. It's the unloading of what Bondo Bob calls, in between spits of tobacco juice, "spoilage."

"Spoilage, that's the problem," Bondo Bob had said. "Live bait ain't live forever—if it were, I'd be a millionaire."

And so I spend most of my morning scooping out handfuls of dead, stinking worms and piles of translucent, pinkish greasy shrimp. I wipe the compartments clean with some blue fluid called Fabuloso, replace the dead, scummy fish with scoopfuls of writhing masses of live bait. The shrimp are jumpy, they hop around like summer crickets, jumping so fast you have to close the door as soon as they're in, or they'll come flying out. Their little legs thrash in my hand, and they're ticklish and I'm getting some kind of funky rash in both palms. The shrimp make a squishy wet crunchy noise when you accidentally step on them. They make a noise like a scream and they disturb the hell out of me.

The worms are slow and kind of gentle the way they loll all over one another and, if you forget what they are, comforting to watch. Kind of hypnotic, but then I haven't eaten or slept in a while. I'm bent over, dividing worms into a compartment that they live in until their number's punched. From behind me, a car blares its horn and I jump up and hit my head on a sharp edge of the machine. I turn around and see Sergei's SUV. He leans out from the driver's side. The sun glares on the windshield, so I'm guessing that Maggot Arm Joe is with Sergei, but I can't quite make him out.

"Nick Ray?" Sergei says. He gets out of his car, not bothering to pull fully to the curb or close his door. Cars swerve and honk and he gives them the finger. Maggot Arm Joe gets out of the SUV.

I'm rubbing my head, stars are swirling, and I hear a high-pitched scream that I'm not sure whether it's coming from the shrimp or inside my head. I feel sick. The ground's swelling, people are changing shape.

Sergei steps up beside me. "What the shit is going on?"

I try to clear my head by shaking it, but I just end up on my knees throwing up. My puke smells like stale tap beer and Chinese food.

Sergei sidesteps the puke without moving his arms and he looks like the guy from *Riverdance*. "Be careful. These six-hundred-dollar shoes."

I nod and it takes most of my strength to stand up and avoid falling.

Maggot Arm Joe says, "Shit, Nick. What's wrong with you?"

I tell him the general story—lack of sleep, lack of food, a vicious headache, the whole tainted-bait thing. Sergei tells me I should have come to him. I tell him I did. That I looked for him in several places.

"No, Nick Ray," he says. "You couldn't have. Home all day—all you need to do is ring, I answer."

He's lying, but I don't have the energy to pursue why.

Maggot Arm Joe helps me up. "You okay?"

"I've got to eat," I say.

Sergei says to get in the car, he'll buy me breakfast. Then we have work to do.

"Throw bike in back," he says.

Maggot Arm Joe starts to load the bike in, but Sergei makes a face. "What smell?"

"Bait," I say.

"No bait in Sergei's car," he says. He tries to take the cooler off the bike, but it's held in place with thick strips of metal that look like the earthquake bracing they use on water heaters. He struggles with it for a moment, then he lays it down in the street and starts kicking at the cooler. He kicks at it for a while, but that doesn't seem to do much. I'm leaning up against the SUV, and I feel awful, it's like I can feel my organs doing their work, they're knocking and pinging like a bad engine, begging for attention. My stomach rumbles like old pipes in a wall. I think I could be dying. Maybe I'm overreacting, but how *do* people feel when they're dying?

Sergei's pissed off—breathing hard and ready to lose it. He's stubborn as a tick—not ready to give in once he starts. I file this away, memorize the way he looks right before the steam valve blows. He takes his nine-millimeter out of his shoulder holster and he shoots the bracings off the bike. The bullets ricochet off the pavement and end up God knows where. I flinch. People die this way. I think of the kid killed up north in L.A. last week—some clowns were shooting up into the air, into nothing, and one of the bullets came down on a kid walking home from school. This happens. There are repercussions to this. There are families, haunted mothers, a world of sadness and lost hope and memories.

The cooler explodes and worms and shrimp and mackerel pour out the top and funk up the asphalt. There's a fishy burning smell and I start to get sick again.

Sergei picks up the bike and puts it in the back. He tells Maggot Arm Joe to get me in the car. Maggot Arm Joe tosses me in the backseat like a bag of laundry and gets in the front. He says to Sergei, "I wish you'd knock that off."

"What?" Sergei says.

"That fucking gun," Maggot Arm Joe says. "Guns are—no

need to be using that gun." He pauses. "On a fucking *cooler*."

Sergei waves him off. "Guns not to be scared of. Gun like people—except gun have no legs."

I'm wondering if I heard that right. Voices aren't reaching me. I'm driving in the mountains and the signal's weak. I close my eyes and pass out.

My guess is that I've been out a couple of hours. Across the sky, halfway up instead of overhead, which is how you tell it's winter in California, the sun's knocking on noon. We're in a parking lot outside of the Long Beach Diner on Ocean Boulevard. Sergei's sitting next to me smoking a cigarette. He's wearing another lace shirt, forest green, with what looks like black leather pants that make a wet farty noise as he moves in the leather seats of the SUV. I look around—Maggot Arm Joe's gone and the bike's not in the back anymore. Sergei gives me a Pall Mall.

"We have much work to do, Nick Ray."

I light the cigarette, thinking it'll settle my stomach, but I take one hit and it flubbers its way down and back up. I swallow hard. There's an acidy puke burn eating its way into the back of my throat and nose.

"Much work to do. Cannot have sick and throw up people." Sergei takes a knife that's wide as a credit card out of his belt holster. He's got a loaf of Wonder bread next to him and he takes out a slice and carves off the crust, or what passes for a crust in Wonder bread. When he's got it cut down to just the white part, he packs it in his palm until it's the size of a golf ball. He holds it in front of my face. "Suck, Nick Ray."

I look at him.

"Good for you. Good for stomach, Wonder bread." He shoves it in my mouth and, oddly enough, I start to feel better. "Don't swallow," he says. "Suck like candy."

I do as he says, the bread gets sugary, and we sit quietly for a moment. He sighs like an old man, like a dog. "This very big deal. Very big. You need to be better."

"I'm feeling better," I say. "Need some food."

"Suck bread."

"I need *food*," I say.

He gives me three twenty-dollar bills. I take them and thank him.

"You cannot be a puke man," Sergei says. He says it as if he cares and I think for a moment that maybe I can trust him. Then it flashes on me that he wasn't in this morning when he said he was. Or maybe he was—who the hell knows?

"I'm okay," I say. "Tired—but okay."

"We have to meet man. You can't be puking bait."

"I hear you." I pause, looking around. "Where's Maggot Arm Joe?"

"Setting up meeting." Sergei points across the street and I see Maggot Arm Joe on a pay phone at a Chevron station. He's writing something down.

"With who?" I say.

"Mr. Fudge."

I pause. A small bug zips by my face and I swat at it. "Mr. Fudge?"

"That his name."

"That's the name the government gave him?" I say.

"Government not name Mr. Fudge."

"He's not a relocated witness?"

Sergei shakes his head. "Oil tycoon. Very rich man."

Maggot Arm Joe begins to walk back across the street. He's got a nice suit on, black pants and jacket with gold silk shirt with a darker shade of gold tie. He looks like a movie star, like Denzel Washington, maybe, and for the first time I get a glimpse of his pre–junkie/lawyer life. I look at Sergei. "How does this Mr. Fudge fit in? If he's not on our list?"

"I told you," Sergei says. "He very rich man."

"So?" I say. The bread ball is getting gooey, so I swallow it. "So's Bill Gates—we're not meeting Bill Gates. Lot of rich people we're not meeting. Why him?"

Maggot Arm Joe gets in. Sergei gets out of the backseat and into the driver's seat.

"What is story?" Sergei says.

Maggot Arm Joe says, "We're on. The man wants to meet at the observation bar on the *Queen Mary* at five."

I'm getting frustrated. Shit has been going on behind my back. "Who the fuck is this guy and why are we meeting him?"

Sergei looks at me in the rearview. He looks as stoic and self-important as a head on Mount Rushmore. "Maybe if you don't have bait side business, you keep up better, Nick Ray."

Maggot Arm Joe says, "He's Mr. Fudge—his daddy made a fortune in oil."

"That much I know," I say.

"But not enough of a fortune for Mr. Fudge—who got involved with some very bad people. Major-level real estate fraud and such. S&L shit—white-collar bad boys. Some of said bad people turned on the man and he did a stint at some Club Fed jail in Connecticut. Leona Helmsley, Mike Milken, and this Mr. Fudge all played golf on taxpayers' nickel, right?

Anyway—now the man's out, he's still rich, and he wants to pin some people to the wall for talking about him to the feds." Maggot Arm Joe shrugs. "Problem is—he can't find these people."

"How do we fit in? How do we even know about this guy?" I say.

Maggot Arm Joe says, "My firm defended him." He looks out the window. "I defended him. I got him a choice deal. Man should have been put away for ten lifetimes. He loves me."

"You defended him against what?" I say. "What charges?"

Maggot Arm Joe shakes his head. "We don't have time for the list. Mr. Fudge has his fingers in a lot of pies. He's got more pies than he's got fingers, this guy."

"We agreed we'd sell the witnesses the lists."

"We didn't agree on shit. We can make one score and leave the nasty business to the nasty men, this way."

"No," I say.

Sergei says, "We did one Nick Ray's way. We do one Maggot Arm's way. We see what works better, no?"

I need for this to not last very long—there's a temptation to go for the quick money. "I'm not comfortable with him buying names from us," I say.

Maggot Arm Joe says, "We're not even sure we have the folks he's looking for. Remains to be seen—me and you gotta check. For now, the man's checking us out—see if we're doing business. Tonight, we're just talking, but we're not *talking*. He wants to meet on the *Queen*—he's some sort of boat nut—only does business on water or something."

"Why can't we just blackmail the people *on* the list?"

"What difference?" Sergei says.

"The difference is when you go to the people who want the list—you're getting the people on the list killed."

Maggot Arm Joe says, "Not necessarily."

"Pretty much," I say.

"How do you know?"

And that's true. What the fuck do I know about these people?

"Fuck them," Sergei says. "I businessman. Businessman go where money is. People who want the people have more money than people who want to hide."

"We can get rich without anyone getting killed," I say.

"You don't like terms, you sell fish in machines, Nick Ray. That good life."

"Fuck you," I say. He glares at me from the rearview and I try my best to stay tough and not back down.

Maggot Arm Joe looks at both of us and leans over the seat. "Look—this guy's loaded and we don't even know if we're going to hook up here." He looks over at Sergei and then back at me. "So let's all calm down, okay? Nothing's been decided. Plus—this guy's not some mobster—he's an oilman. He's not going to kill anyone." He pauses. Sergei nods and I look away. "Are we all cool, now?"

Sergei lights a cigarette. "Sergei cool. Never not cool."

I feel trapped. Claustrophobic and prickly. "Yeah," I say. "I'm cool."

"Good," Maggot Arm Joe says. "Now we got some time to kill."

Sergei puts the SUV in gear and barrels out into the traffic without looking. "Look out, little fucking people," he says calmly.

I look at my watch. It's right around noon. "I need a shower."

"You certainly do, my friend," Maggot Arm Joe says.

"I love supply and demand," Sergei says, and he looks genuinely happy, as if he's forgotten the tension of a minute ago, which is, in its own way, as scary as the anger itself.

A Floating City Awash in Elegance

I shower and get a little sleep and eat five dollars' worth of food at Wang's, which is a lot of food, even if it's not very good. I check in at the desk and Hank Crow tells me Tara left a message. I call her back and it's good news, for me, at least. Someone in Jenny's family's died back in Michigan and so Jenny has to stay all week, instead of two days, and Tara's free for the rest of the week. She asks if she can come over and I tell her later—I have to take care of some business first. I'm thrilled, there's no way she's coming over for sex, since she's wrung out and exhausted enough to have called into work, so she's coming over to hang. I give Hank Crow the phone.

He gives me a look. "What business you got that's more important than a lady friend?"

"None—if you put it that way."

"You put it that way when you made the decision to put the lady off." Hank pauses. "This business—it have anything to do with Sergei?"

I tell him it does.

"That boy's as bad an idea as a traffic circle, son." He

pauses. "You're making trouble for yourself if you do business with him."

"You bought a TV from him," I say.

"If you'd just bought a TV from him, we wouldn't be talking. You should get out and get out now."

"Thanks for the concern," I say. "But we can't be having this talk right now, okay?"

Hank holds up his hands like I'm robbing him. "I'm just an old man at a desk. God forbid my years of learning how this world works might help some of you younger folk."

I start to feel guilty. "I'm sorry." I pause. "So, how does this world work?"

"It works against you. Just watch your back around that crazy Russian, okay?"

"Okay," I tell him.

I walk over toward Sergei's place to hook up with him and Maggot Arm Joe a little early so Sergei can take the walking tour of the *Queen Mary* before we meet with Mr. Fudge and find out if the people he wants to suffer are people who were unlucky enough to end up on our lists.

We walk up toward the entrance of the hotel deck of the *Queen Mary* and a huge banner announces:

WELCOME TITANIC HISTORICAL SOCIETY CONVENTION!!

Under it is a smaller sign:

Welcome Rubber Stamp Convention!

We wait in a line for a few minutes. There's only one desk clerk on and we're next in line behind the one guy at the check-in.

"I need to stay another night," he says.

The clerk clicks her way around the keyboard and shakes her head. "I'm sorry, sir," she says. "The conventions and New Year's have us booked."

"But I'm held over on business," he says. He looks desperate—one of those guys that travels on business in one of those soul-sucking jobs that leaves you crushed as wood pulp by your fortieth birthday.

"I'm sorry, sir."

He slaps his palm down on the desk. He turns and looks at the ceiling. He's trying to remain calm and he reminds me of Billy Jack right before he kicks the shit out of the rednecks that threw the flour on the little Indian kids. He turns back to the young woman. "You have to understand. I'm in lumbo here."

She looks sad. "I'm very sorry, sir. But I'm in lumbo, too."

And I'm thinking: *Lumbo?*

The guy slumps his way toward the elevator, or "lift," as they call them in an attempt to keep the British theme to the *Queen,* and we go up to the desk and get directions to the walking tour.

The *Queen Mary,* a woman in her early thirties tells us in a monotone flat and dull as white latex wall paint, was:

Nothing less than a floating miracle,
a marvel of technology that reminds us that greatness is
    possible,

the apex of luxury
part of the shared consciousness of the glory days of
the early twentieth century
unlike anything the ocean had ever known
a floating city, awash in elegance.

Sergei nods at that last one. "Floating city awash. Very nice."

I look at Maggot Arm Joe, who's frowning and looking bored. "Not your thing?" I say. "Floating cities awash in elegance?"

"Floating city awash in *white* people," he says. "Not part of my shared consciousness."

"Oh, now," Sergei says. "Don't make race issue of *Queen Mary*."

"Listen to you," Maggot Arm Joe says. "I'm not *making* shit—I'm *observing*. I'm stating facts—look at the pictures—you see any black people?"

Some *Titanic* people are turning and looking at the three strange men in the back of the tour. Most of the people on tour are older white guys and they're *Titanic* conventioneers. They have name tags with the silhouette of the *Titanic*. The monotone woman stops. "There will be a question-and-answer period after the tour," she says. "Please hold your comments until then."

The decks are overrun with *Titanic* people. Because of this, the tour runs long and we don't have time for coffee before we have to meet Mr. Fudge in the observation bar, which we do, at the appointed time.

He looks as hard to take down as a rhino, but to hear him

tell it, Mr. Harry Fudge is a sick, sick man who has piss the color of Prestone radiator fluid and shit the color of Florida oranges. He could go south in a hard way any day now. We listen to his health problems for half an hour before he tells us that he's not there to tell us about his health and how the hell did we get him started on that anyway?

Finally, he gets around to telling us that you could call Mr. Harry Fudge many things, but you could not, among those many things, call him a patient man.

"And yet," he says, "I have waited—I have waited these many months since my release to settle scores."

"I understand," Maggot Arm Joe says.

Fudge looks at him hard for a moment. "You were a fine lawyer once. Are you still capable? Or has your lifestyle damaged you?"

I see Maggot Arm Joe bristle a bit. But he plays it cool and says, "I'm fine now, sir. Tip-top."

That seems good enough for Fudge. "This is a question of honor," he says to us. "There are things a man cannot let pass."

Maggot Arm Joe and Sergei nod like a couple of bauble-head dolls. I'm thinking you can let anything pass, forgive and forget, let it go. They didn't touch his millions and it's not like he did time in a real prison.

Mr. Fudge turns to me. "You don't agree, son?"

"With what?"

"With what I said. What the fuck do you think I meant? You don't agree that there are things you cannot let pass?"

There's a pause. "No," I say. "Honestly—I don't agree."

Mr. Harry Fudge looks at me. He's backlit by the sun going down and he squints and reminds me of Clint Eastwood.

Somehow he's not one of us. He looks tough enough to have a shell, an exoskeleton, like some six-foot scorpion. Rap your knuckles on Harry Fudge and expect to hear a clank and get a bruise. Harry Fudge is at least sixty-five, but when he leans forward, I lean back.

"We're different men," he says.

"I think that's true," I say.

"About the list," Maggot Arm Joe says.

Mr. Fudge lets out a wet-sounding cough. "You'll get that fucking list—but not tonight. I meet people, I consider if we'll do business, and I act accordingly. But I'm making a point here and I will be heard." He takes a couple of deep breaths and I see his face turning color a bit and notice the hollow suck noise he makes to breathe. It's like, with each breath, he takes in a little less than he lets out.

He gains some control of his breathing and he says, "Among the names on my list—that you may or may not get— are some former associates of a man named Durrell."

"Spencer Durrell?" I say.

"You know him?" Mr. Fudge says.

"Only by name," I say. "A little reputation."

"I can tell you the reputation is well earned. You've heard all those Vegas stories—the bodies left for coyotes and so on?"

"Sure," I lie. I shrug it off, like it's billboard shit, like it's stuff everybody knows. Like it's a sign for who's on *Oprah* tomorrow. *Oh yeah, bodies left for coyotes—no big deal.* I'm proud of myself for playing along for a minute. I think I'm pulling this off in some way and it's kind of exciting.

"Spencer Durrell is a man to be left alone." Mr. Fudge wipes the corners of his mouth with a *Titanic* hankie. "Anyway,

I did business with some of his associates in some landholdings. They acted"—he pauses and looks to the ceiling—"they acted inappropriately. Unbusinesslike."

"Not to be forgiven," Sergei says. "Must face wrath."

Mr. Fudge brings his glass up in a toast. "Exactly." Sergei seems to have been picked as the leader. The sympathetic ear to Harry Fudge and his revenge fantasies.

Harry Fudge looks at me. "You don't think this is right?"

I hold my hands up. "None of my business."

"That's true," Mr. Fudge says. "It's not your business." He says this, but there's no malice, he's not mad, he's not afraid. He's like the government, too big to be afraid. Money does this to men.

I look at Harry Fudge and I feel every finger that's ever poked me in the chest. Every fist, every elbow pushing me out. Every step back I've taken. This is the stuff of job interviews, of cops, of bank managers, those situations we go through every day without ever pausing to register the fear and menace that pulses through them like electricity. I think of the pleasure it would give me to hurt him and this scares me. This is something primal and raw and I wonder if I've crossed some line. Or, if not, how close I might be.

I'd like to reach into his throat and pull on his tongue like some stubborn weed until it let go and flopped down on the floor. It's hate, what I'm feeling, for him and his kind.

"But, if it were your business," Harry Fudge says to me, "what would you do?"

"I suppose I'd let it go and try to enjoy my life," I say. I think I should stop talking, but I don't—I say, "It's not like you're feeling it. You still have millions."

"I lost millions as a result of these men's actions."

"But you still *have* millions."

"You're not listening," he says. "I lost millions—you have no idea how that feels."

"No," I say. "I don't suppose I do."

"You have a problem with money?" he says. "I can read people and you are some kind of hippie, aren't you?"

"Hippie?"

"You hippies and your Jack Kerouac, living in his mommy's basement. You have a problem with money."

Maggot Arm Joe and Sergei sit there all uncomfortable looking at me like I'm about to drop the ball. "I don't," I say. "I have a problem with rich people."

"What do you know about rich people?" he says.

"Enough to know I'm not too fond of them."

Mr. Fudge considers this. "But you're not so stupid as to cross a rich man. To cross *this* rich man, are you?"

"Not that stupid," I say.

Sergei says, "I love rich people."

Mr. Fudge winks at him. "I like the way you think, son."

"Would like to be rich so as to have food taster," Sergei says.

"What's that, son?" Mr. Fudge says.

"Hire boy," Sergei says. "Hire boy to taste food."

It begins to register and Mr. Fudge doesn't say anything. It looks like he's making a mental note to hire himself a food taster. "I need a cigar." He stands. "Let's walk the decks of this beautiful ship." As we're getting up to leave the observation bar, he points back to the city, toward downtown Long Beach. "All those people there with nothing? They're fine. Having nothing is easy. It's losing everything that's hard."

I want to tell him how wrong he is, how he doesn't know what he thinks he knows, but like so many times before in my life, I just look down and tell a man I agree with him when I really don't.

Just a little longer, I tell myself, and I can leave this shit behind. Make the money and get away from this life. It can be done, I think, just because it doesn't happen often doesn't mean it can't happen.

The Borrowed Dog

It's the night of freaks.

I'm on night desk and I came in a little early because Hank Crow's been so cool the last couple of days covering for me. Tara's due by at eleven and she's bringing chocolate almond ice cream and some Buster Keaton videos and we're going to chill at the desk.

Around nine, I'm relaxing, feeling good and listening to South San Gabriel's amazing *Welcome, Convalescence* album, when Tony Vic and Willie What's His Name stop by and try to sell me a lazy Susan. The two of them are always selling something. You name it, whatever useless crap someone tossed aside, or they stole, they've got it and they'll try to pass it to you.

I met Tony Vic the day he tried to sell me a wheelbarrow full of sod.

"You want sod?" he asked me.

And I looked at him. I mean, he knew I was night manager at a hotel. We don't have any dirt—nothing but concrete. I didn't think it required an answer.

"Well?" Tony Vic said.

I said, "What the fuck do I want with sod?"

That's how it started with us, and while I've never bought a single thing from Tony Vic or Willie What's His Name, they keep coming around and this time it's a lazy Susan.

They come in the front door and the blown-glass wind chime I got at the downtown craft market clinks its little announcement and I look up.

"Hey, hey, my man Nick," Tony Vic says. Willie What's His Name shadows him like a Muslim bride, three steps back and quiet as dust. Willie What's His Name has two habits: he rolls his toothpick over his tongue, sharp end to sharp end, and he smokes plastic-tipped Swisher Sweets that foul every room he follows Tony Vic into and out of. He has the last Afro in Long Beach and looks like Link from *The Mod Squad.*

"Gentlemen," I say, and I shake hands with him and Willie. "What can I do for you?"

"Not what you can do for me, but what I can do for you—let me tell you what I got."

"I'm not buying," I say.

"What you're not doing is listening," Tony Vic says. He looks back at Willie. "How can a man do business in a world that won't listen? It's a crime."

Willie nods.

Tony Vic leans in. "You know those spinny plates?"

And I know right off what he means, because I can see it out on the sidewalk under the streetlight—but I'm bored and I decide to play with him.

"Spinny plates?" I say. "Like *Ed Sullivan,* you mean."

"What the fuck are you talking?" Tony Vic says.

"Like jugglers? Plate spinners?"

He shakes his head and waves with both hands. "You're

way off. On Mars. On Pluto, Nick, my man." He takes a breath. "You're having dinner—but before dinner, you put out a dish of nuts. Say one dish of M&M's and some other things—you put the three dishes and they all fit on one spinning platform together."

"A lazy Susan," I say.

He snaps his fingers like it had slipped his mind. This is one of Tony Vic's little things. He acts like he's a moron so you'll feel smart and flattered and buy from him. Trouble is, he really *is* a moron and so it's not that flattering to realize you're smarter than Tony Vic, so the technique doesn't take. You can't feel good about seeing where Tony Vic's headed any more than you should feel proud about outsmarting a puppy. "A lazy Susan," he says. "That's right, Nick my man. Always knowing the name of things."

"I don't need a lazy Susan," I say.

"You haven't seen this one."

"Don't need to."

"It's a beauty," Tony Vic says, and Willie rolls his toothpick rhythmically.

"I'm sure it is. I just don't need one."

"You don't entertain?"

"Not enough for a nice lazy Susan," I say.

"You're killing me, Nick, my man."

I tell him I'm sorry, but facts are facts and I'm not a lazy-Susan guy.

He looks disappointed. You'd think he'd just bought a flatbed truck of these things. I tell him I'm sure he'll find a buyer.

"Not here, man. Not in the LBC," he says. "I'm seeing that this is an Orange County item."

"It's a suburb dish," I say.

"You pick up on what I'm putting down, Nick, my man. A suburb dish—true words. Truer words have not been spoken." He starts to leave. Willie What's His Name pivots, waits until Tony Vic is three steps ahead, and starts to follow him out. Tony Vic turns around.

"I got something else," he says.

"I'm tapped out," I say.

"I hear you, but maybe you can help me? Spread some word and I can help you out for your troubles?"

"I'm listening," I say.

Tony Vic looks deep in my eyes, this is serious, he's milking this, and I begin to think he might have a major score, maybe coke or heroin, but more likely he tripped into some crystal-meth garage and needs to move fistfuls of the crap. He's close enough for me to feel his breath from his nostrils and intense enough to bother me.

Finally, he says, "Fetal pigs."

He isn't moving, so I roll my chair back. I have no idea what to say.

"I got a great deal on fetal pigs," he says.

"How would you know?"

"I was thinking you could help me, Nick, my man."

"I'm not your man," I say. "Not your fetal-pig man."

"You know people," he says.

"I know people who need pigs?" I say. "Who needs pigs?"

"Sometimes there's a need and you supply a product— sometimes it's the other way around," Tony Vic says.

Willie What's His Name takes his toothpick out of his mouth. "Pet Rocks." He pops the toothpick back in and rotates it.

"Pet Rocks is right," Tony Vic says.

"You want to create a need for fetal pigs?"

"Now you're just being obstinate," Tony Vic says. "Help a man, here."

I don't say anything.

"I'd help you, Nick."

"Look—I don't need lazy Susans—I don't need fetal pigs. I don't need anything you've got."

"I'm hearing you, Nick. But help me out here—you don't need what I'm selling and that's fine. It is. But what say you spread the word?"

"You leave me alone?"

He salutes. "Scout's honor, my man."

"I'll spread the word you have fetal pigs for sale."

That makes him happy enough to leave and Willie slugs out behind him, picks up the lazy Susan, and follows Tony Vic down the street.

Tara comes in about fifteen minutes early. She's wearing a gray sweatshirt with paint stains, purple Chuck Taylors, and a floppy pair of old 501s with a rip in the knee that shows black stockings and she's looking as cute and goofy as bowling shoes. My insides uppercut themselves when she walks in the door and I feel myself smile.

"Hey stranger," she says, and holds up the bag.

"I scream, you scream," I say.

She nods and slides behind me, kisses the back of my head, which shoots warm and chills simultaneously through me, and sits next to me. "And what's new in the world of the lovely Lincoln Hotel?"

"I can get you a deal on fetal pigs," I tell her.

She bends down and shoehorns the ice cream in the dinky freezer section of the minifridge me and Hank Crow keep by the desk. "Bad break," she says, sitting up. "I just ordered a whole bunch of fetal pigs off the Internet."

"Really?"

She nods. "Fetalpig.com. Can you do better than fetalpig.com?"

"Probably not."

Tara leans back in her chair and looks over at me with a friendly, confused smile. "What the hell are we talking about?"

I fill her in on the situation.

"Do you get some points?" she says. "Something on the back end of this fetal-pig venture?"

"I don't think so."

"Finder's fee? If I want a gross of these pigs, what's your cut?"

"Tony Vic promised to leave me alone if I told people he had the fetal pigs."

She pauses like she's doing math in her head. "That's not a bad deal," she says. "But he'll never keep his end of the deal."

It's around one in the morning. Tara and I are watching *Sherlock Jr.* when Scooter closes the video place, comes in, and says he needs some advice. Scooter wants to make movies, wants to be a director, and he was all psyched when he found out Tarantino had worked as a video-store clerk—as if there was some cause and effect. It makes him feel better, the way all the shitty painters of the last hundred years have gotten all pumped up by the fact that van Gogh couldn't give his stuff away.

"What can I do for you?" I say.

"Actually," he says, "I was hoping Ms. Norwood could help me. It's a legal matter."

"I'm not a lawyer," she says.

"But you know lawyers?" Scooter says. "Isn't your girlfriend a lawyer?"

"Sure."

The mention of Jenny makes me kind of tense. I say, "Maggot Arm Joe's a lawyer—at least he was."

Scooter says, "Is he around?"

"He's asleep," I say.

"This can't really wait. Things are getting bad," he says.

Tara says, "I'm not sure I can help you, but try me."

Scooter says, "It's about my girlfriend. And what you need to know before you hear the story is that she's a genius."

"It has a bearing on the story?" Tara says.

"People don't understand her," he says. "Understand her vision. She's in film school up at USC."

"What's not to understand?" I say.

"That's what I'm getting to," Scooter says. "It's about a film she made. Now, you need to understand, it's an art film."

"It's an art film," Tara says. "Understood."

"Now there's a lot going on in this film, other than the problem, but the problem centers on this borrowed dog."

And Scooter goes on to tell us about the art film his girlfriend Eva made. It seems she borrowed a friend of hers Labrador retriever and had it, in one scene, lick tahini sauce off her shaved cunt. He uses the word *cunt* and says to Tara, "No offense."

"None taken," she says. "I like cunts. Big cunt fan."

Scooter looks at her and seems unsure of what to say.

Tara says, "So, Eva's a director slash actor?" She's playing with Scooter, but he doesn't pick up on it.

"I told you," he says. "She's a genius." He pauses, as if to let this sink in on us. "So, they show the film at the student festival—and her friend Marsha sees the scene with the dog and she goes apeshit and starts making noise about suing and stopping Eva from showing her film. Now the school's into it and they're talking about kicking her out of the program."

He stops talking.

Tara says, "So what's your question?"

"Do they have a case?"

"Yes."

"Are you sure?" Scooter says.

"What are they saying she did?" I say. "What are the exact charges?"

Scooter looks disappointed. He expected better news. We're authority figures letting him down. This is that little-kid pout that says there's no Santa Clause. No Easter Bunny. People are mean. "Something about dognapping. Animal abuse. Obscenity. Some other stuff."

"Bestiality?" Tara says.

"Yeah, that was one."

Tara's got her feet up on the desk and her chair creaks as she leans back. "That sounds right. The dognapping may be a stretch, but the rest sounds on."

"She didn't abuse the animal," Scooter says.

"She had it go down on her?" Tara says.

Scooter nods.

"People frown on that," I say.

"You're not a lawyer," he says to me.

"You got me there."

He looks back at Tara. "But she's a genius," Scooter says. "You watch the film, it totally works."

"The tahini scene?" Tara says.

"The whole thing. I've got it next door," Scooter says. "You want to see it?"

Tara and I look at each other. I shrug. She says, "What the hell?"

Scooter says he'll bring it over and he heads out and comes back a couple of minutes later.

Scooter puts it in the VCR and reminds us again that it's an art film with a capital *A* and Eva's the great misunderstood genius of modern film. The VCR starts to play and I pick up the remote and begin to fast-forward.

"When does the scene come up?" I say.

"What are you doing?" Scooter says.

"What does it look like?"

"You can't see just the tahini scene," he says.

I say, "But that's all I want to see."

Scooter says, "You can't look at it out of context—that's no way to see if it's legal."

"What are you?" I say. "Clarence Darrow?"

Scooter starts to say something, Tara plays peacemaker. "How long is it?"

"Twenty-five minutes."

Tara takes the remote away from me. She motions for Scooter to take a seat behind us. She starts to rewind back to the start. "Okay," she says. "Let's see what we have here."

And what we have here is pretty much what you might expect. A shitty black-and-white art film with a jumble of seem-ingly unrelated images. Shot on digital video with some cheap-film-grain aftereffect—I'm guessing she edited it in Final Cut or Adobe. It plays like a silly parody of German expressionism, with a dog licking an absolutely gorgeous woman's shaved cunt in the middle. In the scene, she walks in front of the camera and sits, wearing just a black bra. She really is stunning and I wonder what the hell she's doing with Scooter, even if she is some nut job who has sex with dogs.

She stares into the camera. There's a cut and then she's doing her lipstick in a handheld mirror. Another cut and she's staring into the camera. Another cut, and there it is—the dog scene. She still stares into the camera without showing any reaction to the dog. Another cut, and someone's pouring motor oil into a circular bundt-cake pan. Cut to a shot of a flower being picked. Then the flower gets put in the pan with the oil and put into the oven. And so on, until it ends.

Tara turns it off when Scooter gives her the nod. Tara shakes her head. "That was . . . quite something."

"So now you understand?" Scooter says.

"What's to understand?" I say.

Scooter ignores me and focuses on Tara and her legal opinion. "So what do you think now? Do they have a case?"

"Of course they do," Tara says. "Several cases, probably. Obscenity's a matter of opinion—but this is pretty obscene. And there's no argument on the bestiality."

"But it's art. She's a genius."

"What the dog's name, Scooter?" I say.

Tara gives me a dirty look. "Bestiality's a law," Tara says to Scooter. "Across the board. It doesn't say only dumb people can't fuck animals. It's everyone."

Scooter's amazed. I wonder what's going on in his head,

but his devotional admiration for Eva is kind of charming and attractive in its warped way. "You sure?" he says.

"Pretty sure," Tara says. "Plus there's the animal-abuse charge."

"But the dog was borrowed—not stolen."

"Still probably animal abuse."

"No one made that dog do anything," Scooter says.

I say, "I don't think a dog can consent." I pause. "Legally, I mean."

Scooter gives me a look like I don't know anything, which is probably true, but I feel on solid ground here. He snatches his tape off the desk. "This is so fucked up—this whole situation."

"She fucked a dog, dude," I say.

"Fuck you," he says to me.

"Sorry," Tara says.

"I'm not blaming *you*," Scooter says, and shoots me a hard look. "It's just that no one understands Eva." Scooter takes the tape and heads back into the night. We don't say anything and I can hear his boot heels scuff their way down Long Beach Boulevard's sidewalks until it fades.

"Poor kid," she says.

"Why? 'Cause he's an idiot or because he's in love with dog woman?"

Tara tilts her head, raises eyebrows. "Little of both." She cranes her neck, looks at the old Esso clock on the wall. "That's probably enough for me."

"You can't stay?"

"I'm getting tired. Going home."

"You could crash up in my room—I'll be done in six hours. I'll bring you breakfast."

She touches my shoulder. "You're sweet. But you don't have sheets, Nicky."

"Didn't bother you last night."

Tara's being nice, but she can't be budged on this one. "Last night I wasn't sleeping. I'll fuck on anything and I was too tired to go home. But I can't sleep in your room anymore."

"I'll buy sheets," I say.

"You romantic schemer," she says, and flutters her hand over her heart like a mime. "See you tomorrow?"

I nod, tell her to give me a call.

After she's gone, the night gets quiet and lonely again, so I turn on the talk-radio show. And, as promised, they're talking to the guy who talks to plants. The thing is, and these radio people, they're always telling you what the thing is, see, the thing is that plants are okay with being eaten by us. It's their destiny. They feel privileged to play this role in our survival.

The host is treating him like he's her average guest, like he just said he was for low taxes, or some other bland shit that passes for an opinion in this world. I wonder what her life's like, sitting across from the foreskin reconstructor, and the plant guy, a whole life of them, and she's nodding and being polite. The horrors she must dream of.

All-night radio. Web sites. Everyone's talking at once and it's all just so much static and I wonder if there's anyone left who doesn't feel the need to document their existence. Maybe I need sleep, but the last few nights, I've found myself edgy, jumpy and dangerous as downed power lines, and I need to mellow. I flick the radio off.

I put on Wilco's *Yankee Hotel Fox-trot,* which crackles with a ragged beauty and starts to make me feel better. Then I see this white guy across the street lighting a cigarette in the doorway of the old jewelry place. Jeff Tweedy sings about trying to break your heart. The guy across the street's Zippo lights up his face, all squinty and full of young trouble like Marlon Brando about to shake the hell out of some sleepy little California town in *The Wild One*.

The store's been closed for a couple of months, after something like eighty years at the same location, and people tend to sleep in the doorway until the cops roust them. But this guy, I've never seen before. He looks too well put together to be homeless. Blue denim jacket. Tight jeans. Boots. Give him a cowboy hat and a sunset and he's the Marlboro Man.

He keeps looking over here. I watch him through the second song on the CD. And I don't know if it's my lack-of-sleep jitters, but I'm seeing this clown as a direct line to Mr. Fudge. Maybe to Mr. Frank Carr. I'm seeing myself a phone call away from a bad time. I call up to Maggot Arm Joe's room. I can tell he's been asleep.

"Look out your window," I say.

I hear him shuffling across the room. "What am I looking for?"

"A guy across the street." I say. "At Walker's Jewelers."

"I see him." He pauses and I hear him yawn. "What's up?"

"He's out there," I say. "Looking over here."

"You call Sergei?"

"I wanted to know if you knew him."

"The man's new on me," he says.

The cowboy crushes out his cigarette. He looks up at one of the rooms in the Lincoln.

"He see you?" I say.

"Hard to say. I can't see where he's looking."

The cowboy stares up at our building for a second, then he looks right and left, and heads, slow and lazy as smoke, south toward the ocean, down Long Beach Boulevard. I watch him as far as I can from behind my glass.

Maggot Arm Joe says, "He might just be some hustler."

"He might be looking in on us," I say. "Sergei's been talking us up."

"More bad news," he says. "Bring it up tomorrow with the man—see if he knows your cowboy. But let me get some sleep."

We hang up and I go out the front door to see if I can find the cowboy down the street. He's gone. It's cold. My breath steams. Newspapers kick and roll in the wind. I don't see anyone. It's neutron-bomb quiet and I feel like I'm the only person in the world. It's like that scene in *On the Beach* where the last guy alive in San Francisco goes running down the street screaming about how he used to live there. That kind of aloneness.

I wonder if that's how the cowboy felt out here a minute ago. How Mookie feels under the freeway down by the river. I read in the paper a while ago that people who work nights were twice as likely to have serious mental disturbances as other employed people. Five times as likely to kill themselves. Work nights you'll feel it creeping in on you, that despair that no other person can reach, the despair that it takes to kill yourself. An aloneness that has a pulse, a steadiness, like the hum from the streetlights. I take a deep breath and try to stay away from these thoughts.

I walk out into the middle of Long Beach Boulevard, to the train tracks that hook the working poor of Long Beach to the shitty jobs of Los Angeles and vice versa. I look one way, then the other. There's a sound from the harbor, maybe a freight whistle. I lie down on the tracks and look at the sky and it feels peaceful. There's a vague hum from the tracks, but it's not from the Blue Line train, since it doesn't run at night. The lines vibrate and I think again of the talk-radio people buzzing their troubles in my fingertips. All these uneasy hums that reminds us how nothing ever stops, nothing's ever still or quiet.

But, I feel, briefly anyway, good, calm maybe, for the first time in a while. Things seem fine—all the crap, all the violence and loneliness and night suicides and the sad people who talk to plants, they fade for a minute. And, even though I know that things could go very wrong with the whole deal with Sergei and the computer list, I feel calm as a lake. Easy. Maybe happy to be alive. Things feel okay.

I watch my breath mingle with the night air for a minute before I start to feel dumb thinking these thoughts. I look over at the Lincoln and see Jessie, one of the hookers that lives up on the third floor. Jessie and I have a good scam going. She lives at the Lincoln, but she always tells her johns that it's a hotel where she only does business, so, rather than going straight to her room with her key, she checks into a vacant room and she and I split the forty dollars she gets on top of her fee for the room.

She's knocking on the Plexiglas, looking for me at the desk. Jessie's wearing this vinyl minidress and black knee-high platform boots. She's got eyes as green as a pigeon's neck and skin the color of coffee ice cream and she's among the most beautiful women I've ever seen. How she's ended up doing what she's doing, I don't ask, but I know she drinks and she's from one of those rectangular states in the Midwest. Nebraska, maybe.

The two of them keep rapping on the glass. Jessie's dress rides up her ass when she raises arms to pound on the window and I get up and head back inside the Lincoln and check Jessie and the man in. The CD's playing "I'm the Man Who Loves You" and I sing along, absentmindedly, while the guy pays with cash. Jessie winks at me as she heads to the stairwell. I put one of the twenties in my jeans, and slip the other one under the register for Jessie to pick up later. A half hour later, the guy comes down, doesn't meet my eyes, and heads out. I wait for Jessie to come pick up her cash, but she doesn't, so I read my way toward the morning when Hank Crow will come down and relieve me. Every once in a while, I look up and see if the cowboy's still out there, but I don't see him for the rest of the night.

DAY 4
DECEMBER 28

When the Levee Breaks

I close the desk at eight in the morning. Sometimes Hank Crow relieves me at eight—but *relieve* is kind of a strong word since Hank's not really on duty until noon, but he'll come and sit at the desk, which is, it's pretty obvious, better to him than being alone. Hank Crow comes downstairs and he looks older than normal to me—his face looks gray as concrete.

"Anything exciting?" he says.

I give him the highlights.

"Fetal pigs?" he says. "What doesn't that boy sell?"

I tell him he's got me, and we walk out front and Hank offers me a cigarette. I'm trying to quit, but I figure I didn't buy and I need something to mellow me out, so I take one of his Pall Malls. He lights mine first, then his.

It's that kind of sun-washed California day that makes the world look like an overexposed picture. Like everyone's eyes got caught in the flash and we spend the rest of the day blinking and waiting to see things right again. The sun hurts my eyes, but feels good on my forehead and arms and I feel the morning air mingle with the cigarette smoke and get refreshed in some way.

We look out at the people waiting for the Blue Line North train, and the cars stopped at the light on Long Beach Boulevard, which the old men in the town, Hank Crow included, still call by its original name, American Avenue. I'm looking at the faces of people in the cars, pasty and blank as drywall, all going to work at something they probably despise.

"You ever look at people and wonder what they all do?" I say.

"I don't follow," Hank says.

"Just look at them and see them on their way to their jobs and wonder what they think about all day. What they do all day?"

"You mean job people?" Hank says. "Office people?"

"Right," I say. I've painted some offices, but I've never worked in one and they seem about as attractive as POW camps to me. The whole straight world of employment is so alien—and if I was ever going to find out what it was like, it's too late now. A man can't get to his midthirties without ever having had a real job and expect to get one. It depresses me for a moment when I realize how limited my prospects are, but then I realize I'm getting depressed about not having an office job and I feel stupid. It's like when assholes don't invite you to some lame-ass party and you get upset. Not that you wanted to go, but you didn't want to be left out.

I think about back when I tried to do a résumé, this is a few years ago, this is when Cheryl was still trying to improve me, when it mattered to her what kind of person I was. So I do the résumé, it was video editing for some local commercial company, and I lie and I fudge and manipulate enough to make myself look half decent, but I get all hung up on the "Objectives" section. I asked her what it was for and she said the employer wanted to know what I wanted to achieve, what

I wanted from the job. Other than *make money* I couldn't, and still can't, imagine what could possibly go in that line. Why else would anyone ever want to go to work?

"I was an office person for a while," Hank says. "A suit driver." He looks at me. "You know those people you see on the freeway, their suits hanging in the back?"

"I don't see you as a suit driver," I say.

"I wasn't really," he says. "I was a plant—an insider for the revolution. I was supposed to turn the office against the oppressors. I was supposed to act like one of the yahoos."

I hear words like *revolution* and *oppressor* and I think they sound as old and dusty and quaint as *horseless carriage* and I can't believe that people ever had enough faith in anything to think there could be a better world. It's not so much I think they were bad or wrong, I just can't imagine it. It's like believing in God; it's just shit I can't fathom.

I say, "Where was this?"

"IBM."

"Didn't work, huh? Your revolution?"

Hank starts to say something, but the ground begins to rumble and I feel deep vibrations in my feet and figure it's an earthquake. I start to make for the doorway and then realize the Lincoln's a brick building, which is not where you want to be in a quake. Before I make it back from the door, though, there a deep watery hiss coming from the street, or, rather below the street right in front of our curb.

Hank takes a step back and stands next to me under our awning.

It sounds like a waterfall, but I can't see anything and I start to wonder if I'm hearing things, but the morning crowd's coming out of Wang's, and the drivers in their cars are stretching to see what's going on, so I figure it's real, whatever the hell it is.

The rumble gets louder and the sound reminds me of my bus accident so many Christmases ago. Metal groans and snaps. The ground starts to buck a bit, it rises and falls like old wood bleachers do when people jump next to you. The rushing-water sound gets louder until the street opens up and water starts gurgling up.

This isn't some cartoon fountain, this is not James Dean striking oil and getting happy with the mess and yee-haw whooping it up with his cowboy hat and decking the mean Rock Hudson, but more of a slow, menacing fart of city water oozing up out of the street.

A slab of Long Beach Boulevard, not twenty feet from where me and Hank Crow are standing, drops in on itself and swallows the rear end of a light blue Toyota Celica. The guy driving it screams.

"Sinkhole," Hank Crow says.

The guy gets out of the Toyota and looks back at his wheel sunken into the road. More people have rushed out into the street and are looking out windows. Car horns blow. The water's spreading and starting to back up instead of heading down the city drain that exits into the harbor. It rises and starts to lap at the top of the curb and threatens to come onto the sidewalk.

"Water-main break," Hank Crow says. He keeps smoking his cigarette and seems as calm as if this happens every day, regular as a city bus. "This'll slow down the yahoos for a while."

The Cowboy

When I get back inside, the phone's ringing and Jessie's at the cash register wearing a cream-colored robe that shows her outer-thigh tattoo of some Asian writing. I asked her once what it said and she told me, "It's smart to know your enemies—it's truly wise to know yourself." I pick up the phone and toss her the register key. She lifts the drawer, takes her twenty dollars, gives me the key, and heads upstairs. I watch her walk away for a moment before I answer the phone.

It's Sergei. "Nick Ray must be here," he says.

I ask him what the hell he means and he tells me Nick Ray needs to be in his apartment, needs to be there fast, needs to be there yesterday, so that we can head out of town to go see a man he knows about a thing he needs. This is how he puts it—a man he knows about a thing he needs.

"That doesn't tell me much," I say. "Plus—I'm going to sleep."

"Sleep in car."

I tell him I just turned shifts with Hank Crow, and I'm done, kaput, tired, beaten flat as matzo. But he tells me that he's got to go out to the desert and I have to come with him. It's for my own good, he says.

"Is this necessary?" I say. "Totally, absolutely necessary?"

"Yes, Nick Ray." He pauses. "Get Maggot friend of yours and come."

At Sergei's condo, I tell him about the cowboy from last night. He's wearing a paisley blue smoking jacket and his socks have garters. He sees me looking at them.

"Forget, Nick Ray. You cannot afford."

And I think about telling him that's not why I was looking, but figure what's the point and I fill him in on the snooping cowboy. He seems calm about it, nodding as I tell him about how the guy seemed to be on the lookout for us.

"This nothing."

"You sure?"

"I feed him finger—he go away."

"You feed him finger?" Maggot Arm Joe says. "What the fuck does that mean?"

"Mean what say." Sergei shoves his index finger deep into his throat like he's trying to make himself puke. "Feed finger." He nods, confident as G. Gordon Liddy talking about killing a man with a golf pencil, confident as the lunatic he is. "Cowboy go home."

I say, "I don't want to be around for that."

"Who point out cowboy?" Sergei says. "Not Nick Ray— who?"

"He's a cowboy," I say. "How many cowboys are there around the Lincoln? Find the cowboy—feed him his finger, if that's what you think you have to do—but leave me out of it."

Sergei chuckles. "Leave him out." He looks at me like a mean older brother. This is finger-in-the-chest time. This is a lesson. Bad news in a hurry, like those time-lapse sped-up nasty cloud formations on the Weather Channel. Sergei says, "You want money?"

I see where he's headed and I say, yes, I want the money.

"You want cigar? You want to suck tit and swim in pool?" He pauses and holds up a hand to stop me from answering. "You want"—he gestures to his foot like it was gold-plated— "Sergei sock." He smiles. "Then you feed finger. With Sergei. Against Sergei. Nick Ray must pick."

I nod.

"Pick," Sergei says.

"With Sergei," I say. He hugs me, my nose is full of Old Spice, and some medallion the size of a switch plate on his chest is cool against my cheek.

"With Sergei," he says. "Much happy, much happy." He releases me and holds me at arm's length like I'm something he's thinking of putting over his mantel. "Now—go wait in lot while I dress."

Me and Maggot Arm Joe wait for Sergei in his parking lot. Sergei's condominium shares its parking lot with one of those historic reenactment restaurants. It's called "Medieval Madness" or some shit and they dress their poor servers, as if it wasn't quite a cruddy enough job, as feudal slaves. People come and watch jousting and log-rolling contests and they eat huge Henry VIII leg bones and they don't use forks and they spit gristle on the floor and act, more or less, like the morons they are.

I mention this because a couple of waiters dressed like medieval servants just walked by us shaking their heads and swearing. One of them, who looks and talks like a twenty-year-old surfer, says something about "Dude—one more day and one more asshole calling me one more fucking name, you know what I'll do?" he asks the other guy.

"You'll kill him," the other medieval slave says.

Surfer medieval guy nods. "I'll kill him. You got that right." They crush out their cigarettes and head to the restaurant elevator.

Maggot Arm Joe offers me a cigarette. I shake my head.

"Trying to quit," I say.

"Why?"

"Because they kill you," I say.

He lights a Benson & Hedges. "Good plan," he says. "People who don't smoke—they never die."

Sergei struts out of the elevator and stands in front of us, hands on hips, like Superman with the earth and the American flag behind him. He's wearing this blue sparkly see-through shirt and white pants that look like my grandmother's couch from the seventies and he looks like he thinks he's the best-dressed man on the planet.

I wonder what goes on in his head to make him feel and look like he's so invincible. He walks around and it spills out of him, as if with every step he's saying, *What can hurt me you don't have, and what can kill me hasn't been invented.* I wonder what that's like, that confidence.

"Because I am late," he says, which means he's about to give the reason he's late. "I am watching your *Guinness World*

Record show," Sergei says. Whenever he doesn't understand something, he calls it "your" like all Americans know what the fuck's going on, like it's a big club he hasn't been invited into, like we're the Elks, or the Masons, or Mary Kay. We start to get into the SUV, but Sergei stops us.

"Presents," he says. He reaches into the back of the car. "Close eyes," he says.

"What the fuck?" Maggot Arm Joe says.

"Close eyes."

And we do. My hands are out and I feel him place a weight in them, and some gritty sand in my palms.

"Open," Sergei says.

I'm holding a nice little cactus that looks like a miniature of the one Spike, Snoopy's cousin in the desert, leans against whenever he reads his mail.

Maggot Arm Joe's holding what looks like a big clear plastic pocketbook. He holds it away from his body to read. "A blowup chair?"

"Clear," Sergei says. "You see through." He claps twice. "Read cards."

We open our cards. Mine promises me fifty pounds of freeze-dried Vac-U-Seal meat. I look over at Sergei. The cactus is very nice and I feel momentarily guilty for not trusting him. I thank him. "You know I'm a vegetarian, right?"

"It freeze-dried and drained," he says. "More like jerky."

"Still meat," I say—and I don't mean to argue, but I continue with it for no good reason. "I don't eat meat—jerky or not."

Sergei pats me on the back like I'm a naive little fool. "You eat meat when the Armageddon comes. When the world ends, you eat meat."

And who could argue? Sure, when the world ends, I might

eat meat. What the hell? "Thanks, then." I raise the certificate. "I'll save it for the Armageddon."

"That exactly the plan," Sergei says.

"What plan?" Maggot Arm Joe says. "Who are we going to see that's so important? And why—nice as it may be—do I have a blowup chair and shrunken meat?"

Sergei waves a you're-getting-way-ahead-of-yourself hand. "Let us move."

We get into the SUV and Sergei turns to me in the back-seat. "Nick Ray. I am watching your *Guinness*," he says. "And they show record breaking, no?"

"Right," I say. "They show people breaking records." I get the image of Frank "Cannonball" Richards, the guy from Los Angeles who used to get shot in the stomach with a cannonball.

You've seen the film. Few people know who he is, but that black-and-white footage of Frank Richards getting rocked in the gut by the cannonball, everybody's seen that—a still photo of it even ended up on a Van Halen album. The film's from 1922, and shot about fifteen miles from here, by the down-town rail yards up in L.A., near what's now the Toy District where they have undocumented workers from Mexico make children's toys in dreadful work conditions.

But back then, on the dream coast, Frank Richards used to get shot in the stomach, he used to pull railroad engines with his teeth, he let people hit his head with sledgehammers. When my grandfather was still doing sideshow work, before he became a strip-joint barker, he worked with Frank Richards, and he used to tell me that as long as a man had a high pain threshold, he could always make a good living in America, which was what made this country great. People loved to pay to watch other people suffer, my grandfather always liked to remind me, and if I could remember that, I'd never be totally broke.

Sergei says, "I am watching and there man who stick nail in face." He points to his own face and looks. "In face. In brain. Nails."

"So?"

"Take drill and drill up nose," Sergei says. "Into brain."

"Welcome to America," I say.

But Sergei's having none of it. "Show is *Guinness World Record,* no?"

We nod.

"How is it possible that this record?" he says. "What record about nail into face and drill into brain?"

I say, "I saw a guy lift fifty pounds with a pierced tongue."

"*That* is record, no?" Sergei says.

Is it a record? Who knows? Maybe someone's lifted more than fifty pounds with their tongue. Who keeps track of this shit? "I suppose," I say.

"The face man—it fake face, I'm sure," Sergei says. "No real face can be drilled and nailed. That not record. The fake-face man. What record he break?" He shakes his head. "Your country." Sergei says this like everyone drilled into their sinus cavity, into their brains, like we taught it in public school. "Strange place."

He turns the key and the SUV doesn't start. Nothing but a click. I expect Sergei to blow up, but he takes a deep breath, releases it slowly, hissing like a bike tire that picked up a brad nail, and leans back with his eyes closed. "Nick Ray," he says. "Your piece of shit can make it to desert, no?"

"Could be," I say.

Sergei nods. "We must risk." He gets out and we follow. "Bring gifts. Bring them to desert. Very important."

My car, my piece of shit, as Sergei calls it, my Subaru wagon, has not been the same since it hacked and gagged and wheezed its way past the methane-drenched cattle farms on the grapevine on my way out here from my old life a few years back. But it can still, usually, get where it's going. We walk over to the Lincoln to get my car, and Jeanine Clark's out front with her daughter Molly watching city workers clean out the burbling sinkhole in front of the hotel. We stop and say hello.

Molly says, "I don't have to go to the day care today."

"Good for you," Maggot Arm Joe says.

Molly points to the sinkhole and smiles. "My mommy says hell opened up. That's why I don't have to go in."

I look at Jeanine. I hadn't known she was religious, but she's got a calm look on her face, like she meant it when she said that hell had opened up. "Well, that's a pretty good reason for missing day care," I say.

Sergei bends down, and when he does, his gold medallion flops out of his see-through blue sparkly shirt and swings like a pendulum between him and Molly. He pats her on the head and looks up at Jeanine. "Your little girl—she grow fast as tumor."

Jeanine looks horrified. She yanks Molly's arm hard enough to separate her shoulder and drags her away from us. She stares back at Sergei as she walks down the street.

Maggot Arm Joe chuckles and lights a cigarette. "Grow like a tumor."

"What?" Sergei says. "Tumor grow fast, no?"

Sure, I say, tumors grow fast.

Maggot Arm Joe says, "It's just not something we say, man." He starts to say something else, but points and nods toward the Mole's pawnshop. "Cowboy," he says. "Three o'clock."

The cowboy sees us, sees the way we must be looking at him, because we're not two steps walking toward him when he starts to run away. Sergei runs straight after him, south toward the water, and me and Maggot Arm Joe take off into the alley by the parking lot and cut across to the alley. When we turn left, I can see that Sergei's already caught him and has him shoved and bent toward the Dumpster behind Wang's restaurant.

I stop running and walk quickly over to the Dumpster. The air's thick with the smell of leaked motor oil and doughnuts and Chinese food that's spilled onto the alley after the homeless eat what's left that hasn't turned. Broken glass, small and aqua blue and beautiful, like it's from car windshields, flashes in sunlight and crunches under my work boots as we approach the Dumpster.

Sergei holds the cowboy by the windpipe and it hurts me just to see it. "This cowboy?" he says to me, and I'm thankful he's smart enough not to use my name.

I think about saying no, about letting this poor bastard leave, but then I realize he may be a link in a chain that could end up with me dead. "He's the cowboy," I say, and my stomach starts to churn and flip as I think of what Sergei said about feeding this guy his finger. I look up the alley both ways to make sure we're alone and don't see anyone.

Sergei says to me and Maggot Arm Joe, "Make shield." He mimics a semicircle. "Around cowboy."

"What the fuck do you want?" the cowboy says.

Sergei puts one of his hands over the guy's mouth. "I talk. Not you."

The cowboy nods. I look back up the alley both ways and see Mookie pushing his cart and looking over at us. He gives me a little wave, and not knowing what else to do, I wave back. Mookie stares for a second like he's thinking of coming over, but he thinks better of it and takes off.

Sergei says, "One finger? Ten fingers?"

The cowboy looks confused. I'm not sure where he's going, either.

Sergei says, "Your choice. One finger broken? Ten finger broken?" He takes his left hand off the cowboy's mouth.

"One finger?" the cowboy says.

Sergei nods, slaps him on the cheek like a friend. He looks like he's about to dance, happy and bouncy as a Greek wedding. A hot breeze blows and a pretzel bag sticks itself to my leg before tumbleweeding its way down the alley.

"One finger," Sergei says. He looks at me and Maggot Arm Joe, smiling. "Good choice." He slaps the cowboy's cheek again. "There catch. Ten finger—I break. One finger—you break."

The cowboy looks sick, and I can't blame him.

"Understand?" Sergei says.

The cowboy nods and Sergei begins to lessen the pressure on his throat. I see the redness and the fingernail indentations on the cowboy's throat. Sergei lets him go and the cowboy's eyes dart around and make him look like the trapped animal he is. He lifts the metal lid off the Dumpster with his right hand and slides the left hand under it. The lid looks to be about twenty pounds and it should break it if he lets it go. I start to grimace.

Sergei stops him. "No. You break finger with hand." He pauses. "Right-handed?"

The cowboy says yes, he's right-handed.

Sergei says, "You break finger on right hand with left hand. No Dumpster."

The cowboy looks at him for a second. He looks to my eyes, and I look away and study the cracks in the concrete and feel bad. This is a place where a good person would step in—a place where the good stop the badness and walk away with their hands clean. I'm coming up short here. I have been tested and I have failed. That much I know.

My high school basketball coach used to call me a shithead. Used to shout at me—"Hey, shithead, hey, numb-nuts—you got an intelligent cell in that fucking body of yours?" I'm hearing him now. If someone shouted *shithead* or *numbnuts*, I'd raise my hand and turn around.

The cowboy has his left hand wrapped around his right index finger and he's bending it back toward the shoulder. He's pulling hard. He's trying, but this is unnatural, and maybe that's the point, and he's not doing too well.

Sergei is loving it. This is his forum of violence. He's got a grin like a dad whose kid is pounding the shit out of a piñata. "Try sideways," Sergei says. "Break better."

The cowboy slumps against the wall. "I can't." He shakes his head.

Sergei shrugs. "My turn. All ten."

He takes a step toward the cowboy, who leans back into the brick wall and quickly snaps his finger sideways. I hear it, it's a stick breaking, it's hard candy under teeth. That sound. His eyes roll and waggle and he flops down to the ground. His head hits the side of the Dumpster and his tight jeans begin to darken with his piss. Vomit trickles from the side of his mouth. He makes a high-pitched moan that doesn't sound human, sounds like a rusted door hinge opened and closed over and over. I want him to stop.

I can't believe I'm here. I'm part of this. I look at Maggot Arm Joe and think he's thinking the same thing. It clicks on me, Sergei could do this to me, *would* do this to me. Would do it to people I love. I see him standing over me and I'm snapping my finger back. This could happen as much as anything else could happen. I've put myself in this position and I feel stupid and scared. And I know it's too late to get out, so I better follow the right steps.

This is his world, not mine, and while I knew that before, this has made me feel it like a presence. I don't know what I'm doing here.

Sergei bends down to the cowboy's face. He wipes a trickle of puke off his chin and holds it in front of the cowboy's face.

"Lick," Sergei says.

The cowboy licks his puke off Sergei's finger and begins to really vomit and Sergei clamps his mouth shut. The cowboy spasms a couple of times, he's puking and wrenching, but Sergei's still got his mouth closed. When the puke starts to dribble out of the cowboy's nose, Sergei drops him to the ground and he doubles over into a fetal position and spills himself into the alley. Sergei kicks him in the back of the leg.

"You stay away?" he says. "You—we never see, okay?"

The cowboy nods.

Sergei takes the guy's wallet out of his jeans. He takes the money out and tosses it down at the guy, but he keeps the ID and the credit cards. "Say," Sergei says. "Say we never see you."

"You'll never see me again," the cowboy says, and it looks like he's passed out again. The money flutters in the breeze. Me and Maggot Arm Joe follow Sergei out of the alley and toward my car. Pigeons turn as we walk toward them, they start to run and then they take off across the alley.

Colonel Cactus

In my car I have a CD of Glenn Gould playing Bach that's always in the deck and has become my sound track for the last month or so of my life. This is what I do, I play a CD to death for a month or two and then lose it, or break it, and then that part of my life's over. My marriage started during an Iggy Pop phase and ended with the Stones' *Exile on Main Street,* which was fitting, because Cheryl hated that album and I got a little flicker of pleasure out of playing it over and over as I drove west toward my fresh start in life. How I ever thought I could spend a lifetime of happiness with someone who didn't love *Exile on Main Street* is beyond me, but we all make mistakes.

I start the car and the CD clicks on. Maggot Arm Joe says, "You got to play that?"

I say no, I don't, I like it, but I don't have to have it playing and I start to click it out, but Sergei stops me.

"Who is it?"

I tell him.

"This culture?" he says.

"Sure," I say.

"So's Lauryn Hill," Maggot Arm Joe says.

"But this culture?" Sergei says. I nod. "Play, then, Nick Ray. Let us have culture in this piece-of-shit car."

I push the CD back in and we let it go for a minute while I maneuver my way out of town and head east toward Twenty-nine Palms. I watch Sergei in my rearview, his eyes are closed, he's breathing slow and calm, like a sensei. This is a learned pose, this is how you accept culture, it seems. After about two minutes of the prelude from English Suite No. 5 in E Minor, Sergei says, "Where are his words?"

"It's instrumental," I say.

"This Gould person—no singing?" he says.

I shake my head.

"Take off, please. This government music," Sergei says. "Music without singing like watching people swim one-handed." He pauses. "Make no sense."

I flop the CD out of the deck. I put in the Handsome Family's great *Live at Shuba's* and that seems to please Sergei. Maybe because we're all tired, but we don't say a lot until we're free of the smog and inland traffic. After the logjam of Anaheim, we're shooting east toward, Sergei finally tells me, Desert Hot Springs. We get off the 91 and hit the 60 East, which merges with the 10, and the drive starts to get beautiful. For some people, it's the mountains or the woods, but give me a desert and I start to breathe a little easier.

Outside of Beaumont, near the Indian reservation, Sergei has me pull over at some truck stop that sells tourist crap, stereotypical wood carvings of Native American and Mexican figurines and, he's heard, illegal fireworks. We hit the bathrooms, stock up on water for the road. I buy a WELCOME TO DEATH VALLEY coffee mug. Maggot Arm Joe buys a Chuck Berry CD, and Sergei gets a bag full of Chinese explosives. There are three kinds: the Hen Laying Eggs, the Firing Nest, and Frog on Lily Pad.

All three have the warning: "Caution—Emits Flaming Pellets."

Sergei says, "These—cannot wait to try," as he slides into the backseat and we're back out on the local access road.

The man Sergei has to see turns out to be this guy who's introduced to us as Colonel Cactus. If he has another name, I couldn't tell you at gunpoint, and I figure that's why I don't know it. He has a pink stucco shack that looks like dirty cotton candy outside of Desert Hot Springs with one of those old satellite dishes that looks big enough to catch shows from Neptune and a hand-painted sign out front that reads:

COLONEL CACTUS—DELIGHTFUL DESERT DECORATIONS
LIFESTYLE AND LAWN ARCHITECTURE

Colonel Cactus has that old-lady leather skin you see in Miami Beach, skin brown as a detective's shoes and gritty as a cat's tongue. He's maybe in his forties, but the desert ages people differently. They end up tough as the plants and bugs out here. He could be ten or fifteen years younger than I'm guessing. The first thing he says he's got to do is search me and Maggot Arm Joe. He looks at Sergei.

"No offense to you or your boys, Sarge," he says, and I wonder if "Sarge" is short for "Sergei," or a mistake the Colonel's making. "A man can't be too sure out here, if you know what I'm saying."

Sergei nods. "Strip them and stick fingers in. Sergei have nothing to hide."

Maggot Arm Joe says, "Then let the man stick fingers in Sergei."

Colonel Cactus finishes with me and I put my arms down. He pats down Maggot Arm Joe's legs and points to his right arm, which is still wrapped in a grimy gauze circled with athletic tape that's blackening at the edges. Maybe he's missed an appointment with all this excitement, but his arm looks filthy.

"What's the story there, friend?"

Maggot Arm Joe tells him.

"Don't play with me, friend."

"Not playing."

Colonel Cactus shakes his head. "Live long enough, you'll hear anything, I say."

"So we do business?" Sergei says.

Colonel Cactus looks at him, then to Maggot Arm Joe. "Sure," he says. "Let's rock."

Sergei smiles. We follow Colonel Cactus to an old blue-and-white GMC pickup with those half running boards. Maggot Arm Joe and I get in the back with a big German shepherd named Xeno. We pull away from the Colonel's house. I see Sergei in front laughing and smiling. It's not an act, he likes this guy, he's having fun. I've been watching him and one thing Sergei can't do is bluff. So, when he's looking this happy, he is this happy, at least for the moment. I watch him bounce like a kid, laughing at something the Colonel must have said, he's as subtle as opera.

"You okay?" I say to Maggot Arm Joe.

"The Colonel's got a gun. Our buddy's got a knife. We're

here with some killer fucking dog." He laughs. "At least it'll be quick."

"You think we're in trouble?" It really hadn't dawned on me. I'm still the only one with all the names, and I figure that will keep me safe as long as I can protect the list.

"Who the fuck knows?" Maggot Arm Joe says. He looks around left and right. "How far can you run out here before you drop?"

I look around. We've turned onto a dirt-and-rock road and the pickup bucks us up and down. The lug wrench, one of the old crisscross style ones that looks like a big chrome *X*, rattles by my feet. Xeno looks at me, tongue riding in and out of the teeth.

Colonel Cactus pulls the truck to a stop in the middle of the dirt road. He and Sergei get out of the truck. The minute the door latch clicks, Xeno hops out of the back. I look at Maggot Arm Joe and he looks scared, which makes me nervous.

I think of Mr. Harry Fudge's words about Spencer Durrell: *The bodies left for the coyotes.*

My body. Left out here. And, again, just like on that Greyhound bus when it went sliding off the road, I'm thinking, *So this is where it ends.* Me. Out here.

"This is it," Sergei says, but he's not saying it in a mean way. He was pretty friendly when he made the cowboy break his own finger, too.

Maggot Arm Joe's looking around, not saying anything.

"This is what?" I say.

Sergei turns to Colonel Cactus. "We are agreeing on price?"

The colonel nods. "We are—and you wouldn't be getting this price if I weren't expanding, friend."

"Expanding how?" I say.

"I'm expanding is what I'm saying. In every way. Emotionally—with my business. I need space. I need rows. So you guys are getting a deal, see?"

"Rows for cactus?" I say.

"Rows for cactus—rows for me. I don't make these distinctions anymore, friend."

I let that one go. While I do make distinctions between me and cacti, I don't figure it's worth fighting over, especially since he's the one with the gun.

"This first ten grand," Sergei says.

"What?" Maggot Arm Joe says.

Sergei walks toward the desert and motions for us to follow. He goes about a hundred yards in and stops right next to a five-foot-tall cactus. He bends down, and before I can see what he's doing, he pulls open a trapdoor. It's like the desert itself has opened up. We follow him down some metal steps and enter what looks like an old fallout shelter. I look around. The air is musty and smells like an attic and I see there's a small kitchenette and then a pantry and two rooms off of the main living space.

Sergei asks us what we think.

"What exactly is this?" Maggot Arm Joe asks.

Sergei points to his head. "Mel Collins have me thinking. With the terrorist meat problem and the end of world—all this—we need place to be."

I say, "This is it?"

"Yes, Nick Ray. This place to be when the world ends."

"What if the world doesn't end?" I say.

Sergei smiles. "Then still have great place. Weekends. Nights. Could bring date."

Maggot Arm Joe says, "You spent our money on this?"

"Now I spend my money. You reimburse when we get paid." Sergei looks a little hurt, a little angry. "This good deal."

I try to get him swung back to happy. "If you mean ten grand for this, you're right."

He smiles and I feel relieved. "See," he says to Maggot Arm Joe. "Nick Ray understand. You"—Sergei walks over to the corner of the living space—"you could put new chair over here and read." He slaps himself on the chest. "Sergei think of this."

Maggot Arm Joe chuckles. "Thanks, I guess."

Horrific as it sounds to be stuck underground with him after the world ends, this is Sergei being nice. His clumsy version of consideration, and I feel guilty for thinking he was going to kill us a while back. "Thanks," I say to Sergei.

"So this good?" he says.

And we tell him sure, this is fine.

He looks over to Colonel Cactus. "Let us sign papers."

"You're the boss, Sarge," the Colonel says. "You know I was being strictly metaphoric about the signing of paper—this here's a cash deal, friend."

"Best kind," Sergei says, and we climb out of what will be our home when the world comes to an end.

Oklahoma City Looks Oh So Pretty

We're heading back west with the sun leaning hot and bright on the dashboard and Chuck Berry chugging the rhythm, singing about his love for Nadine and his troubles with Mabeline and all about Marla Venus losing her arms in a wrestling match over her brown-eyed handsome man. Who can listen to this and not feel good, I don't want to meet. The CD's short, and we're on our second trip through it. Maggot Arm Joe's still a little pissed about Sergei spending our first ten grand, which we don't even have yet and which he fronted himself, on the fallout shelter. I can't say as I blame him, but I don't see what we could do about it. Mr. Frank Carr, aka Timothy Shay, is supposed to give us the money in the next couple of days. After that, according to Sergei, we're talking profit.

"This American music?" Sergei says.

"You got it," Maggot Arm Joe says. "The American-est."

Sergei nods and leans back listening. In between songs he says, "Let us go to spa. Let us mud-bath. Celebrate our new home. Get massage."

"No can do," Maggot Arm Joe says. He looks at his watch. "I need to get back. Parole meeting." He lights a cigarette and cracks the window. I'm trying not to smoke, but I can only hold out for a few puffs before I hit him up for one. He gives it to me.

"Quick mud bath," Sergei says. "Quick spa. Hot tub."

"I'm telling you, man, I've got somewhere to be," Maggot Arm Joe says. "I didn't need to be coming out to the fucking desert in the first place. I need sleep. I need rest and you got us hopping all over creation meeting Commander Cactus and all this shit."

"Colonel," I say.

"Whatever," Maggot Arm Joe says.

Sergei's laughing. He takes Maggot Arm Joe's anger about as seriously as people do when they're playing with kittens. "You need relax—you *need* spa. You need massage."

Maggot Arm Joe says, "You need to be rolfed, is what you need."

"What rolf?"

Maggot Arm Joe tells him it's this severe type of massage where you get shoved and crammed to the point where they move your organs from the outside. It sounds vicious—something Tara would probably dig if it led up to an orgasm.

Sergei makes a face. "This good for you?"

"People swear by it," Maggot Arm Joe says.

"Crazy people," Sergei says. "No rolf for Sergei. Organs where they belong."

Maggot Arm Joe tells me to watch my speed—he can't afford to get pulled over.

"None of us can afford to be pulled over," I say.

"I can," Sergei says. "Have several persons who are clean—always carry two clean IDs." He takes a driver's license out of his pocket and flashes it up to the rearview. He puts it back. "Maybe three clean IDs with this cowboy man."

The plan is that when we get back, Maggot Arm Joe's supposed to get that list from Mr. Fudge and check his list against ours and sell him any overlaps. I'm supposed to wait by the desk for a call from Mr. Frank Carr. Sergei's going to call some people and see if he wants to add the mysterious cowboy to his list of identities.

Mr. Frank Carr better come through, though, because if the money starts coming in from Mr. Fudge, and not my deal, I'll have a hard time arguing that we shouldn't just sell to the fat cats straight out. But I want, I need, to avoid that. Seeing that cowboy was enough for me. I can't be a part of that.

Light Fuse and Get Away

I drop off Sergei. He gives me, as a gift, a paper bag with three of his new Chinese explosives—two Frogs on a Lily Pad and one Hen Laying Eggs. I head to the Lincoln's parking lot. Maggot Arm Joe shakes hands with me and goes up the back door that only tenants have the key to. I go around the front and my friend Blake is waiting for me at the check-in desk. Blake's a playwright from up in L.A. and he makes his money doing shitty screenplay work. Straight to cable and soft-core porn crap that should have him set up pretty well, but he's got a gambling habit that tends to put him back. When he's going really poorly, moneywise, he does journalism, which he hates. Last I heard, he had some book-length project on the inner workings of the Manson family. Blake's a Marxist and a big blues fan, which makes him one of Hank Crow's favorite people.

Hank Crow sees me and says, "Boy, go and buy yourself a fucking beeper, you hear?"

"What's up?" I say.

He hands me a stack of messages. "I'm not a fucking machine. Much as the government tries, I ain't a machine."

I flip through the messages. Anyone who'd called me at the

desk has already tried my home number up in the room. "Sorry, Hank."

Blake says, "A couple of those are from me."

And I see that. Two from Blake. One from Tara. And, pay dirt, one from Timothy Shay regarding a Mr. Frank Carr.

Blake lights a cigar, and while most people who smoke cigars these days are postyuppie assholes who deserve a good slap, Blake's been doing it for thirty years and actually likes the damn things, so it doesn't bother me so much. He rolls it around his lips, only smokes Cubans and Hondurans and only lights them with long wooden matches, and puffs away until he's got it going. He blows out the match.

Hank says, "You're not allowed to smoke in here."

Blake gives him a look.

"I gotta say it." Hank shrugs. "You don't have to listen."

I ask him how he's been and he tells me he's been having trouble with this ex–porno actress he's been dating.

"You know how it is," he says.

"With ex–porno actresses?" I say. "Not really."

He waves it off. "Troubles are the same."

"How's the Manson book?"

He points to Hank. "Was telling Hank here about it. They wanted a memoir, an inside story."

"Right," I say.

Blake says, "I finished the book—great stuff for hack work—and they took back the contract and cut the book loose when they found out I wasn't actually *in* the Manson family."

I don't say anything.

Blake says, "Who would've thought not being in the Manson family could hurt your career?"

"So what are you doing for money?" I say.

"Nothing. In-between. I may have a gig writing for some reality TV. Like *Cops* or *When Planes Crash*—shit like that."

"You have to write reality?" I say.

"Most of the people that reality happens to can't write," Blake says. He takes a puff of his cigar. "I need a ride."

I'm thinking I'd love to hang out with him, but I need to get together with Mr. Frank Carr. "Can't do it," I say. "What's wrong with your truck?"

"Fumbles died," he says.

Fumbles is, or was, his lizard, some exotic reptile that was bright and colorful as the Las Vegas Strip that he bought for a few thousand dollars when he had it. He got the name Fumbles for the sloppy way he ate. To me, it was just a lizard, but Blake truly cared about and for it. "Sorry," I say.

"Morgan's really upset—she couldn't stand not knowing why—so we decided to get an autopsy."

"I thought you two broke up?"

He nods and puffs his cigar and blows pretty blue-gray smoke around his head. I watch it thin and separate. "We shared custody. Fumbles died on my watch—I need to prove to her that I didn't kill him—so we got an autopsy."

"On a lizard?"

"Had to sell the truck." He pauses and shakes his head.

"You sold the truck to pay for the autopsy?"

"Lizard autopsies will set you back."

"I guess."

"So, I'm riding the Blue Line," he says. "Riding the bus. But I need to get out of town and see some people. So what do you say?"

"No can do," I say. I tell him I'm off to Orange County, but I don't elaborate.

He makes a face. "Orange County?"

"This is what I'm telling you." He looks frustrated, like this might matter more than he's saying. I say, "Let me make my call—I see where I need to be and when, okay?" This helps, he looks happier. I toss over my bag of fireworks. "Keep yourselves entertained."

I go up to my room to call Mr. Frank Carr. My room needs to be cleaned. The kiddie pool's sitting, deflating, shrugging itself toward the carpet. The video camera's still set up near the bathroom and I trip around it whenever I go in and out. There are three computer hard drives near the corner by the window. And, if anyone dropped in, the five enema bags would beg an explanation I'm not ready to offer. I dial the number Hank Crow's scratched out on the Post-it. Mr. Frank Carr answers and I tell him who I am.

"Thanks for getting back," he says. He sounds nervous and I figure he's bringing me bad news. He has no reason to be nice unless he wants me to do him some sort of favor.

"No problem," I say.

"Listen," he says, and I hear him take three quick breaths. There are bar sounds in the back room. The clink of bottles, distant seventies power rock, and a jumble of voices, he must be on a cell phone. "I'm at a place called TC's on PCH. Do you know where it is?"

TC's is a sewer. Walk by at eight in the morning and hear the crack of the pool balls and the smell of puke and piss by the front door. It's by the L.A. riverbed shouldered by a couple a strip joints. I slept with this woman, Shine, one of the bartenders there once. I tell Mr. Frank Carr that I know where it is.

"Good," he says. "Can we talk?"

"We're talking now," I say. "This isn't talking?"

"I'm trying to deal square with you," he says. "I'll be here for another hour."

"I've got someone with me."

"One of your partners?"

"No. He's got nothing to do with this."

"No go," Mr. Frank Carr says. "You and me."

Maybe I can sell Blake on waiting in the car, or dropping me off and coming back. Either way, Mr. Frank Carr doesn't need to know. I tell him he's got a deal. I hang up, look around the room. There's a thin film on the water in the kiddie pool. A winter fly buzzes and thumps between the windowpane and the roll-up shade and I see its shadow bouncing behind the shade. I unplug my light and go back down to the desk. Blake turns when he hears me coming.

"So," he says. "Can I tag along?"

"I'm going to see a man—if you need to come you've got to sit out in the car."

"Crack a window and consider me a dog."

"Done," I say. "Let's move."

"Can it wait a minute?" Blake says. "Me and Hank want to set off the Frog."

I say it can wait, but only for a minute, and I feel like a parent. Hank comes out from behind the desk and the three of us go outside. Across the street I see Tony Vic giving his sales pitch to a couple of women who shake their heads and walk away. Willie What's His Name stands in the shadows and starts moving the minute Tony Vic does. It's amazing—they're like synchronized swimming, those two. Tony Vic sees me and waves and I wave back. Willie What's His Name gives a nod that's meant to signify the fact that he saw me and that he's the coolest man on earth.

Hank Crow and Blake are like a couple of kids, bent down and crouched over the explosive Frog while Blake twists his cigar around the fuse and blows lightly on it.

"C'mon," I say. "I've got to move."

Blake looks over his shoulder at me. "Dude—Frog on a Lily Pad," he says. "How long can that take?"

Tony Vic and Willie What's His Name seem interested and they walk across the street. Blake and Hank hover over it for a while longer, but nothing happens. Hank tells him to light it with a match, but they can't. I toss over my Zippo, but it doesn't take, either. Blake stands up, gives me back my lighter. "You've been taken."

"They were a gift," I say.

"Gift of crap," Hank Crow says. We walk in and Hank sits behind the desk. I tell him I'll be back as soon as I can and he gives me a good-natured hard time about it. I'm bending down to grab a Diet Coke out of the fridge and I hear a loud pop that sounds like gunfire followed by a high-pitched wail. I look up out the Plexiglas and see Tony Vic running away and Willie What's His Name standing over where the Frog on a Lily Pad was and he's clutching his hand and screaming.

"Fuck," Blake says, and he runs out the door. I follow him and call back to Hank Crow to call 911.

In the street, Willie What's His Name is turning circles and clutching his bloody hand and arm. The blood's running fast down his arms as he holds his fists tight up under his chin. Me and Blake approach him and get drips of Willie

What's His Name's blood thrown on our pants and shoes. I know I shouldn't, but all I can think of is protecting my eyes and mouth from what his blood might have. He's crying like a kid, sobbing and spilling all over me.

"Hold him still, goddamn it," Blake says.

I tell him I'm trying, but he keeps turning with more power than I can grab. He's strong and anguish makes him stronger, kicks in extra gears, and Willie What's His Name is a handful at the moment. He's still screaming, his eyes are wide open but he doesn't seem to be seeing anything. When his mouth opens as he screams, I see the chewed toothpick riding the cheek and molars and I worry for a second that he might choke on it.

Finally, I get him to stop spinning, but he keeps crying and taking in quick shallow breaths. Blake pries his top hand off the left one and looks.

Hank Crow comes out the front door and says the paramedics are on the way. "How is he?"

Blake sounds surprised. "It doesn't look that bad." But then he looks at what he must have thought was the good hand, the right hand. Blake pulls the right hand away from Willie What's His Name's chest and I see his right hand and forearm are missing a chunk the size of a golf divot. Stringy white-and-red shit's dangling out of the inside of his palm and wrist and it smells like burned sulfur and hamburger. Willie What's His Name looks at me and starts fighting with me. He tries to push me away, he spits in my face.

"Let go, let go, let go!" he screams. He tries to bite my nose. I tell Blake to help me.

Blake gets behind him and tries to keep him still.

Willie What's His Name looks right at me, into my eyes

like he's talking to me, and says, "There's no sanctuary for you here, Ramon." He head-butts me and I hear and feel the dull thuck in my head. He does it again, above my left eye, and I'm momentarily blinded and I think a piece of toothpick stabbed me. When my eyes close, he does it again. I feel something hard on the bridge of my nose and the nose resists for a second, then gives way with a crunch. I fall down in the street and try to blink my way back to sight. Hank Crow helps me up. I stand on shaky legs and the world looks like I'm under a couple of feet of water and about to surface. Everything's wavy and borders of objects and people are fluctuating and merging in ways that aren't right.

The red paramedic truck pulls up and they run over and take Willie What's His Name away from Blake. My sight's getting a little better. I'm blinking hard and often and figure I must look like Benny the Mole right now.

A paramedic comes over to me and she says, "What happened?"

My head's clear enough to remember that fireworks are illegal in Long Beach. "I don't know," I say. "We were inside and heard an explosion—we came out and Willie was bleeding."

Blake's standing over her shoulder looking at me. "Some kids threw some fireworks out of a car and took off," he says.

She shakes her head, tired and annoyed, she's got that public-servant look that says she's seen enough stupid and mean people do enough stupid and mean things to last her a thousand lifetimes. She's wearing those medical latex gloves and brushing at my eyebrow with what looks like a huge Q-tip. It stings and I wince away. She tells me to hold on, hold on, hold *on,* and when she's finished with the eyelid, she wipes the blood off my face.

"Your nose is broken," she says.

But this isn't news to me. I've broken my nose five times in my life—mostly in bar fights and back when I played high school basketball. The last time someone broke it, I was lucky enough to have it mash dead center, a nondisplaced break, so it didn't need to be fixed. I haven't had health care since college, so broken noses stay where they fall unless I fix them myself, which is far more painful than actually breaking the nose.

My right eye is starting to clear, but my left one's swelling closed, I can feel the pressure building and my line of vision is letterboxing down top and bottom. I can't breathe out of my nose and my voice sounds like Dustin Hoffman when I say, "Do you have anything for the pain?"

She tells me she'll give me some Tylenol in the ambulance. I have less than half an hour before I need to hook up with Mr. Frank Carr at TC's. There's no way I have time for an ambulance or a hospital.

"You must be joking," I say. "You can't give me a drug? A *real* drug?"

Willie What's His Name's still screaming in short, astoundingly loud whoops.

"We've got shock here," one of the paramedics says. My paramedic gets up, she tells me to stay put, and she goes to help the other guy squeeze Willie What's His Name into the back of the ambulance. Blake looks at me and I nod and we take off behind the parking lot. I give him my keys.

"Christ," I say. I touch my head to the side of my face, take it back, and see greasy bright blood.

"Heads bleed a lot," Blake says. "Probably not as bad as it looks." Blake has a good handle on head trouble. One of his best friends is a former club fighter who's punch-drunk, but nice as a puppy and Blake knows boxing, knows club fighters, so he knows head damage when he sees it and I trust him here.

Blake told me once that the last five ring deaths in California were fighters who had their fathers in their corner. Something like 80 percent of all ring deaths had the father as a corner man. I don't know why I think of this now. Maybe the combination of my throbbing head and Blake being here, but that's what I'm thinking about, fathers sending sons out for another round and the sons not coming back. The father pushing, the son backing down, neither of them aware of the horrific implications of what seem like moment-to-moment decisions.

My skin feels tight and stretched against itself like cling wrap pulled. I start to get scared. This could be real trouble. I tell him about the tension, the throbs that pound with my heart in my head.

"Swelling," he says. "You still need to meet that guy?"

I nod and almost throw up from the small motion. "I do."

He asks me where it is and I tell him. We get in the Subaru and he tells me he'll stop at a 7-Eleven and grab me some ice for my head before we go to TC's. We pull into the 7-Eleven at Tenth and Long Beach Boulevard. It's in a minimall, the kind that swell all over Southern California like ground cover, next to a Popeye's chicken, a pawnshop, and a medical supply store. I sit in the car while Blake gets the ice. I start to fade. My head pain comes in sharp waves and I can't hold on to thoughts too well. Blake comes out of the store and I see him up against the measuring stick they have so that the clerks can identify the gunman's height. Blake comes up a bit shy of six-two. He gets in the car and tells me the only ice they have is in those big party-size bags and he drops it at my feet. He sits in the driver's seat, bends down, and punches a fist-size hole in the ice bag. He takes a chunk out.

"Hold out your hands," he says. I do and he drops the ice into my hands and tells me to put it against the eye and the nose. The ice stings, throbs more quickly and harshly. Watery blood gathers in my palms and runs down my arms and drips onto my jeans and cools my thighs as it soaks through. Blake starts the car and gets back out onto Long Beach Boulevard headed north.

He asks me if it hurts bad. I nod.

"Scale of one to ten?" Blake says.

"Twelve," I say.

"Seriously."

"I don't know," I say. "It seriously hurts, okay?" I pull the ice away and touch the cut over my eye. A maroon clot, thick and chunky like congealed cheese, comes off on my fingertips. I close my eyes and lean back.

"No sleep," Blake says.

My eyes are still closed when I say, "I'm not sleeping."

Blake reaches across and slaps me on the chest a couple of times. "Eyes open," he says. "You go to sleep, you could do yourself some damage."

I open my eyes and listen to the rumble of the car for a minute. The sounds of the world come to my attention. Squeaky breaks. A mother screams at a kid from the street corner.

Blake says, "Put your hand to your nose and blow lightly."

I look at him. "Really?" He nods and I do it. It hurts like hell, a toothache of a pain, intense as a flashbulb, then it fades, but still there in a throbby way.

"Look at the fluid," he says. "Is it clear?"

"Clear?"

"Clear," he says. "You got blood in your hand or a clear fluid?"

I look. There's mostly blood, some crusted and blackish, some fresh and bright red. I tell Blake this.

He nods. "Good."

"Blood is good?" I say.

"It means no spinal fluid's pouring out of you. Your skull's in one piece," Blake says. "No risk of meningitis. But don't fall asleep."

A few minutes later, we pull into the lot and Blake asks me if I have any change for the phone.

"I'll make myself useful," he says. "Scrounge us up some Percodans."

"Get some speed, too. I need to stay awake," I say. I dig in my pockets and come up with a half handful of change. I don't look, but some of it feels big, feels like it could be quarters mixed with the rest.

"On me—since it's your head and your car," Blake says.

I hand it over to him and go into the bar. I look at my watch. It's midnight. Mr. Frank Carr should still be here.

DAY 5
DECEMBER 29

The Troubles We Share

The sign above the door is from the seventies. The light's purple fluorescent and a guy who looks like Tony Curtis with a silly ascot flowering out of his collar, he's giving the thumbs-up sign and has a cartoon bubble above his head that says TC'S—A PLACE WHERE THE SINGLES MEET.

I walk inside and the doorman, a guy I sort of know named DJ, holds me back with a redwood of an arm. "We don't want any trouble."

"Neither do I," I say. "I've had plenty." I look at him, but his face is blank. "It's me, DJ—Nick Ray."

I must look bad, because it's taking him a long time to make sure it's me.

"Honest," I say, and walk toward the bar, where Mr. Frank Carr is sitting drinking a tap beer.

I sit down next to him. He turns and looks at me. He doesn't seem shaken by my appearance.

"I should see the other guy?" he says.

"The other guy's in a straitjacket at St. Mary's," I say.

I try to get Shine, the bartender's, attention. She's leaning with her back to the mirrored glass at the other end of the bar.

She wears a clingy silver skirt that looks like some futuristic metal—like its out of a sci-fi movie, a cutoff black T-shirt that shows a muscular stomach with a silver belly stud and a sunburst tattoo that explodes from the navel. She's into bodybuilding—all tension and angles and beautiful hardness and looks like she could be a cartoon superhero. We slept together once—she didn't seem to have much interest in a second time, but Tara's still jealous—she's got a crush on Shine and when I want to hurt her feelings I remind Tara that I slept with her and she hasn't.

Timothy Shay/Mr. Frank Carr doesn't want to hear about my troubles, about my bloody, pounding, suffering head or any other wrong turns I may have taken. "You've got your troubles," he says. "I've got my troubles. Some troubles we share, and that's why we gather and talk."

"So what troubles do we share?"

He takes a sip of his drink. "Two—one is that we're both in contact, or getting close to contact, with Spencer Durrell, which is very bad."

How would he know this? "Who?" I say.

He makes a face. "Don't fuck with me, kid. You're leaning on me, you have to have something to lean *with*. There's only a couple of people who hold a hammer over me—and Durrell's one of them." He looks at me. "So—are we done fucking around?"

I nod.

Mr. Frank Carr says, "I know him—you don't. You do not want a part of this." He looks at me for a minute. "I'm making a decision here—a decision to trust you, okay?"

"Okay," I say, though I doubt that he trusts me—he only wants me to think he does.

"You're small-time," he says. "I say that in the most sincere, nicest way possible—but look at yourself, pal." He holds his hand up to stop me from saying anything. "Sit and listen, let me buy you a beer, and then tell me what's on your mind, okay?"

I nod and hold my hand up to Shine for a beer.

Mr. Frank Carr says, "These people will fuck you up. And if you don't owe Spencer Durrell money, he will kill you. If you owe him money, he may let you survive long enough to pay off—but you? My advice is that you take my ten grand, you split it however you want, and you stop this nonsense as soon as you can."

Shine brings me over a beer. "Christ, Nick," she says, and winces. "What happened?"

I tell her it was an accident. She looks at me like I'm pasta with worms, that kind of oh-my-how-gross face. It doesn't make you feel good.

"Car accident," I say.

She nods a little nod of understanding and she saunters away.

Mr. Frank Carr says, "I'm trying to help you—believe it or not." He pauses, takes a drink, and sets the glass back on the table. "How many names on that list have you contacted?"

"What list?" I say.

"I can add two and two. I don't know how you got it, but you've got my name, and my name isn't alone. And now people talk, kid. People will know what you're doing. You're in deep water. If Durrell doesn't kill you for the list, the feds will arrest you for it. This doesn't end well, this movie you're making."

Fear cracks and pops inside me like ice in a drink. "Why should I tell you?"

He looks at me like I'm an idiot—it's the same tired shake of the head I got an hour ago from the paramedic cleaning my cut eye. "Don't be cool," he says. "Don't be hip. Cool is stupid and hip will get you killed. I'm trying to tell you something here."

I tell him I'm listening.

He says, "You think this is the way to make it in this life, but you're wrong. You hang out with losers, you lose. It's easy math, pal."

I ask him if he's got a cigarette and he tells me he quit when he left Mr. Frank Carr behind him. He says, "I know— you look at me and what do you see—some fucking boring straight life in Orange County, right?"

"Pretty much," I say.

"Kid, you couldn't pry me out of my life with a crowbar. And that's what you and your people are doing—you see, I've got things I care about, things I'll fight you for. Things I'll kill you for, understand."

"No offense," I say. "But I don't see what you've got to bargain with."

"You're a phone call away from Spencer Durrell knocking on your door."

And I'm wondering, *Why?* "You would call him? Wouldn't he come knocking for you?"

He shakes his head. "I've already changed everything— names, jobs, history. I don't want to again, but I know how. By the time he came looking for me, I'd be somewhere else. Some*one* else."

"It's that easy?" I say.

"It's not easy," he says. "It's what I'm prepared to do. I'm your fucking Vietnam, see? This is my homeland and you're an outsider. You need to know what you're doing. What you're up against. I know small-time—I was small-time. When the pressure hit, I blew the whistle and talked to anyone who'd listen. I'm trying to save you time. Get out and go away. Have some kids that like playing ball in the backyard. Find yourself a woman who's fun to talk with who likes sucking cock and being ass-fucked and get a barbecue and a sunset and enjoy life."

"That's the secret?"

He looks hard at me. "I'm not kidding—you fuck with what's mine and I'll kill you and enjoy hurting you. I'll wrap your body in a carpet and you'll just be another Nevada body drop. My wife, my kids—that's my life. You and your friends? You're flies on the world's windshield. No one misses crap like you."

He gets up and throws a twenty on the table. "You'll get the ten grand," he says. "But if I hear anything from you or about you after that, or if I hear anything squirrelly about you, the deal's off and you're dead." He puts his hand around my shoulder and to anyone looking, I'm sure it appears that the nice-looking handsome Orange County-ish looking guy is saying a quiet good-bye to the bloody guy, nice and friendly. "I've got a human stake in this. You've got money. It's not a contest." He pats me twice and walks away. I watch him in the bar mirror. He doesn't look back at me. There's plenty of change from his twenty and I order another beer and think about how he said no one misses crap like me and I'm not sure I could mount much of an argument.

I drink a beer and start sinking down into remorse and self-loathing, the stuff of broken knuckles, empty hotel rooms, and weepy country music, and I figure it's time to go. Cut myself off before the depression settles, takes root and grows. Part of it is drinking alone and looking at Shine standing twenty feet away and acting like we don't know each other. Dylan's song "She Acts As If We Never Have Met," the live Halloween 1964 version, snaps into my head. Shine's working not to look over my way and she's flirting heavily with a muscular, good-looking guy with dual barbed-wire tattoos on his biceps. I know it's probably because she's fucking the guy and she doesn't want trouble—but it feels like more. It feels like me erased, feels like, not only would crap like me not be missed, but that some people would breathe a sigh of relief and feel good about it. I'm not sure why, but I leave Shine a nice tip and take the rest of Mr. Frank Carr's money and decide to go outside and see if Blake is back with the painkillers.

Waiting for My Man

I'm sitting in the parking lot of TC's in front of an empty parking space off to the side of the building. Faint oompa-mariachi music from the bar throbs in the distance. I sit on a creosote-swabbed cut telephone pole that's in front of the oil-stained space. Broken glass and guava leaves sit in the oil—some of which is fresh and slick and wet, some of which is old and dry and gunky. The air smells of fish tacos and roofing tar and the creosote on the wood I'm sitting on, which they do to keep the termites at bay.

I close my eye that still opens and closes, the other one's glued shut, and I hear the hiss of cars on PCH and the music from the bar gets louder when the door opens and closes. The bar music gets drowned out on occasion by some car blaring rap or salsa as it zips by, then the car music fades, and the faint bar music swells back up.

After a while, it strikes me that Blake's been gone too long. That maybe he's not coming back. I dismiss the thought. I know Blake, he wouldn't leave me here.

But it nags. It pokes and prods. Doubt cuffs me on the ears and I'm left with the ringing. How well do I know Blake?

I'm going down this list in my head and I'm coming up with nothing. Names, facts, nothing special. Blake likes hard-luck stories, he's the best-read man I've ever met, and he's got nothing to do with a university. He pisses through money like no one in the world. He'll buy, on some twisted impulse, the rarest bamboo on earth, and then he'll let his dog piss on it. He bought a three-thousand-dollar bird once. Fumbles, the dead lizard, set him back five grand, and this is before the autopsy.

I realize I know little things, but I don't *know* him. And he's a friend. On my side in the world, one of not so many people, and I see now that I probably don't know much about anyone. Don't know Tara, don't know Sergei, don't know a thing about any of them.

I think about my ex-wife Cheryl and realize that this probably starts when we ended. My life's been fused wires and shorted connections ever since.

Once, she broke down crying in the shower on this vacation we were on in Mexico. This was a big shower, she's sitting on one side and I'm on the other, and she's shaking, crying, and I ask her why and she tells me she's just so overwhelmed, so in love, so whiplashed and knocked by love that she can't handle it.

"I love you, so much, Nick," she says.

And she meant it. She meant it and meant it and meant it until she didn't mean it anymore. And then it got taken over by something like hate, you could tell, near the end, that she looked at me and wondered what she'd ever been thinking to fall for a loser like me.

Near the end, she said to me: "Living with you? It's like a scrum. A bunch of pushing and wrestling for no fucking reason. I don't even know who you are."

And I could have said, *Neither do I,* but I didn't. I slumped out of that life and came to this one.

So who do I know? What do I know? My life is wrapped and tangled with strangers.

I shake my head and the pain rattles and swells and throbs. I see sharp bolts of light behind my closed eyes.

I tell myself it's the head injury, the pain, the beer, twisting my head like wreckage, like a car barreling into a chain-link fence and nothing left is recognizable. These are not good thoughts. These are not productive thoughts. Thinking like a loser makes you a loser. It's like a lightning rod for a sucker's luck.

Doubt is weakness. That I know. Let it crack your surface and you rot from inside like a rusted-out quarter panel. I used to play chess every day for about a year with a chess master and all it takes to lose, sometimes, is to think that losing is a possibility. To prepare for it is to pave the road and build a parking lot for all the bad news that pulls into your life.

My head throbs, but I struggle to hold against these thoughts. *No,* I think. *No, this will not happen. I will not let it,* I tell myself.

I am sitting here waiting for my friend Blake, who will be here soon enough. I say this out loud. I say it again. "I am waiting for my friend Blake, who will be here soon enough." I close my eyes and feel the cool breeze blow over my cuts.

You're Talking to the Wrong Guy

I have no idea what time it is when I wake up to find Blake crouching over me and slapping my cheek while he holds ice to my chest. He pulls me up by my shirt collar and drops some of the ice down my pants.

I say, "What the hell are you doing?"

"You fell asleep," he says. "I told you—no sleep. It's bad for your head."

I nod slowly. I move my head and neck a little and feel the tightening stiffness in the back of my neck. I pry the dwindling ice cube off my balls and throw it onto the parking lot.

Blake slaps my face a couple more times. My head throbs in pain after every slap.

"Enough," I say.

"Good," he says. "Was just waiting for you to fight back." He takes a cigar out of his pocket and begins to light it. "So," he says around puffs. "How'd your meeting go?"

"Fine," I say. "And you?"

Blake reaches into my car and comes out with a Mickey's Big Mouth, which he hands to me.

"Good news," he says. "We're hooked up on some Percs."

"So let's have them."

"We've got a quick stop for that," he says.

I'm starting to wake up and I remember my anger, the fright at him not coming back. "Where the fuck were you?" I say.

"What do you mean?" he says.

"You go off for drugs. You're gone for God knows how long and you come back and tell me we have to take a ride to get them?" I look up at him. "Where were you?"

"I told you before," he says. "I needed a ride. I took the ride. I needed money if I was going to hook us up."

"The ride was about money?" I say.

"Most rides are," he says.

I take a hit off the Mickey's and the bitterness rolls over my teeth and I feel calmness begin to settle on me like a blanket. The years I didn't drink, I swear, I was always on edge. It was living without an off switch and I'm sure I would have crashed and burned if I hadn't started drinking again. Living sober had its pluses. My life would surely be less of a failure without alcohol, but I just never could figure out a way to relax without drinking up and shutting down.

"So you have money?" I say.

"That I do," Blake says, and looks at his watch. "Kill that beer and let's move."

I finish the beer and put the glass on the log. When I stand, I'm more even and balanced than I expected.

When we start to pull out onto PCH, Blake says, "You shouldn't say anything wrong with these guys. They weren't my first choice for the drugs."

"Define *anything wrong*," I say.

Blake tells me we're headed to Pedro, to this abandoned apartment building, to these bad people near the DMV in

Pedro, which people around here pronounce *Pee-dro*. The DMV in Pedro is the most vile and crowded of the Southland since the Long Beach one was burned down after the first Rodney King verdict. Blake tells me he doesn't know a lot about these men, but he's been told to watch his tongue around them.

I tell him this thing Tara told me, that you can get through life with just two lines: *I don't know* and *You're talking to the wrong guy/gal.*

Blake says, "Maybe you shouldn't talk at all."

"That's an option, I suppose."

"Almost forgot," Blake says, and reaches into his jacket and hands me a cassette tape. It's a compilation tape. Blake makes these for me and for Hank Crow. This one's called *Songs from the Point of View of a Dead Guy.*

"You found ninety minutes of songs from the point of view of a dead guy?" I say.

"I had to leave stuff off," he says. "It's a rich tradition." The last tape he gave me was a *He Shot His Woman Down* collection, which was, appropriately enough, songs about men shooting women and was, I'm guessing, even harder to edit down to just ninety minutes of violent-loser-with-a-gun tales set to music.

I thank him and put the tape on the dashboard. It slides across the dash every time Blake turns left, so I put the tape halfway into the player and let the case slide to the floor.

The house is an abandoned fourplex, the kind that speckle Long Beach and South L.A. and Pedro, most of them built in the twenties. There's a masking-tape *X* over the upper left window, and Blake points and nods.

"That's their signal," he says.

"Move the office frequently, do they?"

"More than porno producers," Blake says. "Beeper culture."

"They know you're coming?" I say.

I decide to sit in the car when Blake goes into the apartment. I watch from the outside. There are no lights. Blake gets swallowed up into the darkness of a hallway in the abandoned fourplex, and comes out three or four tense moments later.

Blake starts the car and turns up the volume on the tape. I can see he's a little shaken.

"Success?" I say.

"In a manner of speaking." He drops a Ziploc full of pills in my hand. "Thanks for the ride."

We start the ride home and the first song from the point of view of a dead guy is the Band's version of "Long Black Veil." Blake turns onto the 47, and moves toward Long Beach. The Band is singing, telling their story—a cold wind's blowing, it's night and the woman in the song's visiting the dead guy's grave and she's in her long black veil and she's crying over his bones. A couple minutes later, halfway over the Vincent Thomas Bridge, we enter the Long Beach city limits, population half million, and I pop two Percodans and take a hit of warm beer from a bag in the backseat.

First-Time Caller/Longtime Listener

Blake and I pull into the parking lot at 2 A.M. and Hank Crow gives me some minor hell about coming back so late. After chewing me out, he gives me a note saying Tara called and that she can't come by today or tomorrow.

I give Blake the keys to one of our empty rooms, because the Blue Line doesn't run this late at night. I'm supposed to watch the desk for the rest of the morning, but I feel like hell, so I just leave the "Closed" sign at the window and lock up. Anyone with a key can still get in, we just won't do any walk-by business. The Lincoln is not long for this world, so I don't suppose twenty bucks here or there counts much in the grand scheme.

My room feels funky and musty when I open the door and I figure if I could smell the room, I wouldn't like it much. I don't bother to turn off the light, don't take off my bloody clothes, don't do anything except flop down on the bed, and the last thing I remember before drifting away was someone calling up to say whether they were for or against the death penalty and the host sounding polite, sounding like she cared, like all the opinions in the world mattered in some way.

Nothing to See Here

I wake up to this loud, long whine of a horn outside of my window and try for a few minutes to ignore it, but it's no good. There are sirens. There's a high-pitched wail, there's the murmur of a crowd. For a while, I think I might be floating in the midst of a Percodan dream, but the noises keep up even when I try to send them away. I button up my jeans and go downstairs to see what's going on.

The lobby's full of cops questioning people. I see Maggot Arm Joe shaking his head and smoking a cigarette while a cop writes in a pad. Hank Crow's at the desk staring out at the street, where there are several paramedics in what looks like a football huddle over a body about ten feet off the railroad tracks. There's blood in the street.

I ask Hank Crow what happened.

"I was watching," he says. "Saw the whole thing."

"What whole thing?" I say.

A cop, one of the bike police who looks too young to be a cop, looks young enough to be hanging out and playing video games, taps me on the shoulder and asks me to step away so he can talk to Hank.

Hank points out in the street. "The train just came through and barreled Mookie—just split him up. Just in front of me." Hank's edgy, near tears, and shaking hard.

I think, *Mookie? Hit by the train?* The cop nudges me and tries to shoulder past me and says he needs to take Hank's statement.

"Leave me be," Hank says.

"We need a statement," he says. "It's best to get them quickly before you forget what you saw."

Hank looks up at the cop. "Boy, you couldn't make me forget what I saw with all the guns and badges in your world." Hank stands up with his fists at his sides. "Now leave me be."

I put my hand on the cop's chest and try to reason with him. I feel the slick budge of the nylon-coated bulletproof vest that peeks out from his shirt and has a tuft of chest hair announcing itself above the blue fabric.

The cop looks at me with rage in his eyes. He talks with studied calmness that feels like it's about to blow. I'm thinking about the ways cops can make you disappear with their power, about the kid they beat to death in jail a few months ago, about what the sheriff's deputy told me last time I was in a drunk tank: *Boy, there's a hundred stairs between us and the holding cell and your head could accidentally bounce off every single one.*

The cop in front of me says, "Sir. Get your hand off of me."

"Look," I say. "He's just upset."

The cop grabs my hand, and before I know it, he's spun me around and he's got some vicious pressure on my wrist that's shooting up my arm.

The cop says, "I asked you to get your hand off my chest, sir." He kicks my feet out sideways and pushes me toward the desk. "Are you calm, sir?"

I'm thinking I *was* calm, calm before any of this happened, and it's trickling in on me that Mookie's out there, dead as a deck flounder, dead on the road. Hank said, he saw him split, and I wonder when it happened. How it happened. The cop's pushing on my back. My face is down on the desk, left cheek touching some papers, and I can see Hank at some art-film angle above me.

Hank says, "Get your hands off him—he didn't do nothing."

I tell the cop I'm cool, but he keeps me bent over and spread with the pressure on my wrist.

There are sirens outside. The buzz and hum of official Q & A hovers around.

Hank says, "You want to know what happened? I tell you what fucking happened—the boy out there got harassed by you people and was kicked around like a dog by you people and he wandered and he got killed because you people wouldn't let him be."

"There's no need to raise your voice," the cop says. "I understand you're upset."

"You don't understand shit, peckerwood. You tell me you killed Mookie and I'll start thinking you're understanding things."

The cop lets up pressure on me. He stands up straight, right hand hovering over his holster, and says, "Sir."

"Don't be saying 'sir' to me while you reach for a gun—call me 'boy' with your hand on a gun. Let's be honest about our place." Hank seems to have calmed down, but the anger's still there, it's just under a little control. "You call me 'sir' if you want to hear what happened." Hank pauses and I hear the three of us breathing. Hank says, "Do you want a statement?"

The cop says, "Please don't tell me how to do my job, sir. I'm just trying to get you to tell me what you saw."

I stand slowly so the cop doesn't think I'm about to make any moves. The day's still coming into focus for me. I look out to the street and they're wrapping yellow police tape near the train tracks and across the street. Another cop's outside directing traffic away from Long Beach Boulevard. One cop walks into the Lincoln and shouts to, I'm guessing, another cop, "Keep them moving—there's nothing to see here." I see the door rock closed after he enters.

Hank Crow has a mean calmness. "I want you to write this down," Hank Crow says. "I want it down word for fucking word." He pauses as his voice cracks a bit. "What I saw was a young man who fought in Vietnam for somebody else's interests and who came back here and worked for somebody else's interests and who got harassed and wasted and used and beaten by people in suits and uniforms."

The cop shakes his head like he's only doing his job and why does he get all the nut jobs and why, please God tell him why, can't he just get a statement?

Hank Crow says, "Please. I am doing what you asked."

The cop says he's taking it down.

Hank Crow says, "I saw a young man neglected to death. Actually—if you'd neglected him, he'd be alive. But you wouldn't let him sleep in a park. Wouldn't let him rest at a bus station—outside—on a bench. Wouldn't let him sleep in an alley. Sleep under the freeway. Wouldn't let him *be*. I saw a young man hated to death. And I have lost count of how many black and brown and poor people I have seen hated to death by the very same people who come by afterward and act like they give a shit about what I saw." Hank Crow glares at the cop and says, "That's what I saw. Now, please leave me alone."

The cop asks me if I saw anything. I shake my head and he tells me to never, under any circumstances, lay a hand on an officer of the law. He pokes me in the chest, reminds me of my father the way he pushes me back, and when I tell him I understand, he walks away and outside.

I ask Hank if he's okay.

"I am not even close to okay," Hank says. He walks by me, his eyes and his mouth angry slits, and he heads up to his room.

The Dilemma Faced by Nineteenth-Century Natural Theologians

Me, Sergei, and Maggot Arm Joe are gathering to go over our plans for what happens at Mr. Harry Fudge's estate down in Orange County. Fudge has called us out there tonight at midnight for reasons I'm unclear about. We may be getting his list, but I'm not sure. He doesn't like me and he's taken to Sergei, so I'm on a need-to-know basis, I suppose. Before we head over there, we're supposed to drop by the experimental clinic and Maggot Arm Joe is going, if everything's on schedule, to get the wraps off his arm and be maggot-free for the first time in quite a while. They need to make sure that the maggots have cleaned out all of his dead flesh. If so, they're coming out.

Then we need to kill some time somewhere before we head out to OC and see Harry Fudge.

Sergei puts on a pot of this black-as-tar Russian coffee he likes to force on us. Today, though, I might need some. It smells like oil burning off an engine as Sergei comes back to the living room.

That Mookie's dead is starting to settle in on me as the

three of us sit around Sergei's glass table as he cuts three fat lines of crushed crystal meth. Just one line each, though they're fat as index fingers. This is, as Sergei says, for fuel, not for fun; of course, he's the only one of us who considers meth fun. Maggot Arm Joe's a narcotic guy and I'm a drinker, but we don't say anything. This is for fuel, this is for men who have business to attend to. I take two drinks and then start on water to stay in control for later.

I'm thinking about the last time I saw Mookie, down the alley while Sergei fucked up the cowboy. The last time I talked to him was when he said good-bye to me at the pier after he hooked me up with Bondo Bob Lopez, who's still mad at Sergei for fucking up his bait bicycle. I'm trying to slow down my life, figure out when that was, exactly. It may have been only two days ago, but it feels like it could be a year. My life is dense as a Russian novel, full of names and people that I can't keep any track or sense of.

I can't snort anything with my nose the way it is, so I dump the meth in some gin and juice, just a little, swill it with a dirty finger, and swallow hard. It burns the back of my throat and Sergei hands me a box of snuff and a syringe full of ice water to cool the burn. I shoot the ice water up as far back on the throat as I can, then have him blow a hit of the snuff into the back of my throat. It makes a nice cooling and numbing paste.

Sergei takes the straw and does his line in one Texan snort. He shoots the ice water up his nose and does some of the snuff up his nose, the way you're supposed to, the way guys who can breathe out of their noses do it.

I go quickly to the bathroom to take a couple of the Percodans. I can't let Maggot Arm Joe see them. I know he's trying to stay away from junk and Percs are pretty much a water flume to the pool of heroin.

I wash my face, try to clear some of the scabby blood away from the lips and my eyelid. My bad eye is swollen shut and full of pressure and looks big as a bloody walnut.

Mookie. Death is something I just can't get around. It leaves me openmouthed and frightened. It sticks in me, pushing against my insides, and it doesn't get small and it doesn't dissolve. I think maybe someday I'll be old enough or maybe wise enough or maybe plain and simply tired enough that it will just seem like everything's okay, but that's not what I'm feeling now.

Death is slippery and death is big and it sits on my chest and I can't get a grip well enough to get it off of me. I dry what I can of my face, patting over the cuts gently, leaving pink blots on Sergei's face towel, and go back out to the living room.

Maggot Arm Joe bends over to do his line. Sergei asks if I'm okay.

"I'm still processing the whole thing with Mookie," I say.

"Mookie in better place, Nick Ray—don't worry about Mookie—worry about Nick Ray."

Maggot Arm Joe takes the syringe and shoots ice water up his nostril. "Better place—you believe that shit?"

"Not shit." Sergei plugs one nostril and blows meth-laced snot into his hand and then rubs his gums with the snot. I look away for a second and my stomach tumbles. "Was not allowed by state to have God," Sergei says. "My father had secret prayer meetings—men went to jail. This not shit."

"We go to a better place?" Maggot Arm Joe says.

"We do," Sergei says. "God make all and all good."

"I just can't believe you're religious," I say. "What about that cowboy?"

"Cowboy was evil—good fight evil."

"You're the good?" I say—I don't mean to be nasty, but this has me kind of floored.

Sergei looks at me. "I do much good. And I repent for not good things. Everything is good."

"Fuck, Sergei," Maggot Arm Joe says. "You sound like a natural theologian."

"Fuck you, Maggot man—I don't call you names."

"Not a name, man—it's what you are. You believe everything is God's work? That every sparrow's wing is brushed with the hand of God and every grain of sand is counted, right?"

Sergei nods.

And Maggot Arm Joe tells us about these nineteenth-century theologians and how they were on a mission to prove that God was good and that there was a reason for all the pain and suffering of the world. Lions killed wildebeests, sure, but they killed them zippy quick, no suffering, and it prevented starvation and disease in the herd. There was a reason for all pain, all suffering, and all the evil that infected the earth was put there by people, they reasoned.

But they couldn't come up with an argument for the so-called ichneumon fly, which was actually a composite creature representing the habits of a giant tribe of wasps: the ichneumonoidea.

Maggot Arm Joe says, "Dig—the females, they locate a host to house their eggs for larvae, right? Usually a caterpillar or a butterfly. And they convert that butterfly or caterpillar into a living food factory for their young. The mother paralyzes the host—she dumps hers eggs in it. The eggs gestate inside of the paralyzed host. Then, as they develop, the larvae eat the organs selectively so that host stays alive for as long as possible for them to eat off it. If they ate the heart or lungs, or whatever, the host would be dead—so they eat the fat cells and the digestive organs and leave the poor little butterfly alive."

I make a face. "Man—that's fierce."

"What's really fierce is that the victim is alive through all of this—while these things develop inside of it, eating it from the inside. Eventually—when they're ready to hatch, they eat the heart and central nervous system."

"So?" Sergei says.

"So, some things don't fit. The nineteenth-century theologians couldn't come up with any explanation why God would create the ichneumon wasp. Some shit is just pure ugly in this world and you can't make it nice and go away. Mookie lived on the street. Mookie ate garbage and Mookie suffered. And he died. No lesson in it." Maggot Arm Joe gets up and walks to the balcony, taking out a cigarette as he slides the door open. Sergei didn't used to let us smoke in his condo, but now he lets us light up on the balcony. I walk out and bum a smoke off of him.

Sergei says from the couch, "Believe what you believe. But Mookie in better place."

Maggot Arm Joe says, "Mookie got hit by a train and Mookie died. That's all we know."

My head hurts. My cuts are throbbing and dry and cracked and I feel something like a migraine coming on. I want to stop it all, these troublesome and problematic irreducible stories we tell one another to make it through our days. I want to shut out the world. I take a drag on the cigarette and look out off the balcony, past the harbor, past the oil islands, past the breakwater that I can't see but know it's there, and try to find Catalina, which you can see on a clear day. But today isn't a clear day, so I try to find where it would be if I could see it.

Medical Ingenuity

I've got nothing to do, and I'm too nervous to sleep, so I end up driving. Sergei's SUV is still dead, and he's staying with me and Maggot Arm Joe, for reasons of his own. I'm guessing trust is eroding here, and none of us will talk about it. I'm still mad that they want to deal with Fudge, but no money's shown up as a result of my plan, either. On the way over to the experimental clinic, which is down by the city's storage yards by the old railroad tracks, Sergei starts talking about Harry Fudge and the lists we are, maybe, going to sell him.

"I think tonight I talk to Mr. Fudge," Sergei says. "Get best deal."

Maggot Arm Joe says, "Best deal how?"

"Bluff rich man into better price."

Maggot Arm Joe laughs.

"What?" Sergei says.

"Dude, you couldn't bluff your way out of a kindergarten game of Go Fish. You are so easy to read."

"This not true." Sergei seems surprised and hurt.

"Tell him," Maggot Arm Joe says to me.

I try to think of a nice way to let Sergei know that his

emotions are as bold and awkward as a drag queen doing Joan Crawford. "You've got a pretty bad tell," I say.

He looks confused.

Maggot Arm Joe says, "A *tell*—a tic or series of tics that tip everyone off when you're about to bluff."

"This not true," Sergei says. He pauses. "Nick Ray—this tell—when do you see it—where?"

I decide to tell him the truth. I take my right hand off the steering wheel. "You tip your index finger up and down." I'm still wondering how it became decided by these two that we were dealing with Fudge. I sure as hell didn't sign off on it, and if they think it's been decided, they're way off base. Then it hits me that maybe *they* have decided—behind my back.

"Can keep hand in pocket," he says. "Keep hand under table—around cigar."

Maggot Arm Joe says, "You can't keep your eyes under the table. The man might think it was strange."

"Why didn't you tell me about tell?" Sergei says.

"Because we win money off you," I say. "You never tell your opponent about his tell."

"What do I do with eyes?"

And I want to say what don't you do with your eyes, but I'll keep it simple. "You twitch them," I say. "A lot. Around the eyelid, into the right cheekbone."

"You're like a fucking contortionist," Maggot Arm Joe says.

"Something must be done," Sergei says as I turn off Oregon Avenue, and curve around what used to be the Los Angeles River before they cemented the whole thing in about a quarter mile west of here. I park in a dirt-and-gravel lot near the clinic.

When I get out of the car I think about how this used to be a river, the ground I'm on, and it'll someday probably be a river again. You can nudge nature, but you can't control it. The next big earthquake, the cement riverbed will pop loose and the river will come right back to Oregon Avenue, where it was a hundred years ago.

And that next quake will come. We all know that here, we just don't talk about it much. We're in what seismologists call a "seismic siesta" and the next one might rock and shake the world enough to make future generations wonder just what the hell people were thinking when they plopped down five hundred thousand bungalows dead center on the fattest fault line on the continent.

I ask Maggot Arm Joe if he's excited about the arm getting unwrapped.

"Don't want to get too excited," he says. "Could still be bad news."

"Then what?" I say.

He shakes his head. "Got me. Surgery, I guess."

Inside we meet Maggot Arm Joe's doctor, who insists we call him Arlo and not Dr. Gonzales because Dr. Gonzales is so formal and Arlo just can't stand formal people. He invites us into the examination room, and I say no, but he presses and Maggot Arm Joe doesn't seem to care, so we follow them in. Sergei and I sit in these little chairs against the wall while Maggot Arm Joe hops up on the high padded table and starts to unbutton his shirt.

"So," Arlo says to Maggot Arm Joe. "How have we been feeling?"

"Not bad," he says, and takes his shirt off. I see the gauze wrap on his arm and get a greasy feeling when I realize he's had those maggots eating his flesh for weeks. "A little itchy."

Arlo nods. "Of course. But no fevers? No surface heat?"

"Nope."

"Good," Arlo says. "Now let's see what our little friends have been up to, okay?" Arlo puts on a pair of medical gloves and uses those dull-end stitches scissors to cut the white tape. After a couple of snips, the tape and the gauze flop away, still bent and elbow-shaped, to the floor. Arlo's back is blocking my view of Maggot Arm Joe's wound.

Arlo says, "Nice. Nice. Very good." He turns back to me and Sergei. "This is amazing, really. Years ago, this would have been a gruesome operation. Cutting into live muscle. Very painful. Very hard on the patient."

I'm wondering how this isn't gruesome, but I let it pass.

Arlo picks up the gauze wrap and says, "They're all near death. Very slow, very sluggish." He looks back to the arm. "Here, too—very sluggish."

"So?" Maggot Arm Joe says. "No surgery."

"I should say not," Arlo says. "Thanks to our friends." He takes out a blue curved dish and what looks like a paintbrush and starts swiping up and down the arm. Maggot Arm Joe looks away.

Arlo says, "Just another minute. Then we'll get some ointment on there for the itch." He sweeps the arm a few more times, then scrapes the gauze wrap into the blue dish and turns with the dish toward me and Sergei. He carries it over and holds it in front of us. He says, "There we go."

Inside the blue dish are a bunch of plump maggots that are as yellowed as old newspapers left in the sun. Most look dead. A couple of them move with very slow pulses of their entire bodies.

"Isn't that something?" Arlo says. "Medicine today, gentlemen—it's quite something."

"It is," I say.

I walk over and take a look at Maggot Arm Joe's arm. The inside of his arm looks like someone took a chunk of it out with a mellon baller. There's a big recess, and the skin's all slick, it catches the light, shiny as a latex miniskirt.

I say, "So that's healed? That's how it'll look?"

Arlo says, "That's close. Some muscle will fill back in. But when you destroy muscle, you change the shape of the body."

I look down at the slick recess in his arm.

Maggot Arm Joe says, "It's not so bad."

"You are a lucky man," Arlo says. "Medical ingenuity— there should be a thank-you section in Hallmark for medical ingenuity. The scars that a surgery would have left in that beautiful arm of yours would have been just savage. There would have been a big ugly hole in that arm."

I look down at what looks like a big ugly hole in his arm.

Arlo says, "The man that invented local anesthetic—you know how he proved how it worked?"

"How?" I say.

"He operated on himself. Took out his own appendix and filmed it. I have a still photo of it." Arlo goes into an adjacent room and comes back a moment later with a framed grainy black-and-white photo of what looks like a man slouched over with his shirt open sleeping off Thanksgiving dinner—but when you look closely, you can see he's cut himself open and he's carving around inside of himself.

"Gruesome," I say.

Arlo shakes his head. "Not gruesome. Medical ingenuity. That's what you're seeing there. What a profession—it's a blessing, I tell you, a blessing to do what I do. To be in such a blessed profession."

Sergei says, "Is there something medical ingenuity could give to someone with tic?"

I hand the photo over to Maggot Arm Joe, who looks at it, winces, and places it facedown on a countertop.

"Tic?" Arlo says. "Like Lyme disease?"

Maggot Arm Joe says, "I think he means a facial tic."

Arlo says, "I *see*. You mean to stop the facial tic?"

And I'm thinking does he have anyone who wants to increase their tic?

"Yes," Sergei says. "To stop tic."

"There is something relatively new—something quite wonderful. It's called botulism Toxin A."

"Toxin?" I say.

"It's the toxin that causes botulism," Arlo says.

"Doesn't that kill people?"

Arlo taps his temple, points at his diplomas. "Dosage, dosage, my friend. Proper training. Medical ingenuity, you see."

"It stop tic?" Sergei says.

"It would," Arlo says. "Would you like to make an appointment? I'll need your medical records sent over in the interim."

Sergei shakes his head. "Need to stop tic today. Give me your botulism."

Arlo says, "It's not possible. This is a state-run clinic. There are rules. There is paperwork."

"Give hundred dollars for shot."

Arlo chuckles. "I'm afraid that's not possible. This is a state-run clinic."

Sergei says, "I give five hundred. All I have." I see his twitch and realize he's carrying more than five hundred. Any five-year-old could read his tell and I don't suppose Arlo has missed it.

Maggot Arm Joe says, "How much money would it take for my friend to benefit from your extensive training and medical ingenuity?"

There's a pause. Arlo puts down a pair of shiny scissors and they clang lightly on the metal tray.

"Two thousand," Arlo says, and points to me. "And I'll throw in an ointment for his face."

"We have deal," Sergei says. He hops up on the table in the center of the room. "Let us do this."

Arlo stands by his desk. "Not that I don't trust you," he says. "About the matter of payment."

Sergei shoves a hand deep in the pocket of his leather pants. "Yes, yes," he says, and counts out two grand in hundreds. While his money's still out he gestures to me and Maggot Arm Joe. "How much for friends?"

Before Arlo can answer, Maggot Arm Joe says, "Fuck that—no way the man's shooting me full of botulism."

"Oh no," Sergei says. "Man has maggots in arm but doesn't want a little shot." He shakes his head. "Nick Ray like to fix face?"

I tell him no, I'll stand pat.

Sergei gives Arlo the two grand, sits back, and closes his eyes. Arlo goes into his cabinet, gets a little bottle with the rubber top. He pulls some fluid back into the syringe and walks up to Sergei. "Now this'll be a bee sting."

Sergei opens his eyes, winces, as Arlo injects a series of shots, skin popping, put in at an angle in a skin fold, like people do when they're afraid to shoot into veins, under the skin all along the hairline. When he's done there, he injects one shot in each of the crow's-feet around Sergei's eyes. Blood seeps from every injection site.

Arlo says, "That'll do it."

Sergei smiles. Frowns. Smiles. Frowns. It looks like he's doing community theater and the director's saying *Happy-sad-happy-sad.* He says, "Can still move face."

"Of course you can," Arlo says. "It'll take five days for the poison to be fully absorbed." He pauses. "This is muscle tissue we're talking about."

"Need new face tonight," Sergei says.

Arlo shakes his head. "It's not possible."

Sergei stands, he hovers over Arlo. "You fix," he says. "Need no tic by tonight."

"Sir, please calm down," Arlo says.

"Give back money," Sergei says.

Arlo says, "There is *some*thing I could do." Sergei stops leaning into Arlo. "But it's rather unusual."

"It fix tic by tonight?" Sergei says.

"It could."

"Then do it."

Arlo tells us that a combination of a higher, though still medically prudent, dosage and some minor electric stimulation of the facial muscles could do the trick. He reinjects Sergei's face; from the looks of it, he's tripled the dose. I wonder how much of this toxin a person can take before it causes botulism.

"Electromuscle stimulation," he says. "You've, no doubt, heard the benefits for weight loss, for sports medicine. You electronically stimulate the muscle thousands of times—hundreds per minute—over and over and it's like doing exercises without effort. It's quite ingenious."

Arlo starts hooking little wires, small, like they're from the crystal radio sets I built as a kid, onto Sergei's face. He tapes them down with clear tape. There are two wires up near Sergei's forehead and two more on the upper cheekbones. The wires connect from Sergei's face into a small metal box that looks like the power station for a toy train. It has a circular wheel on it, like a volume knob, and when Arlo turns it to the right, Sergei's face jolts wide open like a flower. Arlo turns the knob all the way up and flicks a toggle switch. "This will set it on a high pulse," he says. "We'll try it for five minutes, and we'll see how we're doing."

Sergei grunts every time the pulse makes his face open and big and he sighs a little every time the charge expires and his face relaxes. Every time the charge hits, his body goes rigid, like he's in an electric chair. Every time the charge ends, his body slumps down.

Ugh. Sigh. Ugh. Sigh.

It looks like a special effect, like it's not a real human face that's expanding and contracting in front of me. I look at Maggot Arm Joe and he shakes his head and looks away. Sergei looks at me, he's keeping his head straight, so he has to look from the corners of his eyes, and he holds out his hand. I don't move. He gestures for me to come over. I walk over to him, and when I get close, he grabs my hand and holds on tightly. I see now there are tears in his eyes and his hand clamps down on mine whenever the charge hits him.

"I think you better turn this off," I say to Arlo.

Sergei shakes his head.

I ask Arlo how much longer and he tells me a minute and a half.

And so, for the next minute and a half, which seems like much longer, I feel the rhythmic pulse of Sergei in pain in my hand when he clenches and unclenches and Arlo sends his charge through Sergei. When it's over, Sergei collapses back onto the table. He lies there, catching his breath, for a minute, while still holding my hand. He takes his hands from mine and I feel the air, cool where his sweaty hand was.

Sergei rubs his chin. He touches above his eyes and his cheekbones. "Yes," he says in a strange, dulled and slurred voice. "That much better, I think." He rubs some more.

"Face hurts," he says. "Hurts much."

"Of course it does," Arlo says. "It's like your face just did two thousand sit-ups. It'll be sore for a while, but that tic of yours should be a thing of the past."

"For how long?" I say.

"A normal dose of the toxin's good for six months," he says. "This is a first—no way to tell how long this will last."

I look at Arlo and wonder if he's even really a doctor. But then real doctors cut off the wrong leg. Real doctors fuck up, too. A kid I knew in high school died on the table while they were taking out his tonsils. Arlo did fix Maggot Arm Joe and he seems to have locked up Sergei's face. Arlo pats me on the back as he follows me out of his exam room.

Sergei tips Arlo $500 as we leave his office. In the parking lot, it's dark. Even though the weather's beautiful, the winter depresses me, no matter where I am. The sun goes down at 4:30 this time of year. Too much darkness too early. Winter reminds me of when I had a family, when I had a life. New Year's

Eve celebrations remind me of another year wasted. Nothing good happens in the winter for me. It's a time to get through.

Sergei moves his jaw back and forth. I ask him if he's okay.

He nods, but doesn't talk.

"Can you talk?" I say.

"Hurts to talk."

I give Sergei one of my Percodans. Maggot Arm Joe sees them, but doesn't say anything. Sergei pops the pill.

"Can you eat?" Maggot Arm Joe says.

Sergei says yes.

"Want to hit the Colonial for the manager's fat-ass special?"

The Colonial is Sergei's favorite place. It's all you can eat, which Maggot Arm Joe calls the manager's fat-ass special. The food's pretty bad, but you can get a ton of it. It's better, I suppose, for meat eaters. All I can get there is a ton of starch that's usually mixed with cheese. I spend most of my time picking what looks like bacon from what might be green beans. But this offer is Maggot Arm Joe being nice, saying thanks in his way for Sergei subjecting himself to this poison, and I'm not about to say no.

"Would like that," Sergei says. He looks like a zombie, like Yul Brynner in *Westworld*, stiff and awkward and without emotion as he wreaks havoc on everything in his path. Arlo's treatment worked—you can't tell what Sergei's thinking anymore and I realize this could hurt us as well as help. It's creepy, his lack of facial gestures. He's like a ventriloquist's dummy—his mouth a slit that opens and closes. He gets in the backseat and closes his eyes as I pull out of the lot, the tires popping and crunching warmly over the gravel and loose dirt.

Lite-A-Line

I eat mostly mushy stuff at the Colonial, since my cuts are stiff and brittle and if I chew too much, they split open fresh. I load up on mashed potatoes and macaroni and cheese and watch Sergei mechanically shovel food into his mouth while the rest of his face remains astoundingly still.

The Colonial is where this local religious cult named The Way always eats. There's hundreds of them, they've got a real Stepford vibe. With his face all stilled, Sergei kind of looks like one of them. The women wear long shapeless dresses with floral prints and the men all look like chubby FBI agents. And they all wear a tag pinned above their hearts that reads DO YOU KNOW THE WAY? You have to be careful. They harass you when you're up getting your soup and gravy. One of them stops by our table and asks if we know The Way.

"My foot knows the way to your ass," Maggot Arm Joe says. "How's that?"

"The Lord Jesus could help you with all that hate—all that anger," The Way guy says.

"You find Him, you send Him over—otherwise leave me alone, okay?"

The guy looks stunned. He will head back to the flock without having saved the three strange men at the table. But for now, he's still standing there dumbfounded with his tray full of food.

"Will you please find *the way* back to your creepy little tribe?" Maggot Arm Joe says.

The religious guy waddles away and sits at a table with a bunch of other Way people who treat him like he's a pinch hit-ter who struck out. It's back pats and reassurances. Next time, you'll get them next time.

After dinner, we walk out in the cool night air, our breath showing a little. Maggot Arm Joe lights a cigarette. He sees me looking at him and he tells me he'll give me one for a Per-codan.

I tell him I'm worried about him doing the Percs, that they might not be the best thing for a recovering junkie.

"I don't stop you from drinking, Nick," he says.

"Fair enough," I say. "But no way is this an even deal."

"Give me the Percodan, and you can have unlimited ciga-rettes."

"Unlimited?"

Maggot Arm Joe pauses and thinks. "For the rest of the year."

This still gives me free smokes for the next two days. I shake a pill out into my hand and tell him he's got a deal. He gives me a cigarette and lights it as I lean toward him.

"What now?" I say. I look at my watch. We've got three hours to kill before we meet with Harry Fudge, which means we've got two hours to kill before we get on the road.

"Lite-A-Line?" Sergei says.

Lite-A-Line is this gambling game down at what used to be Long Beach Pike. It's like a combination of bingo and pinball without flippers. You send your ball up and you hope that it bounces into the right slots to light a line—all the same number, or all the same color. You drop 75 cents a game in hopes of getting back 12 dollars for a winner. At the top and bottom of the hour, they have bigger-stakes games where you put down $1.50 to win $25 or 3 bucks to take $50. Sergei loves the fat games, he'd play two tables if they let him.

Lite-A-Line's in a building that was originally a carousel back in 1911, then in 1941 it became the gambling building. We walk down Elm to Ocean Boulevard and go down the steep hill to the building.

Out front I see Tony Vic with Willie What's His Name and Tony Vic's talking to Billy Mangos, who's known as Billy Mangos because he's addicted to the mango-on-a-stick that the Mexican-American bicycle vendors sell. Billy Mangos is a thief who steals merchandise from the Sea and Land trucks down by the water yard. Actually, he hires high school kids to do his picking, and he stays relatively clean as a low-level crime guy.

We're coming up close to the three of them and I see Willie What's His Name's hand is wrapped up in a gauze and an Ace bandage so that only the last knuckles of his index and middle fingers are poking out of the wrap. The rest of his hand looks like a beige club. I wonder if he's pissed that Tony Vic walked on him when Willie blew up his hand, but I suppose there's an understanding between them that if the authorities arrive, it's time to scatter. It's the only time I've seen them split up, otherwise, they're always together. One moves, then the other—they're hooked, fused, and hot-wired, as wrapped into each other as the feet and head of a pigeon.

Willie What's His Name looks at me, and it's clear that he doesn't remember splitting my face up. I thought maybe I'd say something, but what good would it do?

"I need some toasters," Tony Vic says to Billy Mangos.

"No can do."

"You can't get me toasters? What kind of a thief can't get toasters? I'm not asking for a particularly exotic item."

"Tell you what," Billy Mangos says. "I'll give you some toast and you can backwards-engineer it."

"What the fuck are you talking?" Tony Vic says.

The three of us start to pass the three of them and we do our cool-guy nods and start to walk into Lite-A-Line. Tony Vic grabs me, he holds his index finger up to Billy Mangos, who's staring at my mashed-up face. Tony Vic says, "Nick, my man. How are you?"

"Fine," I say.

Tony Vic looks over to Willie What's His Name, who lowers his eyes like a good kid learning a valuable lesson. He's bringing that hammer he stole back to Mr. Landry's hardware store while his daddy Tony Vic tells him to say he's sorry.

Tony Vic says, "Nick, my man, I'd like to—well, *we'd* like to compensate you for your unfortunate injuries from the other evening."

I hold out my hand. "Give me fifty bucks."

Tony Vic shakes his head. "I was thinking we could barter."

Sergei and Maggot Arm Joe go inside and tell me they'll save me a table.

"I was thinking fifty bucks," I say to Tony Vic.

"Nick, my man. We can barter—like country gentlemen."

"Is that what we are?"

"It's an ideal, Nick. What men like us aspire to."

I could argue that being a country gentleman isn't my ideal, is one of the few things that seems more of a dead end than my actual life, but I'm getting tired of Tony Vic and I want to get inside. "Give me fifty bucks' worth of fetal pigs."

He makes a face. "I was hoping to turn some money on those pigs," he says.

"Bullshit," I say. "How many pigs do I get for fifty bucks?"

"I don't know," he says. "I could give you two."

"Ten."

"That's stealing them, Nick. Ten is a crime," Tony Vic says. "How about five?"

"Done," I say. "Leave them at the Lincoln."

Tony Vic gestures back to Willie What's His Name. "So, we're cool. Everyone here—no one's mad."

"No one's mad," I say. We all shake hands, even me and Billy Mangos, who has slick, hard hands like a farmer, and then I head inside to get my game card and join Maggot Arm Joe and Sergei at the tables.

Lite-A-Line is an experience. It's where the poor of Long Beach gamble at the tables the poor of Long Beach have gambled at for the last sixty years. There's something both ennobling and terribly sad about the optimism of the poor when we gamble. You can't smoke at Lite-A-Line anymore, but you can tell that you could once. Over half the people here have unlit cigarettes, pens, or lollipops dangling from their lips. A buzzer starts the game, then you hear the roll of sixty-four of

201

the little balls as they bounce their way through the tables and light the lights.

The way it usually works is you get pretty close, and then someone else wins. Every hour or so, someone who's been losing badly gets angry and starts pounding on the table glass. Tonight, it's one of the Vietnamese gang kids at table forty, which is my favorite table, the one I've won four or five times on, he's pounding the glass and a big guy in a red "Loof 's Lite-A-Line" shirt comes over and asks him to leave. I don't know this guy's name, but he's sort of the pit boss here and he keeps the order and he says something to the kid and the kid nods and calms down and stays at the table.

For a half an hour, we lose pretty badly—I'm down twenty dollars. The guy who takes the money doesn't seem to notice my face. For better or worse, I fit in here. The woman in the big booth announces that this is a Top of the Hour Game. She says this is the first game on the eighth sheet, which is gibberish that's meant for the people who take the money off the tables, not for the people who put the money on the tables. The Top of the Hour Game is three dollars down for a fat fifty-dollar payout. I sit it out, so does Maggot Arm Joe. Sergei takes a dollar off my table and one off Maggot Arm Joe's and plops the three singles on his table.

"You know, this kind of defeats the purpose of me sitting this one out," I say.

Sergei says, "Have figured table out. It wants to have balls in white."

The buzzer rings and the balls drop and Sergei's playing the whites, he's got the touch down and gets everything but the white 3. He gets the same one, the white 4, three times in a row and the repeats are useless. But several tries in, he gets the white 3 and takes the big-money game. They drop five stacks of ten silver tokens in front of him and he turns to us, his palms up, gesturing to the tokens.

"This," he says, "must bode well for evening."

A few losing games later, we gather what's left of the tokens, cash them in, and go out to my car for our nervous trip down to Orange County.

DAY 6
DECEMBER 30

Harry Fudge's Museum

Harry Fudge lives on top of a foothill in Orange County. One of those lush semimountains that humps itself out of the earth and you see them all rolling and beautiful from the freeway on the days without smog and you wonder who could possibly live up there and live like that.

There's a guard at the gates and I'm about to give our name, but Sergei leans over me to the driver's-side window.

"Advance to go," he says to the guard.

The guard nods and the gate swoops open.

As we climb the driveway the house looms down on us like Xanadu in the opening shots of *Citizen Kane*. It seems huge from a distance, and it only gets bigger as we're up near the front doors, which are bordered by two Roman columns thick as sumo wrestlers and twenty feet tall. A thin man in what looks like the last Nehru jacket in California steps out and is backlit by the light from the entrance.

I stop in front of him and have Sergei roll down his window.

"I am Paulo," he says. "Park anywhere."

"I've got a pretty vicious oil leak," I say.

Paulo considers for a moment, then points over by the

jacaranda tree, which is strung with white lights all along its branches. "Pull it up under the tree—over by the lawncrete."

"Lawncrete?"

I look over, and there's only grass beneath the tree. He points, and I do my best to position it where he wants. I get out and I see what he meant. From a distance, it looks like grass, but it's really grass in diamond-pattern patches on a bed of concrete.

Maggot Arm Joe looks down. "Lawncrete?"

"Who knew?" I say, and the three of us head toward Paulo, who's standing on the front steps of Harry Fudge's mansion.

We reach the steps, which are concrete inlaid with what looks like costume jewelry, round colored stones big as noses.

Paulo says, "This way, you come."

We follow him through an entrance room with twenty-foot ceilings and marble floors. The house is on some huge scale, the hallways as wide as rooms I'm used to, the rooms like gymnasiums, and I feel like I'm in a scene from *The Incredible Shrinking Man*. Paulo leads us to what looks like a study filled with dark woods and stained red leather chairs that creak softly as the three of us sit and wait, as ordered, for Harry Fudge to join us. Everywhere I look, there's something about the *Titanic*. Models, posters, tickets under glass, paintings, you name it, he seems to have it.

Harry Fudge rolls in to the room in a wheelchair a moment later, looking as if he's taken a horrific bad turn since we last saw him. He barely resembles the thick, threatening man I met on the *Queen Mary* just a couple days back. Of course, two days ago, Sergei could smile and my face wasn't full of cuts. Time changes things, sometimes quickly and sometimes for the worse.

Harry Fudge's wheelchair has a caddie on the back for a green hissing tank labeled OXYGEN that leads to a mask that's hooked into this thing that looks like a harmonica holder in front of Harry Fudge's mouth. If he needs a hit of oxygen, he leans forward into the mask and takes a whiny suck that's frighteningly shallow. His face is the color of pickle juice, his fingers are the blue gray of clouds at night and his voice is quiet, and everything he says sounds like he's got something in his throat.

My head throbs and I wish I'd had a drink before we came.

He wheels behind his desk and turns left and right, jostling a bit to fit himself into proper position. "Gentlemen," he says. He nods to Paulo, who unwraps a cigar and hands it to Harry Fudge, who licks it a couple of times before putting it in his mouth for a moment. He takes it out. "Can't light them—I've had an unfortunate attack. The flavor, though—can't live without, you see."

"Of course," Sergei says. "Man need comforts."

Harry Fudge frowns. "What's wrong with your face, boy?"

Sergei says, "Slept on it."

"You say you slept on your face? Who doesn't?"

"Make very stiff," Sergei says.

Harry Fudge looks at me. "And your face, son. What the hell happened?"

I tell him it was a car accident.

Harry Fudge shakes his head, and when he does, his cheeks bump the edges of the oxygen mask and leave little spittle lines on them. He points with his cigar at Sergei. "You foreign boys, you're strange," he says. "When I first got into the oil business, it amazed me how different foreign people were from the people I knew."

Harry Fudge coughs, and even though I can't stand him, it hurts me to watch it. I worked waiting tables in a retirement community once and it changed me, being around that much decay and death. And what I'm seeing now, I've seen before, it's the gray tightness of emphysema and it's killing Harry Fudge and it's something almost no one deserves to have ever felt.

Paulo comes over behind the desk and wipes Harry Fudge's face after his coughing spell. Harry Fudge nods him away, and Paulo takes three steps to the side and stands at attention.

"I don't have long, from what I'm told," Harry Fudge says. "And I need some business taken care of before I go. There is a new sense of urgency. I need you boys—what you have." He nods to Paulo, who takes an envelope out of his breast pocket and hands it to Sergei.

Maggot Arm Joe says, "We may not have what you need. We may not have the people you're looking for."

"True," he says. "But you're my best chance. I will not die without seeing justice done." He looks toward me and takes a big suck on the oxygen while his eyes stare at me and it's disturbing. He gathers himself after moving his head away from the mask. "This has nothing to do with me—this is about setting things right."

I could argue, but it wouldn't do any good. I look over at the envelope Sergei's holding and wonder if it's possible that we could get lucky enough to not have any of their names on our computers. There are a lot of criminals in this world, they don't all have to be on our lists. I'd love to bring Harry Fudge the bad news.

Harry Fudge says, "I will give you twenty thousand dollars for every name you can match from the list I will give you. You tell me where those men are—twenty thousand apiece."

Maggot Arm Joe nods and Sergei, still-faced and wooden with his head full of toxins, does the same. I try to look coolly impressed, but I'm getting tired of this world of men who are like scratch lotto tickets: they swell with the promise of big money, but I'm still broke every time we part ways.

"I want to show you boys something," Harry Fudge says. He jiggles his hand guide a couple of times and his wheelchair kicks and starts and we stand and follow his electric hum down several of his immense halls. We take enough turns that I'm lost. I'd need a guide to find my way out of this house. We come to an elevator that's big and wide, like the ones they take the gurneys onto in hospitals. The doors are brushed metal, like a Viking stove, and I see my bleary shadowy reflection in them before they open.

"Go ahead of me," Harry Fudge says.

We walk in, followed by Harry Fudge and then Paulo, who walks like Jack Webb in *Dragnet*, stick-up-his-ass straight with his arms at his sides. He corners at ninety-degree angles, stiff and military, and he pivots after he's in and hits the down button.

The smell of chlorine and a wash of cold air—like a walk-in freezer—hits me as the elevator doors open on a room that's as big as an airline hangar. There's an Olympic-size swimming pool and I can hear the gurgle of a filter under the sound of our footsteps and Harry Fudge's wheelchair.

Harry Fudge wheels over to the side of the pool, which is dark. You can hear light sloshes against the side. There are lights near the side of the room, dimmed halogens that allow you not to kill yourself walking around. He zips forward and jerks back like he's parallel-parking. He motions us to three chairs set up next to him. I see my breath.

As we sit, Harry Fudge says, "What do you boys know about the *Titanic*?"

"Big boat—hit an iceberg," I say. "Didn't they make a movie about it?"

I can't see his face too clearly, but I'm guessing that Maggot Arm Joe's giving me a dirty look.

"That atrocity of a film," he says, "nearly ruined my life." Harry Fudge goes on to explain that he had spent a good-size hunk of his nest egg, his rainy-day mad money, and boy is he mad, on what he calls a "mass media project" meant to inform the public at large of the greatest story of the century: the sinking of the *Titanic*.

"I had vision," Harry Fudge says between labored breaths. "This was an enormous story—a story too big to bring to the public, you had to bring them to it."

So Harry Fudge, fifteen years ago, began turning his mansion into a *Titanic* museum. This took hours from days and days from what was left to a life but it was, he takes pains to tell us, a calling.

We're still sitting in the semidark in this wet and cold room. The filter hums and gurgles. I think Paulo's still in the room, but I don't see or hear him. Maggot Arm Joe says, "So what's the beef with Cameron?"

"I have studied the *Titanic* for forty years," he says. "It is, among other things, one of the most witnessed disasters of the century. Seven hundred and five people survived to tell a story, and nearly half of those stories are mutually exclusive. Seven hundred and five people were there. Historians, shipbuilders, naval architects, professors of every discipline have studied it—and we know so little about it. More facts are known about the *Titanic*'s sinking than any other disaster, and yet we still don't know what happened that night. You add up the facts and you don't get the truth, you just get story after story after story." Harry Fudge pauses, coughs, and spittles a bit before taking some oxygen. I hear the mild suction when he pulls his face away from the mask.

He says, "It is the most elusive, irreducible, unknowable event of the modern world. You do not take such a majestic tale and make a second-rate love story out of it. Cameron used the greatest story of the century to tell a piece-of-shit, wrong-side-of-the-tracks love story. He cheapened the deaths of fifteen hundred people."

"It's just a bad movie," I say.

"It's not," Harry Fudge says. "It's an event—it occurred. People suffered, people died, because of the decisions and mistakes of others. It's not some story, some movie."

I try to look casually at my watch, but I can't see it and I momentarily curse myself for not getting a glow-in-the-dark face one for a couple bucks more from Benny the Mole. It must be around one in the morning. I'm tired—weighted-down tired—the kind of weariness where sounds blend and roll over one another in waves. What I would like, what I need, is a beer or two and a warm bed.

"How many black people died on that boat?" Maggot Arm Joe asks.

"Ship," Harry Fudge says.

"Ship," Maggot Arm Joe says.

"Honestly," Harry Fudge says. "None. But that shouldn't minimize the event's importance to all peoples."

"Why not?" Maggot Arm Joe says. "The U.S. Army blows the shit out of hundreds of black men—its own soldiers, mind you, not some fucking enemy—and charges the survivors,

charges *them* with treason, for not wanting to let the army finish the job. No one gave a shit about that—no one talked
about its importance to all peoples. Tuskegee—you don't hear
about how all people should be caring about that."

Sergei says, "Shut up—you squeaky wheel, you."

Harry Fudge laughs softly. "No, let him speak his mind."
He pauses. "Point taken, son. You were a fine lawyer, you
know that?"

"I do," Maggot Arm Joe says.

"But sit back and learn something," Harry Fudge says.

Harry Fudge tells this story:

His grandfather, Moses Fudge, was a hired deckhand on
what is known to *Titanic* scholars as the "Undertakers' Ship."
This ship, the *Mackey-Bennett,* was hired by the White Star
Line out of Halifax, Nova Scotia. This is hours after they
learned about the sinking, about all those dead people out
there floating on the surface of twenty-eight-degree water.
Harry Fudge tells us that they hired the *Mackey-Bennett* in
hopes of finding some survivors, but they knew what turned
out to be the truth, there were hundreds of frozen dead bodies floating on the surface, along with tables, chairs, broken
pieces of wood, and—this is among the most troubling for
some reason—over thirty dogs. People were traveling, people
were starting new lives in this great new America, bright and
fresh as factory chrome. Everything was on the surface: their
things, their children, their pets, and them.

The *Mackey-Bennett's* job was simple. They would pluck
the dead from the water and judge, from their clothing and
jewelry, whether they were first-, second-, or steerage-class
passengers. The first-class bodies were embalmed. The steer-
age class were weighted down to drop to the bottom.

Moses Fudge wrote this all down in a diary and then never spoke about it again before he hanged himself in his backyard in Latrobe, Pennsylvania in 1934. The diary, among other papers, was willed to his grandson, young Harry Fudge.

"And as a boy, I read those descriptions of his over and over. How they came across the bodies from a distance in the early morning. The sun gleamed off of the ice field and all the boys on deck were placing bets on which was the fatal iceberg. The first thing they hooked, at least the first thing my grandfather hooked, was a Scottish terrier. When he saw what it was, it scared him and he dropped it and the sound, he said, was like a block of ice. It slid along the deck and slammed into the side of the ship and they chased it down and threw it over. Then the bodies of the passengers appeared on the horizon. Over three hundred people left—left in the water. And, gentlemen, this did not need to have happened."

Harry Fudge claps twice and a bank of lights come on over the far right side of the pool. In the pool is a four-foot model of what I'm guessing is the *Titanic*. There's a tremendous amount of detail, the ship's painted. There are several little people gathered on the decks.

"This is the ship at twelve-forty-five, sixty-five minutes after striking the iceberg. Captain Smith, at this point, knows the ship is doomed. Notice the forward list. At this point, lifeboat number seven, which can hold sixty-five people, leaves the ship with twenty-eight people."

Harry Fudge claps again and an audiotape starts running. There's the clamor of voices and ship's horns and buzzers.

"What you're hearing, gentlemen, is an approximation of the noises that would have accompanied key moments in the ship's sinking."

Harry Fudge says, "Next," and the lights go out and it's difficult to see the model. Then another bank of lights comes on maybe ten feet to the left of the first lights and there's another model of the *Titanic*. It looks worse, farther down, there are several small lifeboats off the sides of it, and there are more little people on the decks. The noise increases from the tapes. There's a swell in the panic of the voices. The buzzing of general fear. Feet scurrying. More horns and buzzers, the desperate croaks of authority and order.

The *Titanic* in the pool looks doomed. The water is up to its name on the side.

"One-ten A.M.," Harry Fudge says. "Lifeboat number eight—there are thirty-nine people aboard in a lifeboat with a capacity for sixty-five. The *Titanic* has one hour and nineteen minutes left."

Along with the sound of people running and moaning and yelling are the gentle cuts of lifeboat oars in the water, a deep, plunky peaceful sound under the human voices.

The lights go out. More lights come up another twenty feet left in the pool. The ship here is even worse off, it's like a time line of despair. If the people on it had any doubts that they were going down, they must have been answered at this point. There's water all over the front of the ship. It looks to be a third of the way down.

The screams and noise on the audiotape are much louder. The people sound more like they know they might die. I wonder how Harry Fudge got all this down. Did he hire actors? The sound system's incredible, the noises get louder with every change of the lights, and now it's rock-concert loud. My ears will be ringing tomorrow. That kind of loud.

"Two-oh-five. Collapsible D is sent off with forty-four peo-ple and a capacity for forty-seven. The boats are filling now—there's a desperation in the crew and passengers that was lacking at midnight. Remember—many people thought this ship could not sink. It was generally thought to be more dangerous to be cast adrift on the Atlantic in a lifeboat."

Around Harry Fudge's doomed model of the *Titanic* are fourteen little lifeboats—scattered like thrown gravel around the ship. Some look far away, if everything's to scale, maybe a half mile or more. The voices on the tape are joined by the industrial suffering of the ship itself, metal racking against metal. Creaks and breaks, thunderous crashes that I can feel inside me, that's how loud it is.

Paulo brings Harry Fudge a microphone, and his voice comes above the noise and damage. "The ship's lights flicker and go out."

The next section of the display is lit, on both sides of the pool, it reads: 2:20 A.M.—SHIP FOUNDERS. It sounds like a thousand car wrecks.

The lights go out and come up on several lifeboats surrounding the spot where the *Titanic* was. The sound of the ship, of the metal, of the crashing and tearing, is gone. All that's left is the steady whine of human voices. It's an unrelenting sound, like an amplified hornets' nest. It sounds a little like when the Grand Prix hits Long Beach, and for three days, there's the constant whine of cars in the distance under everything you hear.

Harry Fudge holds the microphone to his wet lips. "What you are hearing is the sound of those left on the surface. The sound of the three hundred and eighteen dead my grandfather came across the next day. Several of the boats were close enough to go back and pick these people out of the water. None of the voices you're hearing survived."

And I know that the voices I'm hearing did survive, they are actors doing what Harry Fudge told them to, but still, it's eerie. Under the steady but thinning screams of the dying is the *plunk, plunk, plunk* of oars hitting water, taking the passengers farther and farther away from the screams that must have sickened them.

We listen for what seems like fifteen minutes. I feel my heartbeat hard in my chest and ears and fingers. The voices thin, the lack of sound is the sound of people dying. After the fifteen minutes, there are only a few voices under the sound of water, you can make them out. It's hard to tell if they're men or women, it's the sound of near-unconscious pain, but there are three of them left. Then two. Then one voice, moaning in the water, and then none. The slosh of water.

Harry Fudge says, "It's important, if you are to do business with me, that you understand human suffering." He pauses and I wonder if we are supposed to say something. A light comes on at the far left end of the pool. There's nothing to see in the water. It must represent the sea when everything sank.

Harry Fudge wheels over to that end of the pool and we follow. Fudge tells us that this is a saltwater pool, held at twenty-eight degrees. He used the salt because fresh water would freeze at the proper temperature.

"It's essential that you understand suffering," Harry Fudge says. "Know that the men on your list will suffer like this and no one will pull them out of the water. They will know pain and suffering. But know that it pains me to take this measure of justice against them." Harry Fudge coughs and gurgles a bit. I can hear a rattle in his chest. "Know that I understand the nature of suffering before I take my justice against these men. I know what a voice sounds like before it is silenced—know that it hurts me to do this."

He backs up a bit, then jerks forward. "I look forward to hearing from you." His wheels make a rubbery gripping sound on the wet concrete as he pulls away.

A Not Uncommon Occurrence

I'm still cold on the drive back from that nasty meat locker of a room.

It's around 3:30 in the morning when Maggot Arm Joe and I get home after dropping Sergei at his condo. Hank Crow's asleep at the desk as I let myself in. Maggot Arm Joe heads up to his room while I check the desk for messages from Tara. Nothing. I decide to give her a buzz in the morning. Hank Crow's hard to wake up, so I leave him alone. Why wake him up to make him go to sleep? I put up the "Closed" sign so no one'll bother him, and I grab my sport jacket off the back of one of the seats and I take two of Hank's beers out of the minifridge, leave him an IOU note for them, and go to the front stoop.

I put one beer in my sport-jacket pocket and one in a brown paper bag so I can drink it out on the front step. I walk out, the beer in my pocket weighing one side of the jacket down and pulling against my neck. I sit down and the glass bottle clunks on the steps through my jacket pocket and I look up at the blank sky. I'm wondering what I'm going to do with my life. Whether this plan for the money works out or not, there's no way I can continue like this. I'm looking ahead, a year, two years, five, ten, and the years just seem to loom ahead the same forever with boredom and violence and sadness. Every one like the one before it until they stop.

Maybe I should clean out and see what Tara says about a new improved Nick Ray.

I take a drink of the cold beer and feel suffocated as I drink because I can't breathe through the nose.

I finish the first beer and decide to take the other one to bed.

I drag my way up the steps hoping that I can get a decent night's sleep before checking on Harry Fudge's names sometime tomorrow. I open the door and flick on the light and am knocked back in fear and anger when I see that I've been robbed. It rolls in slowly at first. I don't see the video camera, I don't see the television, the window's been broken and is open to the fire escape. Then it hits me: the computers are gone, and with them several names that may be worth twenty grand apiece. I can't believe it. To lose all hope this quickly.

I smash around the room. I throw my keys and the plastic Subaru key ring explodes and the plastic and keys go skidding across the hardwood floor. I try to calm down, to do what someone better than me would do, to assess, to calmly and rationally see exactly where it is we stand. I make a mental list.

Gone:

Television
VCR
Video camera
Computers and monitor
My jar of change by the ashtray

Gone.

I take another deep breath and try to see what's left before I come to any judgments, before I lose control.

They left the kiddie pool, which is sagging and growing a translucent film. And they left a pile of shit on my bed. I look closer and there's two muddy footprints and indentations on either side of it. Some clown squatted and shit on my bed.

I call the police and the woman on the nonemergency line tells me it'll be between one and three hours before the cops come by. I tell her about the shit on my bed and she tells me that doesn't speed up the process, that it'll be between one and three hours before I see a cop. I tell her I could be arrested in five minutes if I tried to sleep in the park and she patiently tells me that maybe I should go to the park then.

I hang up and look around. The computers are gone, it keeps coming back to me, this fact won't go away, it annoys me like a barking dog. We still have the ones Maggot Arm Joe's holding, but they may not have anything, and we could be out a lot of names and a lot of money if I can't find these. I go down to the desk and wake Hank Crow up.

"Boy, what time is it?" he says.

I tell him what happened.

"You say he shit on the bed?"

"He," I say. "She. Who the fuck knows?"

"It's a he," Hank says. "Not a fucking woman in the world would steal from a man and shit on his bed." He rolls his head and his neck cracks a couple of times. He lights a cigarette. "Woman shitting on a bed—I refuse to accept that."

"Was anyone in here looking for me?" I say.

"There was a young fellow with meat looking for you and your lawyer friend."

I look at him.

Hank Crow says, "I signed for it—I signed for meat. Told the fellow I never thought I'd sign for meat, but there it was. Lot of things happen that I never thought I'd see—people taking time to shit on beds when they should be busy stealing. Me signing for meat. It's a hell of a strange world if you live long enough."

Hank gets up from behind the desk and takes me out back, behind the staircase where we keep broken refrigerators and old space heaters. There, on a wooden pallet, is a stack of Mel Collins's freeze-dried meat that's six feet tall and four feet wide. It could fill you up after the apocalypse. Next to it is another pallet of meat.

"You signed for it?" I say.

"I did," Hank Crow says. "I signed for yours and for Joe Cole. You eat meat?"

"Nope."

We stand there looking at this pile of meat for a while and I want to cry. This is what I have in the world.

"The guy that delivered this—did he go up to my room?"

"No. Dropped it off and went away. Saw the truck pull out myself." There's a pause. "Sorry I was asleep, Nick. Wish I could help you with this."

I shake my head. "Looks like they came in and out through the escape—you probably couldn't have done anything." I pat him on the back and he and I go out to sit on the front steps with a couple of beers while I wait for the cops to show up. The night's quiet enough for us to hear the electric lines doing their business.

"You ever been robbed before?" Hank says.

I nod, tell Hank about when I was in Buffalo and someone took all my stuff. This is right after the marriage broke up, when I still had hopes of hanging around and impressing Cheryl with how much better and focused and driven I had become. A month after I moved out of the house, my new apartment got ripped off. They had great taste. I had a collection of over three hundred blues albums from the 1940s and 50s, including all the original Muddy Waters and Howlin' Wolf albums on the Chess label. An ex-girlfriend of mine had given me a framed still, autographed by Chuck Jones himself, from "Duck Amuck," my favorite Looney Tunes cartoon. A pre-CBS Fender Stratocaster worth a couple of grand. This was the last good stuff I had and I thought of it at the time as some sort of message, a message that said, *Don't focus on things.* Time to learn and simplify and understand life, but, like most of my self-improvements, it didn't take. It was only a couple of months later that I was out of Buffalo, and I'd started the drift that would eventually wash me up here.

"Sounds like you had good taste, not the thief," Hank says.

"Thing is, they left the bad stuff—Muddy Waters only cut one shitty album and they left it."

Hank Crow looks out at the street and takes a drink of beer. "Not *Electric Mud?* The psychedelic one?"

I nod.

"You had that?"

"I did." I take a drink of the beer and listen to the power lines buzz. I think of people in my room, rummaging through what little I have. It's a lousy feeling. "Fuck."

"I had a house burn to the ground," Hank says.

"Here?"

He shakes his head. "Back East. Boston—I was coming up from Bridgeport—one of only two cities to elect a socialist mayor."

"No shit?"

Hank looks happy. "And the only United States city to re-elect one—for eighteen years." Hank Crow lights a cigarette and offers me one. It's menthol, and I give it some thought, but I take one anyway, thinking it might calm me down. "That's where I was coming from—thinking socialism would change everything. Working folk would matter—take and share what was theirs—so, I'm supposed to unionize this shelving plant next to the Neco factory in Cambridge. I tell you, the whole street smelled like Neco wafers. Five years of my life smelled like that." He pantomimes a sniff, takes a drag of his cigarette. "Long story short, some men in charge did not share my vision of a united workforce. They burned my house down. Shot my car out. Called me all their names."

I think of what that could mean, to lose everything when you actually had something to lose. I think everyone must have had a harder life than me, which comes from my father. Whenever I cried as a kid, he'd show me a picture of this sideshow geek, the Human Torso. The Human Torso, according to my dad, he painted with a brush between his teeth, he was an auto mechanic, he married and fathered seven kids. *Look,* my father would say, and he'd poke a picture that looked like a huge worm of a naked man, *look at him, he's got no arms and legs and you don't see him crying.* I say to Hank Crow, "What did you do?"

"I moved, son. I left the East—came out here."

Some newspaper tumbles down the street and gets stuck in the fence of the condemned building across the street and flutters its edges in the wind.

"Could be worse," Hank Crow says.

"True," I say. "But that doesn't do me much good."

"I didn't say it would do you much good," Hank says, and laughs. "Just said it could be worse."

"I still have my meat," I say, and smile.

"There you go—that's the spirit, son."

Neither of us says anything for a moment and the night sounds announce themselves in the quiet space. There's a couple fighting diagonally across the street at the Mark James Hotel. I see their frustrated shadows against the shade every now and then. Car horns sound. Horns from the harbor.

"What are you going to do when they close the Lincoln?" I say.

Hank shrugs. "I got family in Oregon. I could stay here. I like the sun. I'm an old man, Nick. I may write my life story."

"Really?"

Hank laughs and takes a drink of beer. "Why not? Not every book can be about Elvis and Princess Di."

And I think, but don't say, that no one would be interested in Hank Crow's story. The American public doesn't much care to read stories about good people who work hard and have nothing to show for it. They don't want to hear about poor people who stay poor people. Start in a log cabin and end in the White House? Cool. Start in a log cabin and end up renting another log cabin, you're shit out of luck, no matter how much you may have helped the working conditions on any number of assembly lines. People don't like to hear the world isn't fair and it isn't nice, and they're sure as hell not going to pay to hear it.

Hank wipes his mouth with the back of his hand. "How about you? You're a young man—what the hell are you going to do?"

I tell him that I may have some money coming in, but that

the robbery may have set me back. I fill him in without going into too much detail.

"Money with the Russian?"

I say yes.

"Fool's gold, son. You got nothing if you're relying on that boy."

"Could be," I say. "But then I've got nothing either way." Then it hits me that maybe Sergei stole this shit. I don't know him that well. He could have done it. Hell, Maggot Arm Joe could have. The two of them have been going at me with their plan since the get-go. Maybe I'm being taken out of the deal? I close my eyes, and feel the sting of my cuts opening fresh. I can't think this way—they are my partners. They wouldn't do this. But still, it keeps coming at me like a popcorn kernel in my throat—they might. Greed makes people do shit.

A cop car pulls up in front of the "No Parking" section of the curb in front of the Lincoln. Hank gets up and says quietly to me, "I'll take my leave of you now, if you don't mind." He takes our beer and goes behind the desk, slinking away from the cop, whose name, his name tag says, is O'Hara.

"You call about a robbery?" Officer O'Hara says.

I nod and lead him up toward my room. Our feet clunk heavily on the old wood stairs, which give just a bit under the weight. This is a pretty beat-up building, maybe it's best that the city's closing it down.

I open the door, and gesture for Officer O'Hara to go on ahead of me. He walks into the room and kicks into the kiddie pool and sloshes a little funky water over the side.

He looks at me. "You have children here, sir?"

"No," I say.

He takes out a pad and pen and points to the kiddie pool with his pen. "What's this for, then?"

I'm too tired to make anything up, so I say, "My girlfriend and I had sex in it."

He shakes his head. "If you're not honest with me, it'll be hard to help you, sir."

"Look," I say. "That's the truth, but it's got nothing to do with the crime."

He asks me what was taken, and I tell him about the change jar, the VCR and TV, and the video camera.

"What'd you have a camera for?" he says.

I point to the kiddie pool and he rolls his eyes and clicks his pen on and off a couple of times.

"Okay," he says. "What else is missing?"

I tell him about the three hard drives and the monitor.

"Why do you have three computers?" he says, and makes it sound oily.

He gives me a look that says he thinks I'm small-time bad news and why can't he just get called on to protect and serve the good people?

"I just do," I say. "Look—I was the one robbed here."

He nods in a bored way.

"They were piece-of-shit 386s—they weren't stolen. There's no one to buy them."

"Okay," he says. Two more clicks of the pen. "Anything else?"

And I lead him over to the bed and point at the pile of shit on it. I make careful note of the footprints and tell him that there are probably fingerprints on the headboard where he steadied himself.

Officer O'Hara says, "That doesn't help us."

"Doesn't help you? Isn't this a clue? You're looking for this guy," I say. "This is his MO. He's the shitter."

Officer O'Hara points at the shit and says, "We see this all the time."

"Really?" I say. Somehow this is more disturbing than being robbed. A whole world of people rob houses and do this?

O'Hara's still pointing at the shit. "This is not an uncommon occurrence." He flips his pad shut.

"So," he says. "It doesn't look good."

"What are the odds I can get my stuff back?"

He shakes his head. "Not good."

"What about the fingerprints on the bedpost?"

O'Hara laughs. "You're kidding, right?"

I'm not kidding. Hell, I thought they'd take samples of the shit and do a DNA scan of some sort. The look on my face must suggest that, no, I'm not kidding.

He says, "No offense, sir. But you lost some appliances. They aren't coming back."

He tips his cap and tells me that he has my number, and if anything turns up, he'll give me a call. He ducks out of the room and down the hall and I hear his feet making their way down the stairs while I stand there looking at my room and wondering what I'm going to do.

I know I need to call Sergei and tell Maggot Arm Joe. I need to let them know, and I need to see their reactions to see if they know about this. But I need sleep more than I need anything else. I go downstairs and grab a key to one of the vacant rooms the hookers use and go to sleep there in a strange bed with a strange window and a whole new bunch of noises that would probably keep me up if I weren't so tired.

Hear Ye, Hear Ye

It's three in the afternoon and Freddie Moon is having trouble covering his bets with Kenny Montelli. I know this because Freddie Moon lives next to this room I slept in last night and Freddie Moon is keeping me up as he gets his ass kicked off all four walls of his room. Freddie Moon did some time upstate and learned how to cut hair there and now he makes his living at Manny's Old Fashioned Barber Shop down the road. Freddie Moon begs for them to stop. The wall that borders mine rocks like we're having a quake. I've gotten too tired, too self-involved, to give a shit about what's happening to Freddie Moon. This is my sorrow and my fear and there's no room in my house for other people's trouble. I've got my troubles and they're all I can focus on.

Freddie Moon should have paid his debts.

Mr. Frank Carr should not have sold out his slimy friends.

And whoever the fuck took my things last night, and I'm still tossing coins in my head about Sergei and Maggot Arm Joe, should never have set foot in the Lincoln. Every man for himself and the only side I'm on from now on is my side.

So, fuck Freddie Moon and his cries for help. He's costing

me sleep. I pound on the wall and tell Kenny Montelli's guys to beat him quieter so I can try to get more sleep, but it's not happening. There's things I need to do.

I go down to the front desk and put on a pot of coffee and Don't Mean Maybe's *Real Good Life* CD, which is one of the great undiscovered albums of the nineties and it always cheers me up, but it's not doing its usual trick.

I call up to Maggot Arm Joe and fill him in on what happened. He sounds stunned and weary. If he had anything to do with it, he's a hell of an actor. He sounds deflated and upset. I ask him if he still has his three computers and he says he does and that it's probably time to call Sergei.

"You think he had anything to do with this?" I say.

"I doubt it," he says. He pauses for another second and says, "No. No way."

I feel like a kid with a bad report card who has to talk to Dad; I'm looking for someone to take care of this, but they're nowhere to be found.

I say, "There's some freeze-dried meat down here for you."

"You're joking."

"I'm not. They delivered it sometime yesterday."

"Why can't they just bring it to that dumb-ass bomb shelter?"

"I didn't talk to the man," I say.

"Okay," he says. "I'll think about it later—give me a buzz when you've got a plan."

I tell him sure, I'll call him when I have a plan, but I don't tell him that calling him was half of the plan I had. I dial Sergei's number. I tell him what happened. He doesn't sound very upset, but I'm not sure if that's because the toxins have frozen his vocal cords, too. I'm worried that if he didn't have anything to do with it, I'm not holding much now. They could cut me loose.

"So, I'm not out of the deal?" I say.

"Why out?" Sergei says.

"Because you still have six computers," I say. "You don't need my three to make money, but I lost three."

"Not lost, Nick Ray. Stolen," Sergei says. "This happen." He coughs. "Plus, three computers not lost. Misplaced, Nick Ray."

"You got any idea where they could be?"

"They not take your Maggot friend's?"

"No."

"Then it not someone who knows what they have—or they take both."

I hadn't thought of that. Sergei's sharp, sometimes I forget, but he's made it in several countries and several languages and he's come out okay.

Sergei says, "So check the pawnshops. Those crap computers—those show up."

"You think?"

"They show up at pawnshops. At yard sale," Sergei says— he sounds amused—like this is a bump in his road. I thought this was the end of the world, but he's making it sound like grape juice and grass stains. Strictly kids' stuff. I'm starting to calm down.

"We buy them back—we take twenty dollars out of Nick Ray's cut," he says. He pauses. "Poor Nick Ray with shit on bed. We hurt the men who do this."

I tell Sergei I'm with him on that one.

"Bad form," he says.

I tell him what the cop told me, how common this is.

"Strange country, this country of yours, Nick Ray," Sergei

says. He yawns. "Need to take pain medication now. Check with Mole's pawnshop—see if we get lucky. Let me sleep now."

Sergei hangs up and I'm still pleasantly stunned enough to sit there frozen until a woman's recorded voice breaks in on the dial tone and tells me that if I'd like to make a call I should hang up and try again.

Amputee Hookers

I go out front to grab a smoke and relax a little before hooking up with Sergei and Maggot Arm Joe later to come up with a plan for getting back the stolen computers. The sky's a gray that's as dull and incomprehensible as accounting tables, it's a sad sky, a sky that you can feel on your shoulders. Jeanine and Molly Clark come out of the building. I think about Sergei scaring them away with that "growing like a tumor" line and I chuckle a bit to myself.

"Hi, Mr. Nick," the kid says, and stops next to me on the stairs.

"Hey, Molly, how are you?"

"Smoking's bad for you," she says. "Smoking will kill you."

The schools hammer this into the kids' heads these days. And I could come up with some wiseass answer, but the kid's right, and as propaganda goes, it's not a bad thing to be filling kids with. I tell her I'm trying to quit.

"You should," she says.

Jeanine tells her to move along and not bother Mr. Ray—that they need to catch a bus.

"We need to catch a bus now because my daddy can't pick me up here," Molly says. "He broke his hand real bad and he can't drive. He can't even ride his horses."

"He rides horses?" I say.

Jeanine says, "Out in the desert—Morango Valley. He tends to wild horses and nurses them back to health."

I'm thinking, *The cowboy?* "How'd he break his hand?"

Jeanine shakes her head. "No idea—but it's not so bad that he can't drive. He could drive if he had to—he's just making me go out of my way for his custody."

Molly says, "Daddy can't drive—he *says* so."

Jeanine rolls her eyes and says in a tired deadpan, "And your daddy never ever lied about a thing." She drags the kid away and I'm realizing we probably kicked the shit out of some guy who was watching his ex-wife and kid. A cowboy with a broken hand who won't come around here anymore.

It can't be a coincidence.

Sergei made him break his own finger, the poor bastard. And I only gave him up because I thought my life depended on it. These facts swirl and gnaw and I keep trying to add them up so that I'm not the bad guy, but it doesn't work. I fucked up, and the cowboy's got nothing but pain and fear because of it. I'm wondering if anyone's better off for having come into contact with me.

The phone's ringing and I run inside to grab it and it's Scooter, two doors down at the adult-film place.

He says, "Dude, you have got to come over."

"You couldn't come over here?" I say.

"I'm at work," he says. "I'm on duty."

"On duty," I say. "Like you're a fucking cop. So someone

can't get their porno—like the world's going to spin off its axis."

"I'm telling you, Nick—there is some shit you have to see here."

It's strange, getting a phone call from someone who is less than an eighth of a mile away from you. Hell, he could have leaned out the window and yelled to me if he didn't want to move. But this is California at the start of the century, everybody's on a phone everywhere you go. People in cars, in lines. I see people checking out groceries while they're talking on the phone, they treat the cashiers like they're robots. The way people treat people who are serving them should be a crime. I know this. Someday, I'll see it on the news that one of these cashiers pounded the shit out of someone in a pressed shirt talking on the phone when they should have been courteous and I'll cheer. Put me on that jury and I'll send the cashier roses and a *Get Out of Jail Free* card.

So I walk the twenty-five steps, I count them, from our stoop to Scooter's door. And when I walk in, he closes the door, spins his "Open/Closed" sign, and leads me to a back room where they have three TVs hooked up to a stack of around twenty-five VCRs.

"So?" I say. "What's up—your girlfriend have another art-film problem?"

"Not exactly," he says. He points a remote at the television in the middle and I recognize it immediately, it's the tape that Tara and I made the other night. The camera's mostly on her, it's what she wanted and I can't say now that I'm upset, and it must be early on, because you can only see my hand when I change nozzles from an empty enema bag to a full one. She's propped up on one elbow while she masturbates with the other hand. She's doubled over in pleasure and pain and every couple of minutes she pukes a steady stream of clear water and moans in ecstasy while it happens. She looks beautiful.

"This is fucking amazing," Scooter says. "She should go on the road."

I'm embarrassed, but I'm also mad. "Where did you get this?"

"Some guy sold me the VCR this morning," he says. "I don't think he knew what he had—I didn't know the tape was in it until after I bought it."

"I need that back," I say. I'm thinking, *Some guy?*

"I thought you'd want it," Scooter says. "The original's all yours."

"The original?"

"Dude," Scooter says, "I couldn't sit on this—we've been copying it all morning. This is the best amateur porn I've seen all year." Scooter looks at me like I should be proud. "I watch amateur porn all the time and this is special."

"You taped it?"

"Taped, packaged, and distributed—hell, I've got it in four categories out front."

And it's one of those moments where the curiosity nudges the anger aside and I ask, "What four?"

"Black, S/M, Puking, and Enema."

"You have a puking section? There's enough puking porno to have a whole section?"

He nods. "Puking and Spitting—they're together."

I'm wondering how I'm going to tell Tara. *Hey—you made four sections.* This day keeps getting worse.

"I'll show you."

And Scooter leaves the tape running and takes me out to the floor and shows me the tape in every section. I look at the label and it reads:

PENNY'S PUKE FEST:
    HOT AMATEUR PORN WITH PENNY—A SEXY BLACK NEWCUMER WHO'S INTO ENEMAS AND PUKING—THIS TAPE HAS IT GOING AND CUMMING!

"You know she's Hawaiian?" I say.

"Really?" He looks at me blankly. "Guess it's too late to fix."

I'm not sure why I'm pursuing it, and not sure it matters, but I say, "You could fix it."

Scooter shakes his head. "It was hard enough to write this. I tried to get enemas in the title, but it just didn't work."

"Penny's Puke Fest?"

"You didn't want me to use her name, did you?"

"No," I say. My head aches, but I can't locate and localize the pain. Shards of hard light are jabbing at my corneas— playing stick and move, dancing like a young Ali and impossible to stop. I look next to the puking and spitting section and there's an amputee section. "What?" I say. "You couldn't manage some thematic tie-in there? Couldn't find a way to have my sex life in every section?"

Scooter whistles. "If she would do amputee porn, she could make a fortune."

"What are you talking about?"

"Huge market—amputee porn. Amputee live sex acts, you

name it. Amputee hookers make five hundred percent more for the same sex act as fully limbed hookers."

"Bullshit."

Scooter says, "Look it up, dude."

The fact that he's sold the tape slaps me hard. "This is a major fucking problem," I say.

Scooter shakes his head and points to the video case for *Penny's Puke Fest*. "I'm telling you—that's a special tape— that's going to move some copies."

"I need those back," I say.

"I don't think I could if I wanted to, dude," Scooter says. He's still unclear on how wrong this is. "She's amazing, Nick— she does things on that tape people just don't do."

And I think of telling him I know, I was there, but I figure why bother. I need to let Tara know this has happened. Just once, I want to bring somebody some good news today. I need to be calm. I need to contain this damage. I say, "How many copies of that are there?"

"I made fifty—but I sold them to dealers." He shrugs. "Could be in the hundreds by the end of the week."

I shake my head.

"It's a special movie, Nick."

I want to punch him, but I need some information. Right now, whoever sold him the VCR may be the only person who knows where the computers are. I ask him to tell me about the guy who brought the VCR in.

"Not much to tell."

"Short? Fat? White? Black? Give me something."

He looks at me blankly. "Dude—I tell you and tomorrow it's on the street and no one ever brings me equipment again."

"Scooter, I swear you are so close to me kicking the shit out of you—and you need to give me a reason not to."

"You, Nick?" he says, and laughs.

And that does it. I punch him hard in the face—remembering what my dad told me so many years ago. Don't make the fist until your hand's right near the face. I feel Scooter's jaw resist, then him, then he's in a heap at my feet and I'm about to kick his ribs, but stop myself.

"Tell me something, Scooter."

He looks up at me, doubled over in a fetal position. He looks away. "You're putting me in a tight spot here."

"I can make it worse," I say, and I get ready to kick him. I feel sick—watching myself do this. This is so far away from the man I wanted to be that I can barely recognize myself. I'm willing and, I'm sure of it, able to seriously hurt Scooter. "I swear, if you don't tell me, you're going to wish you never saw that VCR."

"I don't know his name," Scooter says.

"I'm going to fuck you up, Scooter—and when I'm done I'll let Sergei dance on what's left."

The name Sergei apparently scares him more than me hitting him. He closes his eyes. "He's one of Billy Mangos' kids."

"That's it?"

"That's not enough?" Scooter says. "He's a white guy, maybe seventeen, and he works for Billy Mangos down at the shipyards. That's what I know."

I look at Scooter for a second, wondering if I should still kick him, whether or not he gave me the information. I'd be in my rights, looked at from certain angles. I can hear the sound on the tape that Scooter left running, it's Tara's voice, screaming, there's the sound of splashes and her calling my name in a voice that sounds something like love and then some wordless gurgling. It clicks in on me that I have more important things to do than hurting Scooter. I look at him for a moment, then I walk out and go back to the Lincoln, trying to figure out what I'm going to tell Tara.

What Billy Mangos Has to Say

I tell Maggot Arm Joe what's happened. He and I load his three hard drives into the car and bring them to Sergei's place. Sergei meets us in the parking lot wearing a silk smoking jacket with gold jewelry dangling from his neck the size of sand dollars—he looks like Hugh Hefner's personal trainer, just off the boat from Austria and fresh from showing Hef and Jimmy Caan the latest in bodybuilding techniques. I fill him in on what I know.

"Billy Mango must have explanation," Sergei says. "Men never interfere in business of each other."

"Let's get these inside," Maggot Arm Joe says.

"Egg in one baskets," Sergei says as we walk into his condo carrying the three computers.

Maggot Arm Joe says, "We have security here. The Lincoln's too easy to break into if one of Billy Mangos' clowns can do it." He plunks a hard drive down next to Sergei's computer. "Plus, maybe we can gather some names for Harry Fudge. You have the list?"

Sergei says, "Have list. Must get dressed." He walks into his back bedroom.

I shout down the hallway to ask Sergei if I can use his phone.

"Only local call for Nick Ray until we get computers back." He laughs at his joke and I hear him opening and closing his closets.

I dial Tara's number and get her machine. I tell her that I need to talk with her, but I might be hard to track down for the next few hours. I tell her I'll try again.

When I hang up, Maggot Arm Joe says, "Trouble?"

"Trouble," I say.

"Anything I can help with?"

"I don't think so," I say.

"You'll let me know?"

I nod and rub my hand over my face and a ring catches on one of my eyebrow scars and the cut stings for a moment. My hand throbs from punching Scooter.

Sergei struts out from his back bedroom in these pink leather pants with a somewhat matching off-pink leather shirt. He sees the two of us looking at him and says, "What?" He turns and looks behind him, then back to us.

Sergei says, "Is problem?"

Maggot Arm Joe says, "Where did you get that? I mean is there a store for this shit you wear? Or do you have to order it?"

"Fuck you, Maggot Man—this thousand dollars." Sergei spins around like a catwalk model and caresses his ass before turning the full three-sixty. "Man feel good in good clothes—you would not know."

"I've had nice clothes," he says. "They didn't look anything like the shit you drape your crazy ass with, I'll tell you that."

Sergei looks at me. "How I look, Nick Ray?"

I don't see the point in hurting Sergei's feelings, or in

upsetting him when he's been very cool, this far, about me losing the computers. "You look fine—like one of the New York Dolls," I say.

Maggot Arm Joe says, "He looks like a huge fucking tongue."

Sergei pumps his pectorals back and forth, one breast bulges and then the other. He looks at himself in the hallway mirror. "Maybe I change." He looks at Maggot Arm Joe. "Not for you— just don't want blood on pretty clothes." He goes to the bedroom and says, "Unless Mr. Mango has good answer, he must bleed. Cannot bleed on pretty clothes. Bleed on work clothes."

I think about Billy Mangos bleeding and that sends me thinking about the cowboy. I wonder if I should tell them about it. Maggot Arm Joe is punching a bunch of wires— hooking one of his hard drives to Sergei's twenty-one-inch monitor. Sergei comes back into the living room in a pair of black leather pants and a shirt that looks like vinyl.

"Those are works clothes?" I say.

Sergei runs a hand gently down the length of his arm. "Nothing stick to this shirt—much easy cleaning. Like Teflon shirt. Handi Wipe cleaning."

"You know, before we get ahead of ourselves with Billy Mangos, you should know we made a mistake with the cowboy the other night."

Maggot Arm Joe looks up.

Sergei says, "How mistake?"

And I tell them what I think, that we busted up some guy who helps nurse wild horses back to health out in the desert, who's probably Jeanine's ex-husband.

Maggot Arm Joe says, "What the hell was he doing looking up at the Lincoln all night?"

"No idea," I say.

"I do," Maggot Arm Joe says. "Dude was a stalker. We did Jeanine Clark a favor—I'm telling you, I saw enough of those guys in court. Restraining orders don't do jack." He nods toward Sergei. "Our man did a public service."

Sergei smiles. "Happy mistake."

"I don't know about that," I say. "We don't know he was a stalker."

"We don't?" Maggot Arm Joe says. "The man lives out in the desert and he just comes to look at the Lincoln Hotel at two in the morning for what? Because it's so lovely?"

He's got a point. Maybe the cowboy was a stalker. That's nothing but trouble, can't get too upset over that.

Sergei says, "Plus, he cowboy. Cowboys make stupid Americans. Make worst poetry—should all be fed finger."

Maggot Arm Joe says, "Go for it, man—bust up all the cowboys and you can wear whatever the hell you like and I'll never say another word."

Sergei looks happy, like busting up cowboys would be a dream gig. He slaps me on the back. "Nick Ray a worry man. Worry much. Cowboy get what cowboy deserve." He nods with the confidence of the young Mike Tyson about to crack somebody open before the crowd's even been shown to their seats. "Let go talk to Mango."

Maggot Arm Joe says that he'll stay put—that he wants to check the hard drives for any witness relocation names that might match some of the names Harry Fudge wants to put a hurting to. Sergei says that we'll be back soon, it shouldn't be long before we find out what Billy Mangos has to say for himself.

When Business Becomes Personal

Sergei and I walk from Ocean Boulevard back to Wang's Everything's a Dollar in hopes of finding Billy Mangos hanging with some of his kids. If he's not there, logic says he's at Lite-A-Line or, if he's fresh with new money, maybe King's Grill, this first-rate seafood place on Pine Avenue.

I smoke a cigarette as we walk.

Sergei says, "Nick Ray much nervous."

"I suppose."

"Worry much. Everything fine—never work again when you get money."

"That sounds good," I say, though I'm not sure it is. While I've always hated work, hated and resented every job I've ever had, I'm not sure what I'd do if I had a bunch of free time.

"Is good, Nick Ray. Is very good not to work."

"You ever work?"

"Work now, Nick Ray. Not working very hard work."

"No," I say. "I mean straight work—punch-in punch-out kind of stuff."

He nods. "When first came to United States, work as dishwasher." He looks at me as we come to a stop at Ocean and

Long Beach Boulevard. "Work as garbage collector in Russia—pay very well. Then wash dishes when come here." The light changes and we start walking. Sergei says, "Work sixty, seventy hours and man pay me dollar an hour. When I find out about your minimum wage, I choke him and take exactly what owed me out of register."

"You choked him?"

He nods.

"You choked him dead?"

"No, Nick Ray. Just choke to pass out. Then take what was mine. Add up hours, multiply by minimum wage." He sniffs. "Little-boy math."

"So that's all you took?"

"To penny, Nick Ray. What is owed Sergei." He taps his temple. "Always know—always collect—always to penny. Sergei never round up, never round down."

We get to Wang's Everything's a Dollar and do a quick scan, and there's Billy Mangos, surrounded by a few teenage punks who think he's hot shit but they'll grow older and realize what a loser he is. By then, they'll be replaced by another crop of sad-faced, lonely disenfranchised boys. These are the same unrooted kids that the white supremacists like those Metzger idiots recruit. Dumb and pliable as modeling clay.

When we get to the table, Billy Mangos sends the kids away and says, "I hear we have a problem."

I point at his gaggle of deadbeats walking away from the table. "That's our fucking problem. One of your clowns ripped me off."

Billy Mangos is eating Buffalo wings that are the color of Chee·tos. He wipes his mouth with a greasy napkin that's smeared the same orange as the wings. "Now—how do we know that it was one of my boys?"

I start to say something, but Sergei holds up his hand. "Not know. But have hunch."

Billy Mangos says, "A hunch? Fuck you and fuck your hunch. Now let me eat."

Sergei barely raises his voice when he says, "I break your wrist. Stick fork through hand." I check his face and there's no tell. Either he's learning to bluff or the poison in his face is working, or he means it. There's no way to know. He grabs Billy Mangos' wrist.

"Fuck off," Billy Mangos says.

Sergei takes a fork and puts it on the back of Billy Mangos' hand, which he's got pinned on the table. Sergei says, "Stick fork in hand—then spin you around table until wrist breaks." He starts to put slow weight on the fork and I see the skin on Billy Mangos' hand start to gather white around the prongs of the fork.

Billy Mangos says, "I didn't know you had anything to do with that VCR."

"Fuck with friend, fuck with me," Sergei says. "Where the rest of Nick Ray's things?"

Sergei leans down on the fork, and I see blood pooling around the prongs.

Billy Mangos starts to shake, his face turns a pale red, and he's pounding the table with his free hand. The silverware on the table bounces and rattles each time his free hand comes down. Some people are looking over at us and Sergei leans harder and you can hear crunchy noises from the hand.

"Tell us things," Sergei says.

Billy Mangos says he'll tell us where the computers and the rest of the things are as soon as Sergei lets go of his hand.

"Wrong order," Sergei says. "You talk—I let go."

Billy Mangos blurts out that Mario did it, and that the rest of the stuff is at Billy Mangos' warehouse space, which is up in Carson near the Arco oil refineries about ten miles north of here.

Sergei lets go of his hand and tells Billy to give him the directions and the key to the storage locker.

"I'll go with you," Billy Mangos says.

Sergei says no.

"I'm not going to trust you with my locker," Billy says.

I say, "Fine—so you can rip us off, but we can't be trusted?" I push him hard in the chest and his chair slides awkwardly back on the tile. "Is that how this works?"

Sergei pulls me away from Billy and says, "Nick Ray, wait outside." He looks in my eyes and nods—the look says, *Go outside—this is not a matter of debate.*

I go out to the corner, and through the windows I see Billy Mangos hand over a key to Sergei, who says something and shakes the same hand he was breaking up with the fork a minute ago. He takes a chicken wing and starts to come outside. When he gets to where I'm standing on the curb, he holds out half of the chicken wing.

"Want, Nick Ray?"

"I don't eat meat," I say.

"This not meat," he says. "No orange meat in world." He holds it close enough for me to get the smelling-salts wallop of the hot sauce in my tearing eyes. If I could smell, it would probably hurt. I shake my head as my sinuses flood and some blood trickles onto my upper lip. He throws it onto the sidewalk near a pigeon that hops away at first and then approaches the tossed meat, carefully walking sideways. The light changes and we start to cross Long Beach Boulevard on our way, I'm guessing, to my car and to the storage lot in Carson, and Sergei says to me, "Sorry to make you go outside, but never make business personal."

"What you were doing with his hand wasn't personal?"

Sergei shakes his head. "That business. You getting angry."

"You weren't angry when you were busting up his hand?"

"No, Nick Ray—cannot be angry and do business."

"But you can push a fork through a man's hand and not be angry."

Sergei looks confused. "Not personal. When business become personal, bad things happen."

U-Haul

I never knew that Tom Jones did a version of "Green, Green Grass of Home," but here it is on my *Songs from the POV of a Dead Guy* tape Blake made. He's singing about his sweet corn-fed girl, coming to visit after they dumped him under his green green grass of home, and he's as hammy as William Shatner—it's amazing this guy ever made a living with his singing.

Sergei says, "Disneyland New Year's Day, Nick Ray."

I look over at him briefly, then back to the freeway. All the freeways in Southern California are above the cities and the only things at eye level are the tufts of the palm trees that remind me of Dr. Seuss creatures and the billboards that relentlessly advertise movies and TV shows. I'm worried about finding my stuff in Billy Mangos' storage unit and I'm not paying full attention to Sergei.

He says, "Nick Ray too worry. Disneyland cheer you up."

I light a cigarette.

Sergei says, "Happiest place on earth."

"You ever been there?"

"Of course. First thing—Disney very American—must

see." He turns the tape down. "Sad music—this doesn't help Nick Ray's worry."

I drop in the CD of Bennett & Burch's *The Palace at 4AM*.

The first chords of "Puzzle Heart" come on, and by the chorus, Sergei's bopping his head in time with the music. "Much better," he says.

I get off the 405, and after going the wrong way a couple of times, we find the storage unit. It's dark and cold as we get out and cross a wide parking lot and go to the storage-unit office. There's an old man at the desk smoking one of those cigarillos Clint Eastwood smoked in *The Good the Bad and the Ugly*. He wears a baseball cap that reads OLD FART and he's got these glasses squeezed onto one of those old-man cauliflower noses that usually mean he was a club boxer or a soldier. I was worried about security, worried that they wouldn't let us in to Billy Mangos' locker just because we had his key, but we barely nod and the guy leans over like it takes all the effort in the world and buzzes us through.

Indoor storage is an amazing thing. The center opening is wide enough for two Humvees to go through, and then there's all this shit piled up to an airline-hangar ceiling. It smells vaguely of mothballs and I remember the way my grandmother's antique shop used to smell. She opened it up on the Maine coast after my grandfather had to retire from the circus because he'd taken a nasty fall that affected his use of nouns and that he never truly recovered from.

Lucky for us, Billy Mangos' unit is on the floor in the third row. Sergei opens it and leans in and tells me to help. "Where are computers?"

I see my television and the video camera. There are some

computers, but there aren't the ones that were stolen from my room.

"Fuck," I say. If they're out in the world, we aren't the only ones that have the information.

Sergei's tearing the place apart, throwing shit all over, swearing.

The guy with the "Old Fart" cap comes close to the entrance to Billy Mangos' unit and says, "You fellas having a problem in there?"

Sergei and I look at each other and I see fear in his eyes for the first time.

"No problem," I say, and we leave the unit open and take off, leaving my stuff behind.

When we get to my car, Sergei says, "Let's get coffee. Need to think."

We stop at a Spires coffee shop by the oil refinery and sit by the window and watch the open fires out of the enormous tubes lighting up the night.

"Who does this?" Sergei says.

"Billy Mangos," I say. "We should go find him."

Sergei shakes his head. "Billy Mangos gone. Sent us here, gave him time to run away. Someone else."

"Let's go find out who," I say.

"Maybe Nick Ray," he says.

I look at him and I see the calm shark's eyes he had when he made the cowboy break his own finger. "What?" I say.

"Maybe Nick Ray hedging bets. Maybe no one stole computers."

"That's ridiculous," I say. "What would I have to gain?"

"You don't like selling to Harry Fudge. Maybe you don't sell to Fudge. You fuck Sergei instead."

He's looking hard at me, trying to read my face. I could lose a finger here. I could get seriously fucked up. There's a few ways I could play this, but I'm thinking I should go with honesty. At least then I won't need to remember a lie.

"Look—I don't like selling it to Fudge, but I've been honest about that. There's no way I'd take these three," I say. "Plus, Mangos himself told you he had the rest of my stuff."

"Then why are computers gone?" he says. "Only computers?"

It's a good question. "I don't know."

Sergei looks tired. It seems his desire to hurt me is spilling out of him. "This bad turn, Nick Ray."

"We'll find them," I say. "Plus, I have a printout of the names from my main hard drive."

"You have backup?"

"I have a list of what was in one of them, yeah," I tell him.

"Some good news," he says.

"But it's not good that they're out in the world."

"No," he says. "Other people know what's on them, and we lose."

"Chances are they don't know," I say. Saying it makes me hope it's true.

He closes his eyes. "Take me home. Must sleep and think."

Free Delivery

I get back to the Lincoln and Hank Crow's there talking to a huge man in overalls, the guy must be six-seven and well over three hundred pounds. It worries me, maybe he's been sent to talk to me about some of our business. I doubt I could get my arms around him, let alone hurt him in any way. As I reach the desk, Hank tells me he's a plumber. I'm still leery, but if it's a disguise, it's a good one, he's got grease and plumbing slime all over him and his fingers look like he works for a living. I turn to the plumber, who has the name CLARENCE sewn above his right pocket. He shakes my hand and tells me his name is Mo.

I point to the name above his shirt.

"It's someone else's," he says. "Guy I work with."

They have two guys this big? I'm wondering where it is they find these enormous plumbers.

Hank Crow says, "Sewage problem."

"Bad?" I say.

Mo the Plumber says, "Plumbers have a saying. There's no such thing as a good sewage problem."

"You say that?"

"We do," he says, entirely humorless.

Hank Crow says, "Shit was backing up into the toilet and onto the floor. It's a sad mess upstairs. I called Mrs. Carlisle and she said the city's at fault."

What Hank Crow's telling me, and I'm not sure that Mo the Plumber's in on this, is that Mrs. Carlisle isn't paying for this, but he called the plumber, anyway. She doesn't care much for her people, she's a slumlord, and Hank Crow would love to give her a headache that would last. The city's claimed the Lincoln under eminent domain, so she's pretty much let it rot into the ground since she knew she'd be losing the building.

Hank points to the plumber. "Our friend here has it fixed."

"For now," Mo the Plumber says.

"For now?" I say.

"This is just the beginning of your sewage problem. You've got some real trouble under your building and it's doubtful the city's going to take responsibility."

"What about the water-main break?" I say. "Could that have affected this?"

Mo shakes his head. "Sewage and the water main have nothing to do with each other."

Hank Crow says, "Thank goodness for small favors."

"Why won't the city take responsibility?" I say.

"Sewage is a gray area," Mo says. "They own it when it enters beneath the city streets. Under the building, the owner owns the sewage. Between—under the sidewalk? It gets dicey."

"No one owns the shit between the building and the street?"

Mo nods. "The waste under the sidewalk is in a kind of limbo." He pauses. "It causes us a fair amount of trouble."

"I could see that," I say.

"But not forever," Mo says. "Everything's being privatized—fresh water, prisons, police forces, schools—I don't expect waste will remain public for long."

"Who would own sewage?" I say.

Mo shrugs. "Someone—there's big money in sewage—someone will see that."

"No doubt," Hank Crow says.

"My shower's been stinking up," I say. "Are you telling me I've been showering in sewage?"

Mo the Plumber shakes his head. "You're talking different pipes."

"The showers really stink," I say.

Mo the Plumber says, "When was the last time you flushed the water heaters?"

I look at Hank, who looks back at me with what I imagine is the same blank look on his face that I have on mine.

"Of course," Mo the Plumber says, full of self-righteous satisfaction. "You never have, have you?"

Hank Crow says, "I've lived eighty years and I've never heard of flushing a water heater."

Mo the Plumber tells us that the crap I'm smelling is a buildup of what he calls calcites and they grow like a fungus, like an evil film, and they infect the hot water with what he calls a "sewagelike smell to the untrained nose."

"Really?" I say.

"You know who should flush their water heaters?" He pauses. "Everyone. You know who does?"

"No one?" Hank Crow says.

"Plumbers," Mo the Plumber says. "You shower at a plumber's house—you'll never smell those calcites—you'll never see that nasty white film on their shower door."

"Great," I say. "You know any plumbers whose house I could shower at?"

"You think it's funny now, and that's fine—but you've got a serious sewage problem under this building. Not a funny thing down there."

Mo the Plumber has Hank Crow sign some papers on a clipboard, pulls a pink copy away from the yellow and white copies, and hands it to Hank. He tips his cap and heads out the door and down the stairs.

Hank looks at his watch. "'Bout time you take over."

I tell Hank I'm not taking over, that I'm going to bed.

"Who'll watch the desk?"

"Who cares?" I say. "This place is getting the wrecking ball."

Hank nods. "True enough." He doesn't move. "I'll stay up, though."

"Don't make me feel guilty," I say. "Why don't you go to bed?"

"I'll stay here," he says, and waves an arm. "You go on—don't worry—not being a martyr here." He turns on his nine-inch TV. "Nothing in my room I'm missing out here."

I go upstairs and outside of my door are five mason jars with fetal pigs floating in them. There's only a forty-watt bulb dangling in the hallway, but I can see that they have little anguished faces and they look brown as pottery clay with black spots. There's a note on them that reads "Free Delivery" from Tony Vic.

I open my door and carry them inside in two trips before closing my door and realizing that I've yet to clean the bed after the robbery. The window's still broken and the room's freezing. The toilet was backed up and the floor around it is speckled with semidried sewage. I leave the room and decide to go back down to the desk.

When I get there, Hank Crow says, "You don't need to feel bad—I'll stay up."

I tell him about my room. I sit next to him in the lower chair and I feel like a guest on a talk show, with Hank Crow in the high chair looking down on me in a friendly way.

Hank starts talking to me, but the words start merging and blurring around like amoebas, like those psychedelic color film backdrops behind the Velvet Underground on the back photo of the first album with Nico, until they become words that are just sounds and then I fall asleep with my head on the desk.

DAY 7
NEW YEAR'S EVE

The Weakening of the frog

I fell asleep at this desk when it was dark and I woke up and it was dark again, which is always a strange feeling. It's like when you're in a car in the parking lot and the car next to you moves, but for a moment, you think it's you and it shouldn't be happening and your heart mule-kicks in your chest. I'm edgy and jumpy, it's like I'm forever at that moment when you think you left your keys in the car. That's me, patting my pockets and looking worried for the rest of my life. I need to calm down. I put on the Flying Burrito Brothers' *Gilded Palace of Sin* and close my eyes and let the fragile beauty of the Parsons/Hillman harmonies wash over me.

I think it's Thursday. There are several newspapers on the desk and the least yellow one is Wednesday, so maybe it's Wednesday, or maybe there's no today's paper yet.

I look around, but no one's here. I could call Hank Crow, but he's probably sleeping. There's very little noise from outside. Papers flip-flop their way down the street. I think about calling the Time Lady, but I don't know if she exists anymore.

I turn off my CD, and turn on the radio and it's Larry

Mantle's *Air Talk* on Pasadena NPR and they're talking with some scientist about the weakening of the frog.

I think, *Weakening of the Frog?* I put on some coffee and the scientist is talking about how these kids in Minnesota were on some field trip back in 1995 and they were supposed to be learning about the swamp, or some shit, but things took an ugly turn. Seems these kids slogging around in their knee-high swamp boots keep coming on these deformed frogs. The scientist, she says these frogs were missing back legs, had one leg on the left and three on the right. This is circus shit, this is grotesques and horror-show frogs, and she's saying this is bigger and badder than it sounds, though I'm thinking it sounds pretty bad as it is.

Larry Mantle says, "How many did they find that were in this state?"

She says, "Half—over half of the frogs in Minnesota—had some severe deformity."

Maggot Arm Joe comes down the stairs and sits down behind the desk with me. He looks like he's about to say something, but I shush him and point to the radio.

The scientist says, "And reports started coming in from the Philippines, from Australia, from all over the world, that they were finding severely deformed and mutated frogs. This has become a global catastrophe that we need to study."

"Any idea on what's causing this?" Larry Mantle says.

"There are theories—the most troubling is that it's caused by us—by what we've done to the environment."

Maggot Arm Joe shakes his head.

The scientist says, "The implications are troubling, to say the least. Frogs are what we call an indicator species."

"Which means that this could just be the beginning of something?"

"Exactly," she says. "These deformed frogs could be an environmental canary in a coal mine. We could be looking at us in a hundred years."

"But there could be other causes?" Larry Mantle says.

"Yes," she says. "This could be the end of world as we know it—or it could be something else entirely. This is why it's imperative that we study this."

And Larry Mantle says they need to go to Steve Julian and check out the traffic, but that they'll be right back to talk to their guest in the studio about the implications of the genetic mutations of frogs.

Maggot Arm Joe and I go out and smoke a cigarette on the porch. Across the street there's a homeless guy I don't know poking in a Dumpster. One of the bike cops comes by and harasses him, tells him, I guess, that it's illegal to steal somebody else's garbage. This guy Gordo is selling dime bags of pot across the street at the Mark James Hotel. Gordo's up from Mexico and without papers, so he doesn't make a big show of himself. He and Scooter are hovering out of the range of the security lights.

You sit on this stoop long enough and you see so many of the quiet horrors of the world and it all just seems so very big and it leans on you and you feel like you can't move under the weight of all of it.

Tony Vic and Willie What's His Name juke by and Tony Vic says, "Nick, my man, you got the delivery?"

"I did," I say.

Tony Vic opens his trench coat and points to the inner pocket. He says, "Phone cards, gentlemen?"

"No thanks," I say.

"I got Pakistan. I got India. Russia."

"Don't need them," I say.

Maggot Arm Joe says, "You got Chad?"

Tony Vic stops walking and Willie What's His Name stops behind him. Tony says, "Chad, Chad" and starts flicking through those little credit cards. He looks up after a minute. "You're playing with me."

Maggot Arm Joe says, "I am."

Tony Vic shakes his head and turns to Willie and says, "No such place as fucking Chad—the man's playing." He walks away muttering to Willie What's His Name, who still has that big cast on what's left of his wrist and now has to smoke his Swisher Sweets with the other hand.

We watch them walk away for a moment. Across the street, the cop is still giving a hard time to the homeless guy. The night gets quiet and we stare blankly at the empty Blue Line stop in front of us. In the darkness, a train pulls up, and all the people inside look so tired and otherworldly—in that specific way people look on public buses and trains at night. That sad, lonely-faced weariness that seems to glow out of us all under the fluorescent light. Maggot Arm Joe says, "Could be the end of the world." He puts out his cigarette.

"Or something else entirely," I say.

Down the street, I see Scooter buy a bag of pot from Gordo and I realize I need to get in touch with Tara before she finds out about that movie from someone else.

Bad News

When I finally get her on the phone, Tara says she can meet me tonight before she goes to the Dry Martini, a place with one of the signs she's using for her gallery show. It's a big blue neon martini glass jauntily tipped, with a blinking green olive inside. She's taking a bunch of pictures of it tonight after work. She tells me to swing by at 6:30 and we'll head over and have a drink and talk. I tell her I've got some bad news.

"Are you okay?" she says.

"Sort of," I say.

"What is it?"

"I was robbed," I say.

"But you're okay?"

I tell her, yes, I'm okay. And I'm touched that it was her first question. But then I tell her everything, about the tape and it being copied and sent out into the world.

She takes in a breath of recognition. Then she laughs.

"Jesus," she says. "What if Jenny sees it?"

I tell her if Jenny were browsing the puking section of a porno-video store, I don't think she'd have a problem.

"I guess you have a point," she says. I hear her breathing

slowly, like she's trying to stay calm. "This is just great," she says. "How many copies?"

I tell her what Scooter told me.

"Fuck," she says, and laughs again. "I can't talk about this now," she says. "I can't even *think* about this right now."

I start to say something and she says, "Look, we'll talk tonight, okay? I'm at work and I can't go into this here."

Before I can give an answer, she's off the phone.

The Garage People Revisited

We're sitting deep and fat in the soft white leather of Sergei's couch while this yellow-and-green bird Sergei picked up at Pet Partners chirps away by the balcony. He doesn't have a name yet, Sergei calls him Mr. Bird and talks to him like he talks to everyone else.

"Don't talk baby talk to Mr. Bird," he says. "Animals hate this."

Sergei puts peanuts between his lips and lets Mr. Bird pick them out. He hasn't been cut yet.

Maggot Arm Joe has compiled a list of the names we have on our computers, plus my hard-copy list, that match the list of names Harry Fudge wants to suffer. The total of relocated names we have is eighty-eight. The overlap is twenty-two names, which is $440,000, which split three ways is enough to move me out of this life. It's not, as Hank Crow says, "Fuck-You Money," but it's leave-the-Lincoln-behind money, and for now, that's plenty for me.

Sergei smiles. "Many thousand money."

Maggot Arm Joe says, "We got a problem."

I ask him what the problem is and he tells me it's Mr. Frank Carr, who has become Mr. Timothy Shay and who's on both lists.

"What problem?" Sergei says.

"We sold Frank Carr back his name."

"Right," Sergei says.

Maggot Arm Joe shrugs. "So we deal him square? We keep him off of Harry Fudge's list?"

"We have to deal him square," I say. "We told the man he had a deal. Unless he reneges, that's the deal. So Harry Fudge gets twenty-one people to kill instead of twenty-two. What Harry Fudge doesn't know doesn't hurt him. Or us."

"That's where there could be a problem," Maggot Arm Joe says. "These names are all there for a reason, right? These are all men that fucked with Harry Fudge—they may have something to do with each other. He may know that Frank Carr should be on this list——and he may wonder why he wasn't."

"He'll just have to wonder, then," I say. "We made a deal with the man."

"You do not fuck with people like Harry Fudge, or Spencer Durrell, Nick."

"Who's fucking with Spencer Durrell?" I say.

"We all are," Maggot Arm Joe says. "And the longer this goes on, the more things that can go wrong. Fucking Frank Carr could have called the FBI by now."

I say, "What'll they do for him?"

"They'll relocate him, asshole," Maggot Arm Joe says. "And then the FBI will know they've been compromised with their witness relocations."

It hits me that they could move everybody, and then our names could be worthless.

"Frank Carr supposed to pay by now, no?"

"It's Thursday, right?" I say.

The two of them nod and I say, yeah, he was supposed to have paid tomorrow.

"Cannot wait," Sergei says. "Must collect now."

I hadn't wanted to tell them about his calling me out to TC's—was hoping it wouldn't be relevant, but it looks like it could be and so I say, "Mr. Frank Carr called me the other night."

"And?" Maggot Arm Joe says.

"And he said he'd pay us—he gave me this talk about how we were in over our heads and he said if we fucked him over, he'd send Durrell after us."

"And this is why you don't want to screw him?" Maggot Arm Joe says.

"No. I don't want to screw him because that would be wrong. I just thought this might be a little extra incentive not to screw him."

Sergei says, "Why send Durrell? Durrell kill Frank Carr. He have nothing to negotiate with."

And I tell them what Mr. Frank Carr said. That he'd take off and make a new life with a new name far away from Spencer Durrell.

Maggot Arm Joe says, "When were you going to tell us about this?"

"I didn't think it was important," I say.

"Well, it just so happens it is fucking important," Maggot Arm Joe says. "And who left it for you to decide?"

"I'm sorry," I say. "The guy called me and didn't say anything that altered the deal, so I let it pass. I would have said something if he screwed us, but he hasn't." I pause and he doesn't say anything. "If I fucked up, I'm sorry."

"You did fuck up, Nick," he says. "Screw this guy—let's just give his name to Fudge. Fuck him—threatening us."

"He knows bad people," I say.

"He *turned* on bad people—he doesn't want to be in touch with them. I don't accept that."

Sergei shakes his head. "Get tiring, this."

"We still owe him the chance to pay us," I say.

Maggot Arm Joe says, "What the fuck are you—Opie Taylor? We owe him jack—the man should have paid us."

"Let's give him a chance."

Maggot Arm Joe says, "I hate Orange County."

"It's worth ten grand if we go."

"It's worth twenty if we don't."

Sergei stands. "We go. Nick Ray right. He pay, we get money. Doesn't pay, get more money. Still good situation."

"We could call," I say.

Sergei says, "Call on way. Element of surprise."

"Dude could not be home, too," Maggot Arm Joe says. "How's that for a surprise?"

Sergei says, "Let us go."

We get up and Sergei goes over and takes the birdcage off its stand.

"What are you doing?" I say.

"Mr. Bird first night," Sergei says. "Can't leave alone. Mr. Bird must come."

"You're joking?"

"Be in backseat," Sergei says. "Not problem."

We're on the 22, heading down south and toward the Anaheim Hills.

On the way down Sergei calls on a cell phone and gets the answering machine.

"Want to turn around?" I say.

"Maybe screen calls," Sergei says. "This last chance—make him explain why he hasn't paid us."

Nobody talks much in the car. The bird chirps now and again. I turn on NPR and they're talking about more end-of-the-world talk and terrorism and the world falling apart. They talk about the way people went flippy at a bunch of other times in history and how this just seems to be the way people are. Give them a major date or cut-off point, the fortieth birthday, the end of the millennium, 9/11, whatever, and they start acting like loons. Things take on a significance they may or may not have. Stuff that's without meaning is taken as signs. Pseudosciences crop up around the turn of new centuries, last time around it was phrenology, now it's the pseudoscience of the savant, which the guest describes as an ignorant distrust of all empirical sciences. This, in turn, leads to cults, like Scientology and all the apocalyptic cults.

"And Christianity," Maggot Arm Joe says.

"Stop with bad-mouthing," Sergei says.

The people on the radio are talking about end-of-the-world cults and apparently one of the big ones is here in Long Beach. They recruit at yard sales; that's their technique. The man on the radio says, "So it behooves you to be very careful at Long Beach yard sales."

None of this ever means much to me. If the world's going to end, my guess is that it will be very quiet and very unannounced and it won't fall on some date and time that a preponderance of lunatics have agreed on.

Sergei's nodding as we listen. "Good thing we have meat, no?"

Maggot Arm Joe stares out the window and sounds bored when he says, "Yup. A lifesaver."

Sergei digs in his pockets and comes out with a couple of key rings with a key on each of them. "Have key made." He tosses one to Maggot Arm Joe in the backseat and puts one in the breast pocket of my flannel shirt. I look at him.

"Bomb shelter," Sergei says. "No end of world for us."

Maggot Arm Joe says, "I'm telling you, let's blow this clown off. He's had his chance to pay off."

Sergei says, "One chance more."

We pull into the guest slot up around Mr. Frank Carr's place in the Anaheim Hills. The guest slot is near the bank of mailboxes and this old guy in his garage waves and says hello as we get out of my car. There's a woman in the garage, too. She's seated in a folding chair, but she's not at the table with the guy. There's a coffee table with a phone next to her. The guy is at one of those folding card tables that peppered suburbia in the sixties and seventies. He sits there with an ashtray and an open notebook. Behind him is a big roll-down map of the world, the kind you see in high schools. There's a video camera in his driveway that seems to be pointed at him and the woman.

Sergei waves. "Hello, garage person."

The guy looks confused, but friendly. He looks beyond his camera and points a handheld remote that shuts off the tape. "Hello."

We keep walking to Mr. Frank Carr's town house and

the garage person says, "Are you fellows looking for the Shays?"

The Shays? Yes, it clicks in, that's Mr. Frank Carr's name now. "Yes," I say.

He shakes his head. "They had a death of some kin in Arizona."

I'm thinking, *Did he say* kin? *Who says* kin?

Maggot Arm Joe says, "When did he leave?"

"They," the garage guy says. "They left this morning. I'm watering the plants, that's why I know." He gestures around to the other town houses. "I'm pretty much the waterer around here. It's an issue of trust." He sticks his hand out and says his name's Gordon Wright.

I know that name.

He points to the camera, then the woman. "You've probably seen the show. *The Wright Report.*"

I think I have seen this show. Local-access cable, the guy sits at his desk and reads the passages he could get from Operation Blue Book. He reads first-person accounts of UFO sightings. His wife sits in the back and waits for phone calls of sightings. I say, "You're the UFO people?"

"That's right," Gordon Wright says. "So you're a believer?"

I've watched his show with the same sort of interest I reserve for infomercials. I wouldn't call myself a believer. I tend to think people like Gordon Wright are as loopy as Deuteronomy, but not as dangerous. I'm not sure what to say, it's like talking to God-people, you can tell them you're not on the same page, but it's flat-out not worth the trouble to disagree, ultimately.

Maggot Arm Joe says, "When do you expect the Shays to be back?"

The phone next to the woman in the back of the garage

rings. Gordon holds his finger up and says, "If you'll excuse us, gentlemen—we have a call." He puts his finger to his mouth and points the remote at the VCR. He says to the camera, "We have a sighting."

The woman in back picks up the phone and listens for a second. She says to Gordon, "A sighting in Borrego Springs."

Gordon gets up and walks over to the side of the garage with the map and with a pointer indicates a place in Southern California. "What kind of sighting?" he says.

The woman listens on the phone for a moment and says, "A silver lipstick object that hovered in an otherworldly way before speeding away."

Gordon nods in that maniac true-believer way and says directly into the camera, "Speeding away too fast to be from this world."

Maggot Arm Joe looks at me and rolls his eyes. He checks his watch and shows it to me. It's 5:20 and I need to get moving if I'm going to meet Tara at the Dry Martini.

Sergei leans over and whispers, "Always to desert, the UFOs—always."

Gordon Wright says to the camera, "Borrego Springs, eighty-five miles northeast of San Diego, lies in the middle of the Anza-Borrego Desert State Park. This is not unusual. We've had several calls and, no doubt, we will get many more. We shall pay attention." He looks over at the woman. "Thank you, caller. Thanks for all the eyes on truth." He holds a plastic look of sincerity at the camera for a moment and points the remote at the video camera.

Once the camera's off, Maggot Arm Joe says, "Any idea when they'll be back?"

Gordon shakes his head. "Could be a while. There's an

estate to clear. The kids are out of school. They left a hundred pounds of dog food."

The three of us start to walk back to our car.

Gordon Wright says, "Keep your eyes on truth, friends." He waves in that picket-fence way that people do around here and we get in the car and pull away.

"Lunatics," I say.

"Yard sales. Garages," Maggot Arm Joe says. "Is nowhere safe?"

I say, "Do you think the man really had family die?"

"No fucking way," Maggot Arm Joe says. "We need to get this taken care of before everyone on that list is moved."

"How fast FBI act on something like this?" Sergei says.

"Too fast," Maggot Arm Joe says.

And I don't say anything, but something seems off. If Mr. Frank Carr wanted to pay us, wouldn't he have called and tried to make arrangements? And if he didn't want to pay us, why isn't he worried about what we'd do? He must have told someone about the computers, but if he told the FBI, wouldn't they have already contacted us?

"You okay?" Maggot Arm Joe says.

"Sure," I say.

"Nick Ray worry man," Sergei says. "Cannot change worry-man habits."

I'm tired. I don't know what to think and I would close my eyes and relax, but I need to keep this car on the road, and right now, that's taking more energy than it should. The image of Mr. Frank Carr telling me that no one would miss crap like me floats into my head and needles me like a collection agency. *Stay positive*, I tell myself. Thoughts like this are inevitable, they don't mean anything.

Plan B

While we're still on the 22 freeway and in Orange County, Sergei decides to call Harry Fudge and let him know we have found twenty-two names on his list.

"But Carr's gone," I say. "He won't find him at that address."

Maggot Arm Joe says, "We don't want it to look like we were holding out on the man."

"But we *were* holding out on the man," I say, though I don't suppose there's any way he would know we didn't intend to put Frank Carr on the list.

Maggot Arm Joe says, "We? Fuck we—*you* were holding out, Nick. And I'm still not sure why."

"What does that mean?" I say.

"Since the start, you've been pulling for Frank Carr—and now we find you're talking to the man behind our backs."

I say, "Behind your back—fuck you. I haven't been pulling for anyone—we made a deal with the man and I wanted to hold to it, that's all."

"And maybe you did okay with that deal, Nick," Maggot Arm Joe says.

"What the fuck does that mean?"

"That means that you met with the man, had a talk, and now the man's safe and sound, just like you wanted all along."

"That's ridiculous," I say.

"Is it?" He stares at me. "Where's the ten grand, Nick?"

I can't believe I'm hearing this. "I wouldn't do that," I say.

"You would, too," Maggot Arm Joe says. "This is business. Anybody will fuck anybody. I just thought your price might be higher."

"Fuck you," I say. "We're done."

"Stop!" Sergei yells. "What the shit is going on?" He turns around and looks at Maggot Arm Joe and then to me. "Cannot happen, this. Same side—same team. No fights."

"Same team my ass," I say.

"Where's the money, Nick?" Maggot Arm Joe says.

"Stop," Sergei says. "Enough."

"Ask the man why he's protecting Mr. Frank Carr," Maggot Arm Joe says.

I look in the rearview and say, "I'm not protecting anyone. Call up Harry Fudge and give him the address. Hell, for twenty grand, I'll drive Frank Carr door to fucking door and let crazy Harry Fudge freeze him to death or whatever the hell he wants to do."

No one says anything for a moment. Mr. Bird squawks and chirps.

Sergei says, "Good. Same page?"

"Yeah," I say. "Same page." And I'm thinking same page, the page that ends up with Mr. Frank Carr dead, with his Martha Stewart wife and his polished kids without a dad, even if he's a weasel. Let's synchronize our watches; let's kill people. I wonder how and why I ever got involved with this. I need to cut loose. Nothing's worth this—surely not money, of all things.

Sergei says, "Same page?"

I see Maggot Arm Joe nod in the rearview, but he still looks pissed.

Sergei says, "Nick Ray do the talk." And he holds out his phone to me.

"Nope," I say. "Not when I'm driving—I'm not going to be one of those phone drivers."

"Give me the damn phone," Maggot Arm Joe says. "I know the man best."

Sergei shakes his head. "Too angry for business."

"Just give me the goddamn phone."

Sergei gives it to him and Maggot Arm Joe dials. The bird chirps a couple of times. Maggot Arm Joe clicks the phone shut. "No answer."

"No machine?" Sergei says.

"Zip."

Sergei says, "Let's go to Fudge house. Things must be dealt with."

Dead-End Blues

We're winding through the rich neighborhoods of Orange County, where the lawns all look like golf greens and the people still have enough money and ignorance and bad taste to think a lawn jockey is a cool thing in the world.

I take a right on this street that looks familiar, and ask Maggot Arm Joe where I make my next turn.

"What am I?" he says. "A fucking Sherpa?"

"I just thought you'd know," I say.

"Take right at sign," Sergei says.

I take a right and then I see the road that winds its way up to Harry Fudge's mansion, which has several lights on in the windows that glow at the top of the hill. When we get to the gate, I roll down my window and Sergei says, "Do not pass go."

The guard at the gate says, "That's not today's password, sir."

We all look at one another for a moment.

Sergei says, "Must see Mr. Fudge. Very important business."

"Mr. Fudge is at the hospital, sir."

"Why?" I say.

"I'm not at liberty to say, " he says.

"Where?"

"I don't know. The paramedics took him away on the last shift—all I know is it's pretty serious. You'll have to call the house for more information. Now please back out, sir."

He steps back into the booth and there's no more talking to him, so I do as I'm told and roll the car back and turn it around and head down Harry Fudge's hill back to the public roads.

"Fuck," Maggot Arm Joe says.

"It could be nothing," I say. "The man could be fine."

Sergei has Harry Fudge's assistant Paulo's phone number back at his condo, so we head back north. The trees and billboards all whiz by and I don't pay much attention to anything except the fact that our plan is blowing up in our faces. But I try to focus on potential good news—people go to the hospital all the time and they walk out with a smile. This doesn't have to be bad. Still, my chest is tight as cling wrap and my breath comes in narrow shards as we get off the freeway and drive through town on surface streets.

When we get to Sergei's condo, the news isn't good. Sergei talks on the phone for a few minutes and it's impossible to read his blank face, but then he hangs up and fills us in. It turns out Harry Fudge has slipped into a coma and he doesn't look like he's coming out anytime soon.

"Looks like probably die," Sergei says.

"That's it," I say. "No chance he's coming out?"

Nobody says anything.

I say, "People do come out of comas."

Sergei nods in a distracted sort of way.

I go to the fridge and get a beer and look out at the lights over the marina and out onto the water. A bunch of boats are on the water, it looks like a regatta, like they should be wheeling Rose Kennedy herself out to wave hello before they put her back to her darkness. The little sailboats bob and wobble in their controlled way, well-off people getting in place to be beneath the fireworks celebration later tonight off the *Queen Mary*, which is where I met Harry Fudge less than a week ago when he looked strong enough to kill me with his hands.

Harry Fudge has to be seventy years old. That's seventy years with 365 days in them at twenty-four hours a clip and then all added up and the fucker couldn't have hung on for another twenty-four hours, another single day to pay us? I down the beer quickly and put the empty on the table.

I tell Sergei and Maggot Arm Joe I need to take off, that I'm overdue at Tara's place, but that I'll call over later.

Neither of them says anything, maybe later there will be back pats and keep-your-head-ups and a series of Plan Bs, but for now they're looking like sad-faced kids. Even Sergei looks drained, all the toxins in the world can't block his disappointment. Some illegal fireworks pop out on the water. My feet clump on Sergei's deep carpet as I go to the door and head out.

Knockout

Tara meets me at her door in a bathrobe and tells me she's about to shower in hopes of relieving her back pain. I see her in the bathrobe, a thigh peeking through, her hair messed up like she's been driving with the top down, and I fall in love with her all over.

She's been to the doctor today, her back was hurting, and so she goes to the doctor and they diagnose her with pleurisy, which I hadn't heard in years. This is a knack Tara has, she gets things I thought had gone the way of smallpox and the dodo bird, things from other centuries, from Brontë novels. Last year she had scarlet fever.

I go up the stairs into her apartment. "What's next?" I say.

"Beats me," she says. "Consumption?"

We get into her place on the second floor and I'm trying to read her for signs of anger about the video, but she doesn't seem upset.

"Are we cool?" I say.

And she turns and messes up my hair and smiles and tells me we're cool, but it's a sad-looking smile and she heads into her bathroom and I hear the water kick in the old pipes. She says, "I'll be out in a minute—then we can get a drink."

She closes the bathroom door and I hear the whine of the hot-water pipes. I put on one of her CDs, The Urinals' *What Is Real and What Is Not*. I do what you do when you're waiting, poke around and read the spines in the bookcases. There's a bunch of architectural theory, stuff on Frank Gehry, some on the Usonium houses of Frank Lloyd Wright, the Robert Venturi book that she loved, *Learning from Las Vegas*, that gave her the idea for the book of signs. There's all of Pat Califia's books, a bunch of Roland Barthes, and a series of comic books called *The Diary of a Dominatrix*. An art book on bowling signs. I check and see if the Java Lanes, Long Beach's cool bowling alley with a hip fifties futuristic sign, is in there, but it's not.

I sit on the couch and flip through a book on string theory, which is a new and unprecedented unified theory of the universe. It seems pretty interesting, but next to it is a coffee-table book called *Fetish Girls from Prague*, which beats string theory hands down. The book has a series of women from, I'm guessing, Prague, wearing rubber dresses and thigh-high boots strutting around with riding crops and sexy bored looks on their faces. The book has a note tucked in it. I open it up and it's one of Tara's fantasy letters, on L.A. County Parole Department stationery.

Happy Birthday

Mistress X's slut, her bad girl, her pathetic toy, is cuffed on her knees. Mistress X puts a dog collar on her slave. Mistress X places her slut in a ring gag. Mistress has a small bowl and a honey bear. She pours some honey into the small bowl and dips a kitchen brush full of honey. She then paints the honey on her slut's tongue and back against the slut's teeth and gums and cheeks. Mistress X then attaches her slut's dog collar to a ring in the floor so that she is bent over inches away from the floor.

She cannot control her drooling and drools on the floor beneath her.

Now, Mistress says, you get a special birthday present, worm. She takes out 33 birthday candles and puts a drop of Krazy Glue on the bottom of each and glues them to her slut's back and ass (*I have tried this—no problem—the glue holds the candle to the skin—they come off easily, then the glue brushes off. Be careful, however, not to get it on the fingers—they stick together. The best way is probably a drop on the back/ass, hold the candle in place for 10–15 seconds, then move on to the next one*).

She arranges these candles however she'd like, then takes a 12" candle and tells the slave she's going to K-Y it and stick it in her ass and light it so that it drips onto her cunt. The Mistress plays with the candle in her ass—humiliating and violating her helpless slut. She doesn't yet light this one, however.

First, she lights the 33 small birthday candles and lets the wax drip on her back and ass. She laughs at her slut's helplessness.

She lets them burn for a while and blows them out. After this torture, she lights the candle in her slut's ass—she tells her to make a wish. She taunts and torments her—calling her names—she threatens to fuck her in the ass with her strap-on when she's done with the hot wax. Mistress tells slut to lick her boot. To humiliate her slut, she steps on her head with her boot, grinding her face into the drool on the floor. She blows out the candle and takes it out of her ass. If she's in the mood, she fucks her slut into further humiliation.

Then Mistress tells her she's going to whip the 33 birthday candles off her. As a final present, she gets 33 paddles with a long-handled palm paddle before she's allowed to please her Mistress.

I read it twice. *Mistress? Strap-on?* It is a fantasy, after all—and it's not like I don't know where Tara's tastes run. Maybe it's an early draft. Maybe they all start out with a Mistress before I get my copy. I'm not sure I could do this one, though, but I guess I'll wait and see it when I'm supposed to and see if it's the same.

On Tara's built-in desk is a box of little birthday candles and a minitube of Krazy Glue. I hear her singing from the shower—high notes swelling above the steadiness of running water—and I feel like I could spend the rest of my life keeping up with her if she'd let me. I let myself slip into seeing us years down the road, people make arrangements, not all relationships are the same, people let each other be happy. If she wanted to be with women, maybe I could be the kind of person who could be cool with that. I turn the CD down and I listen to her voice from another room and think that I could listen to that voice for a hell of a long time. When she gets out of the shower, I'll drop it on her, see what she thinks.

Tara turns off the water. The pipes give a wobbly growl. I'm seeing if the whole Krazy Glue/birthday-candle thing works. I put a few on the inside of my forearm and she's right, just a little drop holds them. I take a Zippo off the desk and light a few candles. When the wax drips down, it stings, not terrible, but it must really sting when thirty-three of them are lined up and lit on your back. I wonder where she thinks of these things.

Tara says, "What are you doing?" She's wearing her bathrobe with a towel around her head.

I turn around quickly and the four candles on my arm throw wax down. I blow them out. "I was just seeing how this worked," I say.

She closes her eyes and quietly says, "Shit." She looks over at the coffee table where the fantasy letter's open on top of the book and she stomps across the room and picks up the letter and puts it back in the book.

She looks frustrated, so I just blurt it out. I tell her I'm sorry for reading it, but that I know her, that I love her, that I'll let her be anyone and anything she wants if she'll stay with me.

She doesn't say anything for a minute, for too long. I hear the drips of water into the claw-foot tub. The gabble of TV from her neighbor's apartment. The beginnings of an early New Year's party from across the alley.

She says, "Oh, Nick," in a way she would say it if I told her I had inoperable cancer. She's got tears, but they aren't happy ones. And she says, and somehow makes it sound kind, if not good, "No, Nick." She takes a deep breath and tells me that she called me over because after I called about the video, she'd done some thinking.

She says, "I'm leaving Jenny."

"Not that many people will see that video," I say.

She shakes her head. "I'm not upset about that. I was, but

then I tried to understand why I was upset and the reasons weren't good. I'm not hiding who I am anymore—I can't be ashamed of myself anymore."

"You haven't seemed ashamed," I say.

"Not around you," she says. "In general. With the rest of the world. No one at work knows about me. My family. People like that."

"You're telling them?"

"No, but I'm not lying, either. I want to live a totally honest life."

"You're telling me this is a blessing in disguise?" I say.

She chuckles. "Not telling you that," she says. "It would be a hell of a disguise."

"Does Jenny know?"

She nods.

"How'd she take it?"

"Not good. I'm hoping worse than you," she says.

"What does that mean?"

"Nick, I need to be alone for a while. I need to figure some stuff out."

"I love you."

"Don't say that," she says.

"But I do."

"Nick. *Please* understand this. I need some help here."

"With what?"

"I need time to figure shit out. I care about you, you know. Deeply."

Not love, but not tossed out the door, either.

She says, "I need you to be my friend."

And I'm sure I will. This is one of those moments in life where you can see ahead and know that this is the way it had to turn. That this is a friend being a friend and letting you down easy and the right thing to do is to understand, but you don't, not right off. There will be understanding, but for now there's hurt.

I look down and realize that I've still got four candles on my arm and I wonder if I've ever felt dumber in my life. I knock them off and stand up. I sit back down. I have no idea what to do here. How could I be so dumb?

I'm six years old and I hear my parents fighting and it takes a few minutes until I realize they're fighting about me. And my father says, "It's not like having the kid was my idea." And my mother says, "It wasn't my idea, either—you think I wanted to be a mother? I had a *life*."

That's what I'm remembering here. I could hear them because their closet was always full and my father would hang his dry cleaning over the bedroom door, so the door never shut, so I found out that I, in some foundational and essential way, was wholly unwanted in this world. And I felt it as a physical sensation, a cold buzzing all over the skin.

Everything else has been a reminder, ever since.

I fall to her chest and I feel my face against the terrycloth robe and against her rising and falling chest and I think that this is pretty much how things end. Most of my endings are full of hugs and tears and full of people swollen with sadness and an inability to make better what they desperately desire to make better.

I don't know what else to say, so I say what I think I'm feeling. "I love you," I say. "Why not me?"

She looks at me. "Nicky, you're such a fuckup." She smiles. "You're great, Nick. You're kind and good, but be honest— would you want to share a bank account with you?"

"Not if you put it that way," I say.

"You're not a long-term plan," she says. "I'm sorry."

"But I love you," I say again, and feel dumb repeating myself, but it feels like maybe one of these times, it'll do the job.

She holds me tight, with something that feels very close to love itself, and she says, "I know." She kisses the top of my head. "You still want that drink?"

And struggling not to sound desperate for the drink or her company, I say that yes, I'd still like that drink.

The Dry Martini

Tara takes my picture outside the Dry Martini. I'm under the sign next to a bunch of smokers huddled near the building. You see them outside of every bar since California enacted a no-smoking-in-bars law. As Tara takes the picture, I see myself years away and small and distant and four-by-six in a photo in a book Tara's lover is flipping through and she'll ask who's that in the picture and I suppose Tara will bend over and say, that's Nick, a friend from a long time ago, and before you know it, the page will be flipped. The people next to me smoke away and their faces change color as the lights on the sign come on and off.

Tara and I sit at one of the outside tables. People are already drunk, are already making asses of themselves. Whooping and yelling and screaming. A guy across the street is screaming, for no apparent reason, into the face of another man. They don't seem angry at each other. It seems to be some gesture of friendship.

Our cocktail waitress, whose name tag reads THUNDARA, comes out and asks us what we'd like to drink. Tara asks for a martini, dry.

"How dry?" Thundara asks.

"Dry enough for cactus," Tara says.

I ask for a Bass ale, then I say, "Save yourself a trip. Bring me two."

Thundara shakes her head and clicks her gum. "No can do."

"Why not?"

"State law," she says. "One drink per person."

"What about a double?" I say.

"What?" she says.

"A double," I say. "Twice the amount."

"A double ... beer?" she says. "The glass would already be full."

"Then bring me two," I say.

"I can't," she says. "You're a one."

"I'm a what?"

"You're a one—one person. If you were a two, I could bring two drinks. If you were a group, you could have a pitcher."

"Look," I say. "I'm having a hell of a day." I see Tara look down.

Thundara gives me an it's-the-rules shrug.

"I'm a group of people having a lousy day—how about a pitcher?"

She says, "You're a one." She looks hard at me. "A one gets one drink. I'll get you one drink."

I don't know why I'm giving her a hard time, but it's like when you fall down and you want to stop it, but you can't. Control has momentarily slipped. "Is your name really Thundara?" I say.

"You want a drink?" she says.

"Fine," I say. "Get me a drink."

And I feel instantly like shit. The way you judge people is by how they treat food-and-drink service people and I have failed in some way.

I look over at Tara. "Sorry," I say.

She shakes her head. "You okay?"

"No," I say. "But I will be—don't worry." I pause and wonder if I should ask what's on my mind, and curiosity gets the better of me. "Do you have plans for later?"

Tara nods.

Loneliness clubs me. I resist saying *I thought you needed time alone.*

But we're adults, we'll get through this, we'll be able to talk sensibly about this, I suppose. We know the rules here, as easy to follow as those dance-lesson charts. Step here, step there, that's the way through this dance. I used to think it was easier to get dumped than to dump someone, but I've learned they both suck in ways language can't reach. Just a flat rusty sadness that can't be approached and the easier side is the side you don't happen to be on this time around. Plus, Tara's dealing with dumping Jenny, and she loved her, too, even if it didn't work out. She's got her troubles and I've got mine, and like Mr. Frank Carr said, we gather to talk about the troubles we share.

A woman with very short platinum-blond hair walks by in thigh-high boots, fishnets, and a black miniskirt. She's wearing a gray top with spaghetti straps and she's muscular and her shoulder blades are perfect, like two parentheses. Tara and I watch her walk by, her ass sweeping like a pendulum all the way to the pool tables in the back.

I shake my head.

"Hot number," Tara says. "You should go for her."

"I don't know," I say. "I'm having a little woman trouble."

"The fillies getting you down, sailor?"

"You must be reading my mail," I say.

She smiles and it feels momentarily good. We're still tight. This is a shift, not an end. There's still a history here, still words to use that don't sting.

Thundara comes out with Tara's martini and my beer and she treats us like tourists, especially me. She goes away quickly, all pouts and anger and superiority.

Tara shakes her head. "Bad form."

"Well, I wasn't at my best."

"Still, she's rude."

"Not a crime," I say.

"It should be," Tara says. "She should be shunned."

"Shunned?"

She nods. "That's my new thing—I think we should bring back shunning."

We sit for a couple of minutes, and I knock back the beer and want another one as soon as it's gone. We go back and forth on our who-to-shun list, which so far starts with Thundara and ends with Jewel, Fiona Apple, and anyone from that hideous band Creed, since pretentiousness is a shunnable offense, according to Tara.

I'm trying to find Thundara, or anyone else, to get another drink, when I see Sergei coming across the street. He makes it to our table, breathing hard and looking nervous.

"How'd you know I was here?" I say.

"Checked desk at Lincoln. Checked room. Start looking at bars."

It staggers me that I'm that easy to find. At work. In my room. Or drinking. I need to get more interests. I ask him what's going on.

He looks at Tara.

"It's fine," I say. "What's up?"

"We have trouble. Need to talk."

"It can't wait?"

"It can't wait."

Sergei says, "FBI called us."

Tara says, "The FBI?"

I tell her it's okay, though I'm sure it's not.

I take Sergei out of her earshot, out by the sidewalk, and I say, "How the fuck did the FBI get our number?"

"Probably Frank Carr."

"Fuck," I say.

"We must go."

"Where?"

"To bomb shelter, Nick Ray. Let this blow over. Need not to be here when FBI starts looking."

I tell him I'll meet him at his place in five minutes.

"No time, Nick Ray."

Five minutes, I tell him.

"No," he says. "I wait here."

I go inside and tell Tara I need to get going.

Tara asks what's going on, and I tell her I can't talk about it, but I try to act like everything's cool and that this is minor, this is a speed bump, this is nothing to get excited about.

"Doesn't sound okay," she says.

"It's nothing," I say. "Some people who need to be shunned—that's all."

She looks scared, which must mean I look scared, and she says, "You'll call me tomorrow?"

"What if I told you I was going away to straighten up for a

while and that when I come back, I'll get a job and try to prove to you I'm someone worth you being with for good?"

"Is that what you're doing?" she says. "Straightening up?" She looks really worried about me, and I just want to kiss her for caring.

"In a manner of speaking, yes," I say. "What if I did that?"

"Call me, Nick."

"We can talk about this?"

"Are you okay?"

"I'll be fine. Can we talk about this? About us, when I call?"

"We can talk about this, yeah."

I kiss her on the head before snaking my way through the crowds with Sergei.

What Sergei Knows

"When are they coming here?" I say.

"They are here. Tore apart the Lincoln," Sergei says.

"Have they gotten to your place?"

"No," he says. "Frank Carr have your address. My phone."

But it won't be long, if they're asking around the Lincoln, until they add up some easy math and come to Sergei. We need to get Maggot Arm Joe, who's back at Sergei's working on names, and we need the computers and we need to leave.

One day. If we'd just been able to get a list to Harry Fudge yesterday, just yesterday, Mr. Frank Carr would be dead in Harry Fudge's pool and the FBI would be doing whatever they do. We fucked up.

The street is swimming in people headed down to the beach. People carrying chairs and families with kids and nothing but noise and motion going that one way down to the beach and down to the marina. You can lose your footing, get carried by other people's bodies, and it becomes frighteningly obvious how those people die in soccer crowds, how those eleven people were crushed under human feet at the gates at that Who concert in Cincinnati.

I shake my head.

Sergei says, "Bad."

I nod.

"We go away. They not find us."

I look at the mob tromping by outside and wonder if we can get there in time, but then I remember that this is my town and I might know a shortcut or two that the FBI might not know.

Parking for Medieval Madness Patrons Only

We take the alleys, sidestep garbage and old boards with rusty nails and various alley hazards, and slink our way over to the condo, sneak back up the rear entrance through the parking lot that Sergei's condo shares with the Medieval Madness restaurant, which is packed and having a New Year's jousting contest. We head up the back stairs that people usually take when the elevators are out and we get up to the sixth floor and turn the corner carefully toward his hallway. The walk to Sergei's door is slow and frightening. This is that noise in the middle of the night, the unknown shadow. This is real fear. I can hear parties all up and down the hall. People talking, the sound of televisions blaring from speakers.

Sergei's door is closed. He knocks and we step back to each side, though I'm not sure why. There's no answer. He knocks again. I can feel my heartbeat in my neck and hands. Still no answer. Mr. Bird chirps. There's the faint noise of the stereo playing.

"Hello," Sergei yells.

Maggot Arm Joe swings the door open. "What the fuck are you knocking for at your own door?"

"Was worried," Sergei says.

"Well, welcome to the fucking club," Maggot Arm Joe says.

The two of them have already packed some duffel bags, and the computers are stacked in a pile.

"We take as much as we can carry," Sergei says.

"Hold on," I say. "Why don't we just give them the computers and walk?"

Maggot Arm Joe looks at me like I'm an idiot. "First of all, these may still be worth something. And secondly, they'll put us in federal prison."

"I bought those computers," I say. "Not a crime."

"And then you tried to blackmail a government employee—which is what federal witnesses are—with the information. That's a felony."

I say, "You never told us that."

He stops loading himself down with bags and says, "I'm sorry, Nick. Did you think this was all on the up-and-up? What we were doing?"

"Well, no," I say, searching for something better.

Sergei says, "Enough. We have clothes in bags. We have meat in desert. We take computers and stop on way for drinks."

I'm swept up in their wave, and before I know it, I'm holding two leather shoulder bags and three stacked computers and heading down the service elevator with Sergei and Maggot Arm Joe. Mr. Bird sits on Sergei's right shoulder and makes this whilling noise every few seconds. We get to the parking lot, dump the stuff in the back of his SUV, and start to pull out.

Somebody Walkin' in My House

KROQ, aka K-Rock, is counting down the top hundred rock songs of all time, the way they do every year. The list doesn't change much—sometimes something decent like Nirvana cracks the list, but it's mostly moldy old cock rock, and I get struck by this awful feeling that this is all we'll have to listen to for a while.

"I need you to swing by the Lincoln," I say.

"Nope," Maggot Arm Joe says.

"I need some stuff."

He says, "Look, I'm stuck for who knows how long wearing Sergei's fucking clothing. If I can spare not going back, so can you."

Sergei says, "You lucky man to wear Sergei's clothing. Enough of your bad mouth."

I'm thinking of the music that keeps me sane. Living underground in a box without some headphones. No way.

"Sergei, swing me by the Lincoln. I'll be in and out."

Sergei nods. He says, "You be very quick, Nick Ray. No dawdle time."

He swings a left on Long Beach Boulevard and starts to

pull into the loading zone when I see three guys in suits talking to Hank Crow under the fluorescent glow of the front desk. They couldn't look more FBI if they were auditioning for the part in a movie.

"Sorry," Sergei says. "Must go, Nick Ray."

"Right," I say.

We keep going, north to the 710. I'm in a funk, thinking of all I'm leaving behind. There's not much stuff. Except for my CDs and some of my favorite clothes, I guess it's all pretty much crap. I can replace the CDs. I start making a mental list of the ones I absolutely need. The bigger stuff, like the Stones and the Beatles, I can get in the desert, probably. Maybe I can get Wilco at Borders or Barnes & Noble. The smaller stuff, Bennett-Burch and the South San Gabriel and stuff like that, I need to order off the Internet. But I probably can't do that because I'd need a credit card and they could track us that way.

I wonder how long this hiding's going to go on.

Maggot Arm Joe and Sergei are sitting quietly in the front seat. Sergei merges onto the 91 East. The long boring part of "Free Bird" drones and stomps slowly to its ending on the radio.

"How long are we going to be underground?"

Sergei shrugs.

Maggot Arm Joe says, "A month at least. See if Harry Fudge gets better. Still try to turn a buck on this."

"You don't think the FBI will keep looking for us after a month?"

"Dude, I've worked with the FBI. They don't catch anybody. That anthrax scare. The Olympic bomber. Those loonies that derailed the train in Arizona."

"They got the Unibomber," I say.

Sergei says, "No Nick Ray negative thinking."

Maggot Arm Joe says, "They needed the fucking Uni-bomber's brother to turn him in. McVeigh's family turned him in." He laughs. "They're fucking stooges. We lay low for a while, and we'll be fine. They don't know our names. We just need to stay under the radar for a while."

We get quiet for a while. I sit in the backseat and watch the lights and hills blur once we're outside of Green Valley. I fall asleep as Sergei takes the 60 toward Indio.

I wake up at 11:30 when we're outside of a Stater Brothers supermarket in downtown Twentynine Palms.

"How far are we from our place?" I say.

"Ten minutes," Sergei says. "Let us get some Happy New Year things."

It's just before midnight, and the three of us are sitting in plastic lawn chairs we bought at the Stater Brothers. I also got some energy bars and some vegetables, but I'm wondering how long before I have to eat Sergei's fucking dehydrated meat. The girl at the checkout told us the Marine base has a massive fireworks display at midnight, so we're hanging out in the cold to see it.

I have a bottle of Sapphire Blue Bombay Gin between my legs, and I take a sip and feel the warmth spread through me. I think about maybe not drinking after this bottle. About maybe being a little bit more put together the next time I make my pitch to Tara.

"What are we going to do with your SUV?" Maggot Arm Joe says to Sergei.

"What?"

"Well, it'll look pretty odd. Just having this thing parked in the middle of nowhere, no?"

Sergei takes the bottle of gin from me and drinks. "Tomorrow, let us worry." He points with the bottle to the sky. "Tonight, let us have Happy New Year."

"Fuck you," Maggot Arm Joe says.

I can't believe I'll be trapped in a bunker with these guys for at least the next month. Sergei has a gun. I hope we don't kill one another.

"Calm down," I say. "We've got to be cool."

Maggot Arm Joe says, "Fuck you, too. If you hadn't hesitated, we would have sold everything fast and clear."

"I didn't hesitate. I disagreed with the way you wanted to do it. There's a difference."

"Well, if we'd done it my way, we'd be rich."

"If it weren't for me," I say, "you never would have been included."

He looks around and gestures to the vast emptiness of the desert, and then to his ridiculous clothes. "And look at all that I would have missed."

"Shut up, shut up, shut up!" Sergei says. He points to the sky. "Army blowing everything up pretty."

Some fireworks have started. They're playing music, some hyperpatriotic piece-of-shit Lee Greenwood or Toby Keith slab of jingoistic crap about the greatest country on earth comes all distorted and warbled over the mountains. The sky explodes in green. In silvery lights that flower down like huge electric weeping willows. I can see my breath.

The fireworks go off above me and resonate in the valley. In between fireworks, I hear the distant cheers and oohs and aahs of people who have gathered to celebrate the end of the year, or the beginning of the new one, which, like the deformed frogs, like the floods and the earthquakes, like the end of fresh water to drink, like the mud slides, like just about anything you focus on, could mean the end of the world or something else entirely.

The fireworks keep going and the people keep making their noises. We haven't been found. I will be okay, I tell myself. I will hide here, which is a retreat, a loss, but I will go back to Long Beach with a new plan on the coast where rebirth's a way of life.

My ex, Cheryl, was right. Nick Ray is a loser, but that doesn't mean I always have to be a loser. This is not carved in stone. I think about my options as the people celebrate and cheer the show of lights above me. Light strobes into the sky. Red. Then green. I feel my heart hammering in my skull. Music thunders and weaves around the explosions. I tell myself that I am alive and I have a fallout shelter in the desert and I have a brain and people have made more with less than that to start over with. This is, after all, America.

We'll Keep You in Suspense

First Cut
ISBN 0-06-073535-X (paperback) • On Sale Now
Previously titled *Caedmon's Song* and never before published in the United States, here is a gripping stand-alone thriller from modern master of suspense **Peter Robinson**.

Kinki Lullaby
ISBN 0-06-051624-0 (paperback) • On Sale Now
The latest suspenseful, rapid-fire installment of **Isaac Adamson's** Billy Chaka series finds Billy in Osaka investigating a murder and the career of a young puppetry prodigy.

Night Visions
ISBN 0-06-059462-4 (paperback) • On Sale Now
A young lawyer's shocking dreams become terribly real in this chilling, beautifully written debut thriller by **Thomas Fahy**.

Eye of the Needle
ISBN 0-06-074815-X (paperback) • On Sale January 2005
For the first time in trade paperback, here is one of legendary suspense author Ken Follett's most compelling classics.

More Than They Could Chew
ISBN 0-06-074280-1 (paperback) • On Sale February 2005
Rob Roberge tells the story of Nick Ray, a man whose addictions (alcohol, kinky sex, and questionable friends) might only be cured by weaning him from oxygen.

Get Shorty
ISBN 0-06-077709-5 (paperback) • On Sale February 2005
Elmond Leonard takes a mobster to Hollywood—where the women are gorgeous, the men are corrupt, and making it big isn't all that different from making your bones.

Be Cool
ISBN 0-06-077706-0 (paperback) • On Sale February 2005
Elmore Leonard's follow-up to *Get Shorty* is self-consciously a novel about sequels and the sometimes cowardice that limits the creativity of the American film industry.

Men from Boys
ISBN 0-06-076285-3 (paperback) • On Sale April 2005
A collection of short fiction, edited by **John Harvey,** that examines what it means to be a man amid card sharks, revolvers, and shallow graves—from today's elite crime writers.